IRON AND LACE

Nadine Miller

A KISMET® Romance

METEOR PUBLISHING CORPORATION
Bensalem, Pennsylvania

For Edward, my own true hero.

To my wonderful critique group: Lee Undsderfer, Judy Strege and Mary Alice Mierz.

And to Jim Waddilove, whose knowledge of the great foundries of the past made this story possible.

NADINE MILLER

Imagining herself as part of a story comes naturally to Nadine. She and her husband live on the shore of historic Poverty Bay in Washington State, on the site of the bootlegger's cottage where the Canadian Rum Runners landed their cargoes during the Prohibition Era. Aside from her writing, her chief interest is her collection of primitive African art, which she has acquired on her many trips to West Africa to visit her three grandchildren.

PROLOGUE

"I'm in trouble, Josh—big trouble. You're the only one I can turn to."

A familiar chill crept up the back of Joshua Eddington's neck and he took a tighter grip on the telephone receiver.

"Are you there, Josh? Did you hear what I said?"

"I heard you, Kyle, but I resigned from the guardian angel business when I bailed you out of your last fiasco."

"This is different."

"They're all different," Josh said patiently. "Susan was different, and Ingrid—and Mimi was very different."

"It's not that kind of trouble . . . this time. I haven't even had a date in months."

Josh raised a skeptical eyebrow. Trouble and women were synonymous where his handsome brother was concerned. "What is your problem then?" Even as he asked it, he knew the question was a mistake. The relieved sigh sliding across the long-distance wires said Kyle had taken it as a tentative promise of help.

"It's the family business. The auditor says unless we pull off a miracle, it's going under."

The words exploded in Josh's ear. The last thing he'd expected was trouble at the century-old Eddington foundry. He listened dumbfounded while Kyle continued his startling recital. "Practically every casting the foundry turns out fails inspection. The X-ray costs alone are enough to bankrupt us."

"That's ridiculous." Frustration sharpened Josh's voice. "Eddington employees have turned out topnotch work for three generations . . . and since when do manhole covers and cast-iron sewer pipe have to be X-rayed?"

"We're making aircraft parts now." Kyle swore softly. "Thanks to that fool production manager and his scheme to bring the foundry into the twentieth century."

Josh ran nervous fingers through hair bleached from two weeks in the Caribbean. Leave it to Kyle to turn his first day back at work into a nightmare. "Angus McTavish is one of the best foundrymen in the country," he muttered. "I can't believe he'd take on something he couldn't handle."

"McTavish! That reactionary old fool. I fired him over a year ago. He balked at every order I gave him."

Josh cringed. When his father died, he'd encouraged his grandmother to turn the family business over to his younger brother, Kyle. Josh had never had the slightest interest in managing the foundry or in living in Titusville, Indiana, the industrial town named after his great-grandfather, Titus Eddington. The sinking feeling in the pit of his stomach warned him he was about to find out the idea had been a bad one. "Who's running the production end of the foundry now?" he asked.

"That's the problem. The guy I hired talked a great game. How was I to know he was a phony?"

"Did you check his references?"

The silence on the telephone line spoke volumes, and Josh felt as if someone were stretching steel wires across his shoulder blades. Methodically he massaged the back of his neck to relieve the tension he felt building.

"How did I get stuck with this job in the first place?" Kyle wailed. "You're the oldest son. You should be babysitting the family's white elephant instead of playing politics in Washington, D.C."

"As I recall, you begged for the job." Josh's voice shook with anger. "Are you suggesting I give up my career and rush back to Titusville to straighten out your mess?"

Kyle's bravado disappeared like a puff of smoke in a windstorm. "I apologize, Josh. I don't know what made me say such a thing. I'm just so tired of trying to hold the business together, and I'm worried about Grandmother."

"Why? What's wrong with her? She seemed perfectly happy when I visited her in Martinique last week."

"I wonder how happy she'll be when her monthly checks stop arriving . . . not to mention the shock the old girl would suffer if the Eddington name were dragged through the bankruptcy courts. It could kill her."

Kyle paused, obviously for effect. "Then there's Mother," he continued. She's already called twice this month because her allowance is late arriving at her bank in Rome. Apparently her Italian count has expensive tastes."

A tide of white-hot anger surged through Josh. "Damn it, Kyle," he raged, "I can't believe I'm hearing this. Have you actually run the business so far into the ground you can't even pay the family stockholder dividends?"

"Don't yell at me!" Kyle whined. "I didn't want to take out that loan. I had no choice, and I only asked for enough money to make payroll for a few months until I could turn things around. Now, just because I got a little behind on the payments, that idiot who took over the bank when Charlie Hamilton retired is calling in the loan. He says he'll refuse to honor our checks unless I pay the damn thing in full. Can you believe it? A glorified bank clerk having the nerve to pull a stunt like that on an Eddington."

"How far behind are you in the payments?"

"What?"

"How far behind, Kyle?"

"Eight months . . . but what does that have to do with anything?"

The headache which had been threatening for the last

ten minutes slammed into Josh's temples with hurricane force. He took a deep breath and waited, certain there was more. Something in the tone of Kyle's voice warned he was building up to the coup de grâce.

"And to top it all, that ugly business about Tim O'Malley has flared up again."

The name meant nothing to Josh. "Who is Tim O'Malley?"

"The young guy who was killed in the foundry fire three years ago . . ." Kyle hesitated. "You were in Europe at the time and I guess I forgot to mention it when you got back to Washington. You'd think it would have died down by now, but last week the widow's brother marched into my office and claimed the foundry owed her some kind of compensation. The jerk started tossing around figures that sounded like a recap of the national debt, and naturally the union reps backed him all the way. Anything that makes the Eddingtons look bad gets their support."

Josh groaned. He felt as if he'd stumbled into a quicksand bog and was sinking fast.

Kyle continued his recitation, his voice breaking pitifully. "I'm dying here in this lousy little town, Josh, and the vultures are closing in from all sides. For God's sake, you have to help me."

With grim resignation, Josh replaced the phone receiver in its cradle and gazed around the quietly elegant office he'd worked so hard to attain. With two new firms recently added to his client list, he couldn't have picked a worse time to take an extended leave of absence.

For a few brief moments he wracked his brain trying to come up with some way to put things right in Titusville without spending a lot of time in the miserable place. He couldn't, and with a shrug, he made a mental rundown of the names of the few men who could adequately replace him while he was gone.

He decided on one, pushed back his chair, and rose to

his feet. Squaring his shoulders, he walked reluctantly toward the connecting door between his office and that of his partner. There was going to be hell to pay when he broke his news. Might as well get it over with right away.

ONE

Shayna O'Malley looked up from the nineteenth-century English literature textbook she'd been studying and rubbed her tired eyes.

The night-school course in literature appreciation she'd been hired to teach started on Monday. This was Friday and she felt confident she was as ready as she was ever going to be for the challenge ahead of her. She'd had a number of substitute teaching assignments in recent months, but this was the first time she'd been awarded an entire semester of teaching. A warm glow of satisfaction engulfed her. After three years in limbo, she was finally getting her mind . . . and her life together again.

She glanced out her kitchen window to make certain her daughter was still playing safely in the fenced backyard. Megan was a tiny mirror image of her mother, and in the first terrible months after Tim's death had often been all that kept Shayna sane.

At the moment, black curls bobbing and blue eyes bright with determination, the sturdy little girl was waging an unsuccessful campaign to convince her cat to walk on a leash. Shayna smiled to herself. Parsley was a stubborn cat, but she was betting on her five-year-old. When it came to stubborn, Megan was definitely her mother's daughter.

A glance at the clock told her it was three o'clock. Instinctively, she braced herself as the cuckoo popped from his Black Forest cottage and shattered the afternoon quiet with his raucous announcement. On the last squawk, the kitchen door burst open, and Shayna raised startled eyes to find her mother's ample frame filling the doorway.

"So help me, I could hear that stupid bird as I came through the hedge." Maggie Brenegan sounded breathless. "It beats me why you didn't strangle it years ago."

Shayna shrugged off the familiar complaint. "I could never bring myself to part with the first gift Tim gave me."

Maggie cast a disgruntled look at the bird's tiny cottage. "Tim was a darling, but I don't think much of his taste. Couldn't you at least desquawk the varmint?"

"No!" Shayna swallowed hard. "I couldn't do that."

They'd been so young, both of them seventeen, the day Tim bought the silly thing at the county fair. "When the little bird speaks," he'd promised in his soft brogue, "you'll know wherever I am, I'm saying I love you."

Compassion softened Maggie's weathered features. "Forgive me," she said. "I'm just a cranky old woman who talks before she thinks."

Shayna watched her mother tuck straggling wisps of gray hair into the knot atop her head and smooth the wrinkles from her cotton housedress. Maggie's obsession in life was her garden. She was her happiest with mud on her shoes and twigs in her hair. This unusual fixation with neatness was a dead giveaway. She had something on her mind.

"Any special reason for this visit, Mom?"

"Do I need a reason to visit my own daughter?"

"Of course not. I expect you for morning coffee, but it usually takes a major emergency to pry you out of your garden in the afternoon. Would you like some tea?"

"Yes." Maggie sank onto a chair. "I think a cup of

hot tea is just what I need," she said, drumming her fingers nervously on the table.

"I'm ready for a break, too," Shayna declared. She stacked her books and study notes in a pile, lighted a gas jet on her ancient range, and set a small tea kettle to boil. "What's the matter, Mom? I've never seen you so jittery."

Maggie stopped her drumming and clasped her work-roughened hands tightly together. "The whole town's on pins and needles these days. It's that new fellow who's taken over the foundry. He's like a cat on a fence. No one knows which way he'll jump."

"So I've heard. The rumors at the market this morning were pretty wild." Shayna usually "turned off" when she heard the name Eddington Foundry—the place which had claimed her husband's life. Today, she'd forced herself to listen to the rampant gossip. Like most men in Titusville, her father and two brothers made their livings in the vast smoke-blackened forge of the town's major employer.

"Are Pop and the boys worried about their jobs?"

Maggie's expression darkened. "They're mighty uneasy. Any Eddington is trouble, but this one's really scary. I know you don't want to hear about it, but . . ."

"It's all right, Mom." Shayna poured the boiling water into the teapot and set two mugs on the table. "I can see you need to talk. Who is this man? Where does he fit in the Eddington family?"

"He's Hiram Eddington's oldest son, Joshua. Someone told Pop he's an industrial lobbyist from Washington, D.C., whatever that means. A few weeks ago, he showed up at the foundry and took over Kyle's job. Just like that— and no one dared question him. Pop says he's a big stern-looking man like his grandfather. Nothing like his father or Kyle."

Shayna remembered Kyle Eddington well. He'd made a token appearance at Tim's funeral, mumbled a few words, then roared off in his sports car. She'd hated him instantly. "What happened to Kyle?"

"He's gone, and nobody's had the nerve to ask where," Maggie continued, "and Joshua fired the production manager the day he took over. Pop says neither of them were worth two cents, but it sure has everyone shaking in their boots. Meanwhile, Joshua's poking into every inch of the old place, asking more questions than a new bride in a cooking school."

"He probably has to," Shayna said thoughtfully. "A Washington lobbyist doesn't have much in common with a foundry manager. You have to give him credit for knowing that much. If Kyle had asked a few questions, he might have done a better job when he was running things."

Maggie nodded. "That's what Pop says, and he took heart when Angus McTavish visited the plant yesterday. If Joshua can talk old Angus into coming back, there may be some hope for the foundry yet." She crossed herself fervently. "God knows what will happen to this town if it closes."

"What do the boys have to say about all the changes?"

Maggie shrugged. "As usual, Martin doesn't say much, but Ronnie's full of ideas about how things should be run."

"I can imagine. I just wish he'd zipper his mouth before he gets himself into serious trouble."

Shayna's two brothers were nothing alike. Her older brother, Martin, was a big auburn-haired man with calm gray eyes and a placid disposition. He looked and acted so little like the rest of the volatile Brenegan clan, Shayna had long ago decided he must be a throwback to some ancient Celtic ancestor of theirs.

Ronnie had the same Black Irish coloring as Shayna and the temper to match, but there the similarity ended. As far back as she could remember, he'd been a mischief-maker and conniver, involved in one get-rich-quick scheme after another. So far, they'd all failed miserably, but Ronnie's zeal never diminished. His saving grace was his fanatic loyalty to his family and, despite their many disagreements, Shayna loved her handsome, difficult brother dearly.

Maggie resumed her nervous drumming. "Joshua has agreed to hear any problems the men might have with management, and guess who's heading the Employee Grievance Committee?"

"Surely not Ronnie!" Shayna's breath caught in her throat. If anyone could rub the new head of the foundry wrong, it was her know-it-all brother.

She turned up the gas jet to bring the water to boil again. "I need another cup of tea to digest that news."

Nervously, Maggie tucked a stray wisp of hair behind one ear. "The committee met last night and made up their list of grievances to present at the meeting this morning. Pop just called to say I should tell you about it."

Shayna couldn't believe her ears. John O'Malley had spent his entire working life at the Eddington Foundry. To the best of her knowledge, he'd never before called home during his shift. "Why should you talk to me? Nothing that goes on at the foundry is of interest to me anymore."

Like an orchestrated duet, the telephone on the wall behind Shayna pealed at the same instant steam hissed from the spout of the teakettle. She reached for the phone and gestured for Maggie to lift the kettle from the burner.

"Hello."

"Mrs. O'Malley?"

"Yes."

"This is Eleanor Warren, Joshua Eddington's secretary. He instructed me to make an appointment with you as soon as can be conveniently arranged."

Mrs. Warren's words sent Shayna's startled brain into reverse, until a sudden flash of intuition brought her back into focus. Somehow this unbelievable phone call was tied in with her mother's impromptu visit.

"Mrs. O'Malley?"

"Yes." Shayna's voice cracked. "Why in heaven's name would Mr. Eddington want to make an appointment with me?"

The teakettle slipped from Maggie's fingers and clattered against the tile counter.

"I believe he wishes to discuss the matter of your husband's tragic death."

Shayna's heart pounded and a wave of nausea swept through her. She felt the urge to scream vicious obscenities at this person talking about Tim with such cool detachment, but she forced herself to speak calmly. "I have no desire to discuss my husband's death with anyone."

"Mr. Eddington is a busy man, Mrs. O'Malley. He wouldn't have requested an appointment without good reason. Am I to understand you refuse to meet with him?"

"Yes."

"I believe you might want to rethink that decision." Mrs. Warren's voice was decidedly cool.

"I've done all the thinking about it I'm going to do," Shayna said sharply. Then, remembering the men in her family were employed by the man, she added, "Tell him the subject is too painful for me to discuss with a stranger."

Shayna replaced the telephone receiver and faced her mother. Maggie's ruddy complexion had faded to parchment.

"What's going on here, Mom? You knew Joshua Eddington's secretary was going to call me, didn't you?"

"That's why Pop called. Have you lost what sense the good Lord gave you, girl? You can't say no to Joshua Eddington."

"I just did." Shayna clutched her steaming mug of tea, hoping its warmth would penetrate her sudden chill. "The last thing I need is to rehash that dreadful affair with someone who wasn't even in Titusville when it happened."

"Mr. Eddington's a busy man," Maggie pleaded. "If he's taking the time to talk to you, it must be important."

"Now you sound like his secretary," Shayna said angrily. "Why are you pushing this? Nothing Joshua Eddington could say would interest me in the slightest."

"I think he wants to discuss a college scholarship for Megan." Maggie's booming voice faded to a raspy squeak.

Dumbfounded, Shayna stared at her mother, and one by one, the pieces fell into place—Pop's phone call, her mother's visit, Mrs. Warren's guarded reference to Tim. Good Lord! Ronnie and his Grievance Committee! "What wild scheme has Ronnie cooked up this time?" she asked warily.

"He told Joshua Eddington that Kyle had treated Tim's widow and child shamefully and if the Eddingtons wanted to get back the respect of the men who worked for them, they'd have to do something to make amends . . . like set up a college scholarship for Megan." Maggie's voice was defensive, her gaze riveted on her clasped hands. "Every word he said was true and, to a man, the committee stood behind him."

"How could Ronnie have done such a thing without consulting me? And why didn't you stop him?"

"Because I agree with him, that's why." Maggie raised her chin defiantly as she warmed to her subject. "Why shouldn't the Eddingtons pay for Megan's education? They have plenty of money, and they owe you. Every man in that furnace room would have died if Tim hadn't given his life to save them. He was a hero! That should be worth something!"

"How dare you place a price tag on Tim's death!" Shayna pressed trembling fingers to her aching temples. "I don't need the Eddingtons' money. I have my widow's pension from Tim's social security and his union survivor's benefits."

"Ten thousand dollars! How far will that take you?"

"I finished my teaching degree with it, and that's all the farther I needed it to take me. I'm getting enough work to make ends meet now and I should be able to get a permanent teaching postion in the next couple of years."

Maggie sniffed. "And not one cent has come out of the Eddingtons' pockets. Whatever the scholarship costs, they are getting off cheap. Good Lord, girl, the breadwinner of your young family was struck down in his prime while working in their foundry.'' Maggie's voice rose indignantly. ''Ronnie says a good lawyer could get you a lot more.''

''Ronnie says . . .'' Shayna felt sickened by the knowledge that while her family had been giving lip service to her struggle for independence, they'd been secretly arranging her life behind her back. ''I'm not a charity case, Mom. When the time comes for Megan to go to college, I'll find the money. I don't need to blackmail the Eddingtons.''

''Pop said you wouldn't like Ronnie's idea.'' Bright spots of color stained Maggie's cheeks. ''Your brother is just trying to do his best for you. We all are.''

''Then leave me alone and let me get on with my life.''

The hurt stamped on her mother's face stabbed at Shayna, but anger and humiliation sharpened her tongue. ''You're letting Ronnie do your thinking for you, and I know my brother. He's not half as concerned with my welfare as he is with proving he can outsmart the Eddingtons.''

Hot tears burned Shayna's eyes. ''Tim didn't have a mercenary bone in his body. He'd have hated having people haggle over how much his act of heroism was worth.'' She cleared her throat. ''All I have left is my pride in him and the pride he had in me, and I won't let Ronnie barter that away like one of those junk cars he sells at auction.''

Joshua Eddington slowed his silver Mercedes 560 SL to a crawl and glanced at the street map on the seat beside him. He wondered if his snap decision to visit Mrs. O'Malley had been a wise one. He'd been lost for the past fifteen minutes. It had never occurred to him he could have trouble finding an address in a town the size of Titusville, but he'd never before ventured into the sprawling collection of working-class houses called Titusville Flats.

He checked the street signs. Lombard. Macready. He

must be getting close. At last he spied the one he was looking for. Loblolly. With the exception of its unusual name, there was little to distinguish it from any other street in this section of town.

The houses were squat boxes his great-grandfather had built as company houses and his grandfather had subsequently sold to the men who worked for him. They were small. Any one of them would fit into the library of White Oaks, the Eddington family mansion, with room to spare.

A red-brick chimney sat squarely in the center of each roof and a covered porch spanned the front of each house. Except for an occasional imaginative paint job, they were identical—as if some patternmaker, pleased with his creation, had ordered them all cast from the same mold.

Josh edged his car down the narrow street teeming with children, dogs and assorted tricycles, bicycles and skateboards, and came to a stop by the white picket fence surrounding 820 Loblolly Street.

Resting his arms on the steering wheel, he surveyed the tiny cottage with the sparkling windows and crisp ruffled curtains, trying to envision the woman who lived in it. The newspaper clippings Mrs. Warren had located contained pictures of twisted steel and raging flames and one photo of the young hero from the company archives, but no photos of his widow and child.

What was Mrs. O'Malley up to? Why would she refuse to discuss the settlement proposed by her brother's committee—a settlement Kyle should have made three years ago?

At the thought of Kyle, Josh found himself searching for justification of his brother's appalling treatment of Tim O'Malley's family. It was hard to find. Kyle had dumped the sorry affair in Josh's lap along with all the other problems he'd created in his four years as head of the foundry, announced his nerves were sadly frayed, and fled to Rome to visit their mother and her new husband.

Josh had spent the first week after Kyle left cajoling an irate banker into giving him an extension on the loan Kyle had taken out. If he'd been a religious man, he'd have offered up a prayer of thanks for the powers of persuasion he'd perfected during his years in Washington. They'd stood him in good stead in his dealings with the local banker, and he'd come away with a sweeter deal than any man with his financial problems could normally have hoped for.

Every waking minute of the last three weeks had been devoted to poring through the damning records of his brother's four years as manager of the family business. He'd spent so much time in the ancient foundry office, days and nights had become indistinguishable, and weeks had evaporated into one endless stretch of smoke and grime. Now he had his facts at hand and was ready to start solving the foundry's problems. Mrs. O'Malley was first on his list.

He stepped from the car, pushed open the gate in the picket fence, and gazed around him with interest. He'd been so engrossed in his problems, he hadn't noticed spring had come to Titusville. Tubs of geraniums marched across Mrs. O'Malley's porch—splashes of scarlet against the stark white clapboard, and the flowers bordering the cobblestone walk were a wild and wonderful profusion of pinks and purples and yellows and reds that gladdened his senses.

With a quiet pleasure he hadn't felt in a long time, Josh lifted his face to the warm sun and soaked up the colors and sounds and fragrances of Mrs. O'Malley's flamboyant little garden.

"Hi."

Startled, he searched for the owner of the voice and spied a small, black-haired girl scrutinizing him from the depths of an old-fashioned porch swing. An orange-and-gray calico cat lay across her lap.

"My name's Megan. What's yours?"

"Joshua Eddington."

"That's a long name to remember."

"Why don't you call me Josh? Most people do."

"Mama says I can't call big people by their first names unless they give me per—" A puzzled frown knit her brow.

"Permission," Josh finished for her. "You have mine."

She favored him with a radiant smile.

"I'd like to talk to your mother, Megan. Is she in the house?"

"Nope. She's mowing the lawn." Josh heard a whirring sound coming from the back of the house.

"It's very important I see her," he explained. "How do I get to the backyard?"

"You have to go through the house 'cause there's a fence, but I'm not allowed to let strangers in." She rolled the cat's silky ear between her thumb and forefinger, a thoughtful look on her small, round face. "Does 'walking through' count for 'letting in?' "

Josh struggled to keep a sober face. "Usually I'd say it did, but I think it's all right in this case. I have business with your mother."

Solemn blue eyes assessed him. "I guess that's okay then." Megan wriggled from under the cat and opened the screen door. Placing her hand in Josh's, she led him through a tiny white-walled living room, complete with braided rugs and a sofa upholstered in a flowered print rivaling the riotous display outside.

Beyond it lay an even smaller yellow kitchen. Two loaves of freshly baked bread lay on the counter and the savory smells seeping from the oven of a vintage stove made Josh remember he'd skipped breakfast and missed lunch. He inhaled deeply and his stomach rumbled with hunger.

Following Megan's lead, he stepped onto the porch and surveyed the fenced backyard. A grown-up version of the child clinging to his hand was plodding methodically back and forth across a small patch of lawn, pushing a mower that looked as if it predated her by twenty years.

Mrs. O'Malley was nothing like he'd expected. She was

small, probably no more than five feet three inches, dressed in faded denim cut-offs and a blue T-shirt that hugged her slender form in all the right places. Her black curls glistened in the sun like polished onyx.

At six feet two, Josh had always preferred tall women. They were more comfortable to dance with and he found it easier to read the thoughts of someone who looked him straight in the eye. Still, he had to admit, inch for diminutive inch, Mrs. O'Malley was the prettiest woman he'd seen in a long time.

That was not sufficient reason for the sudden acceleration in his heartbeat. He'd developed a penchant for sophisticated women during his years in D.C., and this pixie with the bobbing curls and scruffy tennis shoes was no sophisticate. Her face was flushed and beads of sweat ran down her cheeks and dripped off her chin, or were they . . .?

Good Lord! They were tears!

Emotion of any kind embarrassed Josh; emotional females terrified him.

Megan tightened her grip on his hand. "Mama's crying," she said. The tremor in his small guide's voice unnerved Josh even further. He kicked himself for barging in on Mrs. O'Malley unannounced. He was prepared to do anything necessary to save his family's honor and keep them from financial disaster, but that didn't include intruding on a widow's private grief.

He grasped the handle of the screen door, intent on making a quick exit. He'd reckoned without Megan. She had the grip and determination of a miniature bulldog.

"Mama . . ." she called, and her clear, piping voice carried easily above the drone of the mower. "Here's Joss, and he's got biznus."

TWO

At the sound of her daughter's voice, Shayna brought the lawnmower to a halt and swiped at her brimming eyes. Thirty minutes of plodding back and forth had left her hot and disheveled, but she still hadn't stemmed the furious tears which had been flowing since her quarrel with her mother. Something was cross-wired in her brain. Normal people didn't face grief dry-eyed and stony-faced, then degenerate into human waterfalls when their tempers flared.

Squinting through the salty blur, she spied a tall stranger on her back porch, hand in hand with Megan. The late-afternoon sun played across his sun-bleached hair and the strong planes of his tanned face. Her gaze slid to his discreet tie and smoke-gray business suit, which obviously had never hung on the racks of Mueller's Mercantile. Whoever this Viking fashion plate might be, he was not your average Titusville citizen.

A light clicked on in her brain. With sickening certainty, she knew the identity of the elegant stranger. Ronnie's committee must have made quite an impression to bring the new head of the foundry to Loblolly Street.

"Joshua Eddington," he said, extending his hand.

Shayna stared at his beautifully manicured nails, and

25

shoved her own grass-stained paw into the pocket of her cutoffs. After a moment's hesitation, he withdrew his hand.

She raised her eyes to the cool green ones staring down on her. He was so tall, she had to crane her neck to look him in the face. Already he had her at a disadvantage. She groaned. Leave it to Ronnie to stir things up, then leave her to deal with the problem.

A new flood of angry tears streamed down her face. Joshua Eddington's horrified look would have been comical if she hadn't been so embarrassed.

"Who're you mad at, Mama?" Megan sounded close to tears herself. "Mama cries when she's mad," she explained.

"Does she really?" Her visitor's deep voice held a note of relief, and the glint in his eyes looked suspiciously like amusement.

Shayna glared at her informative daughter. "Megan, please go next door to Grandma's for a few minutes."

Megan's lower lip trembled. "I want to talk to Joss."

"Do as your mother says, Megan." The no-nonsense tone in Joshua Eddington's voice ruled out further discussion. To Shayna's amazement, her stubborn offspring obeyed him instantly. The indignant bounce of her small rump was a mute protest, but she didn't voice her usual argument. With a last withering look, she slipped through the break in the hedge and disappeared into her grandparents' yard.

Shayna opened her mouth to ask where this arrogant stranger got off disciplining her child, hiccoughed loudly, and closed it again. Everyone in Titusville knew Kyle Eddington had fired Angus McTavish because he dared to criticize him. No telling what might happen to her father and brothers if she insulted this man.

He pulled a handkerchief from his pocket and handed it to her. "We need to talk, Mrs. O'Malley," he said firmly.

Just like that, in the same tone of voice he'd used with

Megan, and no arguments accepted. Shayna dabbed at her tear-stained face, feeling her ''Irish'' rise at the nerve of the man. She sniffed, wishing she could trade the linen handkerchief for a tissue. She desperately needed to blow her nose.

He held open the screen door. It had been so long since anyone had opened a door for her, the sheer novelty of it sent her bolting through before she realized her mistake. In the confines of her kitchen, he looked twice as grand and she felt twice as grubby.

''Please make yourself comfortable,'' she murmured, pointing toward the living room. ''I'll make some coffee.'' Maneuvering cautiously around the elegant giant, she dashed to the bathroom, scrubbed her hands and her tear-blotched face, and stashed Joshua Eddington's handkerchief in the hamper. How and when she could give it back to him was beyond her.

She returned to the kitchen to find him seated at her battered oak table, looking as out of place as a ten-karat diamond in the Titusville Five and Dime display counter. She should have known he'd ignore her directions.

''This is just fine,'' he said.

It might be fine for him. With his sharp eyes boring into her, every nerve in her body tingled and her strangely clumsy fingers spilled a trail of dark grains across the white-tiled counter when she measured the coffee.

Uttering a silent prayer that just this once her temperamental plumbing would perform properly, she gingerly turned the faucet. It was too much to hope for. An ominous rumbling started deep in the bowels of the ancient sink, but no water emerged.

She gave the spout a resounding whack with a wooden spoon. Still no water. In desperation, she grasped the faucet with both hands and shook it. Like the cry of a wounded animal, air screeched through the pipes and a gush of cold water exploded into the sink and onto Shayna.

"My God!" Joshua Eddington leapt to his feet, grabbed the dish towel off its rack, and thrust it into her hands.

"Ronnie promised to fix that," she muttered, dabbing at her water-soaked T-shirt. Mentally she added yet another item to the list of grievances she planned to present the chairman of the Grievance Committee when next she saw him.

"I hope he knows what he's doing." Joshua Eddington sounded dubious. "This thing looks like it needs an experienced plumber. If I were you . . ."

His voice died away as his gaze dropped from her face and came to an abrupt halt somewhere south of her neck. One corner of his mouth tilted wickedly.

Shayna's cheeks flamed. She could feel the wet fabric of her worn T-shirt clinging like a second skin to the most prominent part of her anatomy. What was left to the imagination wasn't worth considering, but to give the devil his due, Joshua Eddington developed a sudden fascination for the cuckoo clock on the wall above her head.

Shayna, on her part, gave a new meaning to the term "greased lightning." In a matter of seconds, she filled the coffeepot, shut off the traitorous faucet, and retreated into the laundry alcove to wriggle into the not-too-clean sweat shirt she'd discarded earlier in the day. She took a deep breath and straightened her shoulders. Coming out of the alcove was a lot harder than going in.

Joshua Eddington was back at the table, calmly removing papers from his attaché case. The only reminder of the sideshow he'd witnessed was a glint of laughter in his eyes. With such control, he must be a whiz in the political arena. The men in her family would have been rolling on the floor.

A hollow silence pervaded the kitchen. Shayna poured the coffee, furtively studying her guest's face while he leafed through his papers. What she saw shocked her. There were dark smudges under his eyes and lines of fatigue bordered his firm mouth. The rumors of trouble at the foundry must be true, and undoubtedly Ronnie's committee had added to his problems.

He'd said they needed to talk. If that would speed him on his way, she'd gladly talk. She just hoped he planned on initiating the conversation. Like all of Titusville, Shayna had spent her life in the shadow of the Eddingtons. Talking to one of them personally was a little inhibiting.

"I understand you refused an appointment with me." Joshua Eddington frowned. "May I ask why?"

"Your secretary said you wanted to talk about my husband's death. Surely you can understand why I don't wish to discuss that particular subject."

"Possibly a poor choice of words on her part, but you must have realized the proposed scholarship for your daughter was what I had in mind." His left eyebrow lifted slightly. "It was, after all, your brother's idea."

"Unfortunately, Ronnie neglected to discuss it with me," Shayna said stiffly.

"You didn't know about your brother's proposal at the time of the phone call?" His shrewd eyes assessed her.

"No, I didn't. My mother told me about it later."

"I suppose that explains your reaction then." He sounded skeptical. "It doesn't, however, explain why you're bristling with animosity now. Most people would be more receptive to the possible offer of a sizable sum of money."

Shayna took an angry grip on her coffee cup. "You should have called before you drove over," she stated coldly. "I could have saved you the effort. I neither need nor want your money. I'm quite capable of providing for my daughter's education."

Her tight-lipped statement took Josh by surprise. Ten years in Washington had left him with a highly skeptical nature and a keen ability to judge people. He'd instantly recognized the need to keep his back to the wall when dealing with Ronnie Brenegan, but this feisty sister of his was something else. Josh couldn't believe she'd actually turn down an offer if he made one, but if this was a pre-negotiation performance, she was one hell of an actress.

"I can't say I liked Brenegan's methods," he stated bluntly, and watched her cringe, "but I have to agree with him that the foundry management has been somewhat remiss in its treatment of you."

No comment. Mrs. O'Malley's gaze remained riveted on her coffee cup. Accustomed to the fast-talking politicos of the nation's capital, Josh found her silence unnerving.

He leaned across the table, compelling her to lift her gaze. "Run this by me one more time. You're saying if a scholarship were offered your daughter, you'd refuse it?"

"Yes."

"Why?"

"I doubt you'd understand if I explained it to you."

"Try me."

"You'd have to have known my husband," she said quietly. "He was a very special man. Aside from the basic needs of his family, money meant little to him. People meant a great deal." Shadows darkened Shayna O'Malley's lovely blue eyes. "The men he worked with told me how he died. He could have saved himself if he'd let eight others die. He didn't, and the idea of profiting from his sacrifice appalls me."

Josh registered the pain in her voice and discarded any doubts he'd harbored regarding her sincerity. The lady was pretty mixed up, but she meant every word she said. Even with his limited knowledge of psychology, he could see she was suffering from a case of survivor guilt. Someone should straighten out her thinking, but he wasn't that someone. She obviously viewed him with the same distrust he'd sensed in the men at the foundry. In the four years Kyle had headed the family business, he'd turned the name Eddington into the dirtiest word in town, and Josh had been tarred with the same brush the day he took over the position.

He shrugged. He hadn't expected to win any popularity

contests when he took on the job of cleaning up Kyle's mess. At least, where the young widow was concerned, he'd made an attempt to right the injustice done her. He should probably thank his stars she'd turned him down, and leave the lady to her guilt trip. God knows the foundry couldn't pay her. The money would have had to come out of his own pocket.

He returned his papers to his attaché case, cursing the voice inside his head demanding he give it one more try. "Believe it or not, I do understand how you feel," he said, "but it makes very little sense from a practical standpoint. Do you know what a college education costs nowadays?"

"Yes, I do. But I still won't change my mind." A smile played across her expressive mouth. "My priest says the only thing worse than my sinful pride is my unholy stubbornness."

Josh returned her smile with one of his own. "There's another thing to consider," he ventured. "Your ethics are commendable, but it isn't your future you're risking. Surely your husband would have wanted his daughter to have every advantage possible. Any father would."

"My mother's words exactly." She frowned. "Why are you so anxious to give your money away, Mr. Eddington? If you're worried about the Grievance Committee, I'll make certain they know I refused the scholarship you offered."

"I don't give a damn about your brother's committee." Josh scowled at the young woman seated across the table from him. "I'm willing to consider any suggestions they might make, but with or without their cooperation, I'm going to turn the foundry into a viable and profitable business." *Then sell the damn thing to the highest bidder and go back to where I stand or fall on my own merit—not on the collective sins of everyone whose last name is Eddington.*

Josh snapped the clasp on his attaché case. "I don't

suppose it occurred to you I might simply be trying to do the right thing.''

She colored fiercely. "I apologize. I shouldn't have said such a thoughtless thing. I do appreciate your offer. I just don't feel I can accept it and keep my self-respect.''

Josh rose from the table. "I'll leave it open . . . at least for now. Think it over carefully.''

Shayna O'Malley stood and held out her hand. "I will," she said, but the determined tilt to her chin told him she'd made her decision and nothing would make her change it.

He grinned down at her. "I've dealt with some strong-minded women in my time, Mrs. O'Malley, but I'd stack you up against the most stubborn female politician in Washington.''

"Now you sound like Father O'Toole." Laughter lurked in her remarkable blue eyes and tilted her soft mouth.

Josh blinked, suddenly aware of her fingers pressing against his. Blood surged through his arteries. He couldn't remember when the mere touch of a woman's hand had triggered such a reaction in him.

"I'll get back to you after you've had time to consider it more fully," he murmured, wondering what her answer would be if he asked her out to dinner. "In the meantime, I have just one more thing to say.''

"What's that?" She looked puzzled . . . and cautious.

"Stay in Titusville," Josh said gently, shocked by the protective instincts her wary reaction stirred in him. The women in his world never dropped their masks long enough to display such vulnerability.

Her fingers slipped from his grasp. "Why do you say that?''

Josh shrugged, hoping she was unaware of his startling reaction to her touch. "You're much too impractical to survive anywhere else.''

A tender look crossed her face. "Actually, I'm disgustingly practical. I'm just dotty where Tim is concerned. I always have been.''

If she'd slapped him, she couldn't have sobered him faster. His pulse was skittering out of control over a woman still bonded heart and soul to her dead husband. Illogically, that realization only intensified the crazy need he felt to touch her one last time before he walked out of the little house . . . and her life. Luckily, the banging of the kitchen door saved him from his folly.

Megan burst into the room. "I'm hungry, Mama!" She climbed on a stool beside the kitchen counter and opened the cupboard. "I'll set the table. Can Joss stay for supper?''

"Mr. Eddington is a busy man. I'm sure he has important things to do this evening," her mother stammered, "and we're having a very ordinary kind of supper.''

"Pot roast? Pot roast's not ord'nary, is it, Joss?''

The expression on Shayna O'Malley's face could best be described as between flustered and frantic. He knew he should extract her from the hook on which her daughter had hung her. Furthermore, he'd have to be into self-torture to consider hanging around here much longer. Still, the idea was tempting. It had been so long since any woman had stirred his emotions, even frustration was a welcome change.

Glancing around the cheerful little kitchen, Josh considered the alternative—dining alone in a mediocre restaurant and spending another evening with the seemingly endless stack of paperwork involved in rescuing the family's floundering albatross. The decision was easy.

"Nothing that smells that good could be ordinary," he said, watching the color drain from Shayna O'Malley's face.

"You're not serious, Mr. Eddington!''

"I'm always serious, Mrs. O'Malley." He grinned. "You're the impractical one. I'm too expedient to turn down a home-cooked meal. Of course, if I'd be imposing . . .''

"You're welcome to stay for supper, Mr. Eddington."
About as welcome as the bubonic plague.

"However, if you have something else planned for this evening." Her voice sounded pathetically hopeful.

"Not a thing."

His behavior was inexcusable. He knew it and, at the moment, he didn't give a damn.

Josh glimpsed a flash of anger in Shayna O'Malley's eyes. She had a temper. Why that revelation should send his temperature soaring was something he didn't care to explore. He simply knew this emotionally sequestered lady stirred feelings in him he'd almost forgotten existed. The temptation to try to lure her out of that self-imposed shell of hers was more than he could resist.

"Please call me Josh." His smile was charming. Shayna was sure he knew it. He certainly knew how to use it.

"May I call you Shayna? I thought it a beautiful name the minute I saw it on your husband's personnel record."

He was smooth all right. Much as she resented the man, Shayna had to admit to a grudging admiration for the ease with which he adjusted to dining at her kitchen table off plates she'd collected with grocery coupons. Dinner O'Malley style had to be a new experience for this scion of the Eddington empire, but he took it in stride.

The question was, why would such a man want to spend an evening with Megan and her? Unless he simply had an urge to see how the other half lived. Whatever his reason, she'd gladly show the self-assured so-and-so the door if the men in her family didn't work in that blasted foundry of his.

Her impromptu entertaining had been a bit hectic so far. She'd shooed Megan and their guest into the living room while she snatched a quick shower, donned a cotton shift, and made a salad. When she called them to dinner, they'd returned to the kitchen hand in hand. The cocker-spaniel look on Megan's face might have been amusing if her hero worship had been aimed at anyone but Joshua Eddington.

Blond Adonises had never appealed to Shayna. The only man she'd found irresistible had been dark-haired and slight of build. Still, she could understand her daughter's fascination. Josh was handsome, if you liked the type, and he was entertaining. Just watching him was an education. He had none of the rough edges of the Brenegan men or— she felt swamped with guilt at the very thought—Tim. His manners were so perfect, it took her a while to realize the quantity of food he put away made her father and brothers look like pikers.

"Joss has his Sunday clothes on." Megan ogled his silk suit. "Grandma won't let Grandpa eat in his Sunday suit." She popped a piece of meat into her mouth and chewed thoughtfully as she watched their guest butter his fourth slice of homemade bread. "Don't you ever spill, Joss?"

Josh's perfect white teeth clamped onto the thick slab of bread; his face went blank. Shayna smiled to herself. Where was his unflappable poise now? Leave it to Megan to knock his props from under him.

"I think he wears suits like this every day," Shayna explained.

Megan's eyes widened. "How come he doesn't work?"

Shayna stifled a chuckle. She understood her daughter's confusion. The men in her family left for work each morning in clean overalls and returned at night in dirty ones.

A flush crept through Josh's tan. He stared at Shayna, inviting her to solve her daughter's dilemma. She smiled sweetly. *He's the glib talker. Let him answer that one.*

"This is what I work in, Megan."

"Honest?"

"Honest."

Megan's brows drew together in a perplexed frown. "What do you wear on Sunday?'

"Jeans and a sweat shirt mostly."

"Wow!" Megan crossed herself fervently, a perfect imitation of her grandmother. "It's a good thing you don't go to our church. Father O'Toole would have your hide!"

Shayna choked, sending a swallow of coffee down the wrong pipe. "That's one of my mother's favorite expressions," she managed when she finally got her breath.

Josh's hearty laugh boomed through the kitchen.

It was difficult to dislike a man who could laugh at himself. As the evening wore on, she found it even more difficult to believe Josh was an Eddington. She couldn't imagine his haughty brother eating pot roast and homemade bread in her kitchen, but Josh was obviously enjoying it. No one could fake such an appetite. She'd almost forgotten the joy of watching a hungry man devour food she'd cooked.

He removed his jacket and tie when he served dessert. "Now you can spill all you want," Megan proclaimed solemnly. "Shirts wash."

Shayna relaxed. If her daughter could handle Josh Eddington, so could she—and it was just one evening. They'd never see him again. The circles he moved in were a social millennium from Loblolly Street. Furthermore, he was good company. For the first time in ages, she was having fun.

He was amazingly easy to talk to. They talked baseball, one of Shayna's favorite subjects. Josh liked the Yankees and Shayna had been a White Sox fan since age six when her father had taken her to her first major-league game.

They talked books. Shayna had read every volume of fiction and most of the nonfiction in the library Titus Eddington had endowed the town that bore his name. She had first call on any new books the library acquired, and once a month she met Mirabelle Pritchard, the town librarian, for a quiet dinner and a chat about their mutual love. Books.

Her family had never understood her passion for reading, nor unfortunately had Tim. Josh shared it. Shayna watched his eyes glow with enthusiasm as they discussed the latest spy thriller, and shook her head in disbelief. The last thing she'd expected was to find a kindred spirit in an Eddington. The thought so astounded her, she found herself telling him her dream of imparting her passion for books to the schoolchildren of Titusville Flats. It was a dream she'd never told anyone except Mirabelle.

When the cuckoo announced nine-thirty, they were still deep in conversation. Megan usually demanded her share of attention. Tonight she'd seemed content to listen wide-eyed until, long past her usual bedtime, she curled into a sleepy ball on her mother's lap and closed her drooping eyelids.

Shayna buried her nose in her daughter's mop of curls. "The evening's over." She heard the regret in her own voice. "I'll have to put her down while she can still maneuver on her own. She's getting too big to carry."

"Let me take her." Josh swept the drowsy child into his arms. "You lead the way."

Megan snuggled her solid little body into his chest and nestled her head under his chin. Her hair was silky and she had a wonderful small animal smell like—he searched his memory—the stray kitten he'd found in the stable at St. Andrew's Military Academy when he was ten years old. He'd made it a bed in an empty horse stall and fed it on scraps from his meals. For one whole month, the tiny ball of fur had filled all the empty spaces in his lonely young heart. Only Kyle had known he'd cried himself to sleep for nights on end when the creature disappeared. A maudlin display of emotion by a son of one of America's captains of industry was simply not tolerated at St. Andrew's.

He hadn't thought of that kitten in years, nor of the solemn vow he'd made to never care that much about anyone or anything again. Odd it should all come back so vividly now.

Josh followed Shayna down the narrow hall and deposited Megan on the white ruffled coverlet of her bed, next to a scruffy teddy bear. She wound her arms around his neck and planted a sloppy kiss on his chin. "Good night, Joss. Will you come see us again?"

"I will if I can," he said, brushing a curl off her forehead to press his lips to the spot where it had lain.

Standing in the doorway, Josh watched Shayna minister to her sleepy child, and it struck him that no woman had ever touched him with such tenderness. A bewildering longing swept through him, and he consciously acknowledged the truth he had subconsciously recognized hours before. This woman and her small daughter triggered feelings in him he wasn't equipped to handle.

The irony of the situation was ludicrous. He'd set out to prove he could draw Shayna out of her shell and he'd ended up proving his own carefully preserved armor was cracking at the seams.

"Good night, Shayna. I have to leave." His voice sounded thin, unnatural. "Thank you for a great dinner and the best evening I've had in a long time."

Without a backward glance, Josh bolted down the hall to the living room, grimly determined to shake the dust of this emotional steam roller he'd stumbled into. Fast!

Grabbing his jacket and attaché case, he headed for the door. The last thing he heard as he reached for the doorknob was Megan reciting her prayers: ". . . and God bless Joss."

THREE

With her guest gone and Megan tucked in for the night, Shayna found her small house depressingly quiet. She tore through the kitchen—sweeping the floor, washing the dishes, setting the table for breakfast—anything she could think of to stave off the feeling of melancholy gripping her.

She couldn't call what she felt loneliness. This restless, hollow feeling was nothing like the aching despair she'd lived with since she'd lost Tim. It was, she decided, simply the normal let-down after the excitement of entertaining an interesting guest.

Her gaze lighted on the chair where Josh had sat, and she found herself wondering where he was and what he was doing. The man had a compelling magnetism that still lingered in her quiet kitchen long after he had gone.

Shayna smiled to herself . . . remembering. With his quick wit and subtle humor, Josh had offered the kind of mental challenge that made her feel vitally alive, and— she cast a guilty glance at Tim's cuckoo clock—at the same time, he'd made her intensely aware of her femininity.

He hadn't flirted with her, nor made the suggestive remarks she was accustomed to hearing from Ronnie's

39

friends. But once or twice she'd caught him watching her, and his narrowed eyes and slow smile had told her more clearly than words he found her an attractive and desirable woman. She shivered, recalling the heady sense of awareness that look had triggered deep inside her and the guilt that had nagged at her each time the noisy little cuckoo had voiced his objections.

She felt foolish and vulnerable and vastly relieved Josh had left when he did. That easy manner of his had almost made her forget he was an Eddington. All her life she'd heard about the notorious charm of the Eddington men and the misguided women who'd become involved with them. It occurred to her she'd been treated to a lethal dose of that charm tonight. The thought was a sobering one that instantly shocked her back into reality.

He'd said he'd call about the scholarship. When he did, she'd make certain her "no" was definite enough to discourage him from pursuing the matter any further.

She was just about to turn out the lights and go to bed, when she heard someone pounding on her back door.

"Open up, Shayna, right this minute." Ronnie's voice was several decibels higher than normal.

Shayna's heart skipped a beat. There must be trouble at the Brenegans'. Visions of her mother or father lying sick or injured in the little house beyond the hedge raced through her mind. Throwing open the door, she stepped aside as her brother pushed past her into the kitchen. His black hair was tousled, his jeans caked with dirt, his hands and face streaked with grease from one of the old cars that were his passion in life.

"For heaven's sake, Ronnie, what's wrong? And please keep your voice down. Megan's asleep."

"What's wrong? Judas Priest, Sis, look at the clock."

Shayna looked. "It's ten-fifteen," she said, staring in bewilderment at her wild-eyed brother.

"You're damned right it is, and Ma just informed me Joshua Eddington's Mercedes has been sitting at your curb since four-thirty. The woman's a nervous wreck. She's had her eye glued to the window so long she's nearly blind. She even sent Marty to the garage to bring me home."

"Oh, that." Relieved, Shayna leaned against the counter and caught her breath. "Don't ever come barging in here like that again unless there's really something wrong. I think you just took ten years off my life."

Ronnie swiped viciously at a lock of hair which had fallen in his eyes and left a wide swath of grease across his forehead. "Well, that makes us even because I'm short a few years myself after what Ma just told me. First you refused to talk to Eddington; then you entertained the guy for close to six hours. What the hell is going on here?"

Shayna struggled to contain her mounting fury. "To begin with," she said stiffly, "Mr. Eddington was here regarding negotiations you initiated. Did I miss something somewhere along the line? I don't recall your discussing a scholarship with me."

"Yeah, well, I can explain that." Shifting his weight from one foot to the other, Ronnie stood poised like a boxer squaring off at his opponent. "I wanted to get the whole thing set up before I said anything—to spare your feelings. I knew rehashing Tim's death would be tough on you."

"Then why didn't you leave well enough alone?"

"Because I figured you were still too broken up over it to see the possibilities. Tim saved a lot of lives. The guys are still talking about it, especially since he was the last person anyone would peg as a hero."

Shayna gritted her teeth. At times like this, she found it difficult to remember he was the brother she loved.

"Tim's act of heroism is not a salable commodity," she said with icy calm. "The matter is closed."

"Are you out of your mind?" Ronnie banged his fist on the table so hard the dishes rattled.

"Control yourself, Ronnie. You know how upset Megan gets if she's waked out of a sound sleep."

"Don't change the subject, Shayna. I've worked my

tail off to get the Eddingtons to cough up big bucks, and all you're worried about is waking up a five-year-old kid.''

He eyed her suspiciously. ''Just exactly what went on here tonight?''

''Nothing 'went on,' '' Shayna said. ''We talked, we had supper, and then we talked some more.''

''You invited Joshua Eddington to supper?'' Ronnie's face was blank with shock.

''Actually, it was Megan who invited him,'' she said calmly.

''Oh, yeah! Is that supposed to explain why a guy who wears six-hundred-dollar suits and drives a car worth twice my year's wages parked his butt in a crummy little kitchen on Loblolly Street for six hours?''

The fact that the same question had occurred to her made it no more palatable when Ronnie voiced it. ''He said I cooked the best pot roast and baked the best bread he'd ever tasted,'' she declared defensively.

''And you were stupid enough to believe that? Judas Priest, Sis, that city slicker sure knew how to get on the right side of a small-town woman like you. You may think you turned down the scholarship on your own; I think he conned you into it.''

Ronnie glowered at Shayna. ''Your problem is you've been without a man too long—and didn't that sharp dude figure that one out fast! He just paid you a little attention, and bingo! You started thinking with your hormones instead of your head and kissed off the sweetest deal our family's ever had its hands on.''

The anger seething in Shayna rose dangerously close to the boiling point. At any minute she'd start that infernal blubbering of hers unless she got things under control. She took a deep breath. Arguing with her brother was a waste of time. He always turned blockheaded when one of his get-rich-quick schemes crashed and burned.

''Maybe you're right, Ronnie,'' she ground out between clenched teeth. ''A man like Joshua Eddington is pretty overpowering for a woman as naive as I am. Perhaps we should discuss this further.''

"Now you're talking, Sis. Just leave everything to me. The deal's not dead yet. First thing Monday morning, I'll tell Eddington you thought it over and changed your mind." Ronnie paced the small kitchen. "I can outthink guys like him every day of the week and twice on Sunday, and don't think I'll settle for some crummy monthly payments doled out fifteen years down the road. I want a lump sum right now. With the ideas I have, we'll double that money—maybe even triple it—by the time Megan needs it. Hell, the whole Brenegan family may just kiss old Loblolly Street goodbye and move up to The Highlands." His grin was triumphant. "I knew you'd see the light sooner or later."

"Oh, I've seen the light, all right," Shayna said. "Why don't I make a pot of coffee and we can talk about it?" She reached for the can of coffee. "Would you mind turning on the cold water for me? The hot water faucet works, but the cold tap is really giving me trouble."

Ronnie looked sheepish. "I'm going to get around to that," he said, crossing to the sink. He turned the handle. Nothing happened. He turned it again. Harder.

The familiar rumbling started in the ancient pipes and Shayna stepped back a few feet. "You have to grab it with both hands and shake it," she said.

Ronnie pulled a paper towel from the nearby roller and wiped the grease from his hands. Then, grasping the faucet in his strong fingers, he shook it with all his might. The geyser of water which erupted from the rusted tap was everything Shayna could have hoped for.

With a gasp, Ronnie staggered backward. Water dripped off his startled face onto his drenched coveralls. "You did that on purpose," he sputtered.

"You're right. I did," Shayna boasted. "I probably should be ashamed of myself, but I'm not. Because, my dear brother, as far as I'm concerned you're all wet in more ways than one."

She opened the door to the porch. "Now get out of my kitchen and out of my affairs before I'm tempted to tell you exactly what I think of you and your disgusting schemes."

It had been a very satisfactory evening, she decided as she climbed into bed. She'd survived Josh Eddington's impressive charms rather admirably for a "naive small-town woman," and she'd set her scheming brother back on his heels. She dropped into a sound sleep as soon as her head hit the pillow.

It seemed only minutes later that the insistent buzzing of the doorbell jarred her awake. A glance at her bedside clock told her it was five minutes to eight. *Who would be calling at this hour on a Saturday morning?*

The buzzer sounded again . . . and again.

Shayna slid out of bed, struggled into her robe, and padded barefoot down the hall to the living room. Whoever was leaning on her doorbell had better have good reason. With Megan sleeping later than usual after her exciting evening, she'd been enjoying one of those rare sleep-ins that seldom come to a mother of a five-year-old.

She opened the door to a tent-size pair of bib overalls topped by two warm brown eyes and a friendly grin.

"Howdy, ma'am. Hope I didn't wake you." The man on her doorstep had a toolbox in one hand and a large cardboard carton in the other. "I come about the kitchen sink."

"The sink?"

"Yes, ma'am. I'm the plumber."

"I didn't call a plumber."

"No, ma'am. He said you wouldn't be expecting me."

Shayna felt a smile start at her toes and work its way upward. Every time her greedy younger brother got so far out of line she had to step on his toes, he turned right around and did some crazy, endearing thing that made her forgive him instantly. He'd outdone himself this time. The Brenegans were a do-it-yourself family. They never resorted to paying an outsider to make their household repairs. Ronnie must be feeling really contrite to foot the bill for a plumber's services.

Her feet scarcely touched the floor as she led him to the kitchen.

"I got orders to put in a new set of faucets and whatever else you need to bring it up to snuff," he said, lumbering along behind her like a blue-and-white striped Sherman tank.

He surveyed the sink thoughtfully. "Yep, just as I thought. I've worked on enough of these old beasts in The Flats, so I knew right off what to bring."

Shayna reached for her coffeepot. "Let me draw some water from the side that works before you tear it apart." She felt so good about Ronnie's reaction to their set-to, she couldn't keep from humming to herself as she set the coffee on to brew and hurried to her bedroom to dress.

She returned to the kitchen to find the faucets completely dismantled. "It's a good thing I come when I did," the plumber declared. "That pipe was so rusted, one turn of a wrench and it fell apart. You could have had a flood on your hands if you'd let it go much longer."

Shayna poured two cups of coffee and invited the plumber to join her at the table.

"Why, thank you, ma'am," he said, wiping his hands on a strip of terry cloth he pulled from his tool box. "Don't mind if I do, but I think I'll just drink it while I work. Mr. Eddington don't strike me as a man that takes kindly to dawdling, especially when he's paying time and a half."

"Mr. Eddington?" Shayna choked on a swallow of scalding coffee. "What does he have to do with my plumbing?"

"Why, he's the one that sent me, ma'am. Called at six o'clock this morning. Thought at first it was my foreman calling me in for overtime—which I sure could use with things as slow as they are. Nearly jumped out of my skin when I found out it was Mr. Eddington."

"Stop right there!" Shayna leapt to her feet. "Mr. Eddington can't order plumbing done in my house. I won't allow it!"

The Sherman tank sighed audibly. "He said you'd put up a fuss. Said you was a stubborn, pigheaded woman, but if I let you talk me out of fixing that sink, I could come in Monday morning and draw my final pay."

"That's monstrous! He can't do that!"

"C'mon, ma'am. You know better'n that. In this town, an Eddington can do just about anything he wants."

Shayna saw red. "You wait here," she ordered. "I'll call the foundry and get this straightened out."

"Won't do no good. Nobody answers the phones on Saturday." He set his wrench on the counter, his friendly grin fading to a worried frown. "Have a heart, ma'am. I can't afford to get him down on me. I've got a wife and three kids to support . . . and it's time and a half."

Shayna didn't doubt the man who'd so shamelessly wangled himself an invitation to supper would say anything to get his own way, but she couldn't believe the plumber's job was in jeopardy. The trouble was, she couldn't be sure. How could anyone be sure of anything with an Eddington?

From the look on the plumber's face, Josh had him convinced, and she couldn't bring herself to add to the poor fellow's worries. She suspected Josh was counting on that and had purposely made the arrangements on Saturday so she couldn't cancel them.

Shayna clenched her fists in frustration. One way or another, she was going to have to find a way to convince everyone, including Josh Eddington, she was capable of handling her own problems and controlling her own life.

Perilously close to tears, she faced the plumber. "Fix it," she said, "but I want to know exactly what this is going to cost Mr. Eddington so I can reimburse him."

"Yes, ma'am!"

Her defiant gesture was meaningless, of course. When the news got out that Joshua Eddington was arranging for her plumbing repairs, her reputation would be muddier than the worst sump hole in Titusville Flats during spring thaw.

Shayna wheeled around so abruptly, she ran head on into the doorjamb. "Damn," she muttered, and fled down the hall just in time to trip over her sleepy five-year-old emerging from her bedroom.

Megan took one look at her mother's face and burst into tears. "Who're we mad at this time, Mama?" she wailed.

The plumber spent three hours completing the repairs. Megan was an enthralled audience until it came time to leave for her Saturday trip to the park with her grandfather. Shayna, on the other hand, buried her nose in a book and tried to ignore the thumping and banging and tuneless whistling that filled her small kitchen.

He was putting his tools away when Shayna heard her screen door slam. She looked up to find Ronnie, complete with toolbox, standing in her doorway. His hair was neatly combed and his hands and face were clean, but his eyes had the puffy look of a man who hadn't had much sleep.

Shayna's anger instantly melted like a chip of ice exposed to the sun. Despite his many faults, Ronnie Brenegan loved his family, and he'd obviously spent a sleepless night after their bitter argument.

Ronnie's gaze was riveted on the shiny new faucets. He blinked. "Judas Priest, Sis," he said gruffly. "You didn't have to call a plumber. I told you I'd fix the faucet."

The plumber grinned. "Hey, Ronnie. I didn't know Mrs. O'Malley was your sister."

"Hey, Orville." Ronnie's smile was thin. "What're you doing here? I thought you quit doing outside jobs when you started working at the foundry."

"I did. Mr. Eddington ordered me to put in some new faucets for Mrs. O'Malley. Good thing, too. They were in bad shape."

"Eddington!" Ronnie glared at Shayna.

"The faucet erupted yesterday when I was making coffee for him," Shayna explained, wishing she'd had the sense to keep her mouth shut when she caught the look of amazement on the plumber's face.

A strained silence descended on the kitchen. Without a word, Ronnie slammed out the back door, leaving Shayna to usher the wide-eyed plumber out the front.

Returning to the kitchen, she poured herself another cup of coffee and sat down to figure out how to untangle her suddenly complicated life. She stared grimly at her new faucets and the debris the plumber had left behind, imagining the furor erupting in the Brenegan household as Ronnie reported his news.

She hated having trouble with her family. Every one of them, including Ronnie, had stood by her loyally during the three years she'd been so numb with grief that she'd turned off on life. Without their loving support, she'd never have managed to care for Megan and finish her teaching degree.

But now at last she was ready to take responsibility for her own life again, and it was obvious she needed to change her image if she hoped to convince people of that fact. What she needed right now was some straight-from-the-shoulder advice on how to go about it. There was only one person she could count on for that, and she knew exactly where she could find her.

On a spur-of-the-moment decision, Shayna changed to a clean cotton skirt and blouse, combed her hair, and started off in her ancient Ford station wagon toward the Victorian hotel that was Titusville's main tourist attraction.

It wasn't until she was walking through the ornate, high-ceilinged lobby of the picturesque old hotel that she remembered she'd let the plumber get away without giving her that invoice she'd demanded.

FOUR

"This must be mental telepathy. I've been meaning to call you all week." Shayna's best friend, Allison Cartwright, greeted her with an enthusiastic hug at the entrance to L'Accent Boutique, the modish dress shop that opened off the lobby of the Victorian hotel.

"I need a favor," Allison said, clearing a pile of dresses off a mauve-and-gray loveseat so Shayna could sit down and dropping down beside her. "Could you help me write a spectacular lecture for the State Historical Society meeting the third Thursday of next month?"

Shayna smiled at Allison's use of the word "help." Allison never read anything but *Vogue* or *Harper's Bazaar* but for business reasons, she had accepted the presidency of the Historical Society, and maintained her reputation as an avid history buff through the speeches Shayna supplied her.

"We're exploring the personalities of the men who shaped our nation," Allison declared in a pedantic tone of voice. "Do you know anything about those jokers?"

Shayna thought for a minute. "I could work up something on Alexander Hamilton. I did a paper on him my second year in college and I still have my notes somewhere."

"The name sounds familiar." Allison raised a questioning eyebrow. "Was he a biggy?"

"Good Lord, Allison, any sixth-grader could answer that question."

Allison studied her nails. "It isn't what you know . . . but who," she said, obviously alluding to her "friendship" with Edgar Schermerhorn, the owner of one of the town's two banks. Their relationship had opened doors for her that would otherwise have remained firmly closed.

"I'll work up the speech and drop it by," Shayna promised.

"Great. You know, some of that stuff you dig up is actually kind of interesting."

"Thank you," Shayna said drily, glancing around the cluttered shop. "What's been going on here? The place is usually so neat."

"The price of success," Allison drawled. "Business has been so fantastic lately, things have gotten out of control. I'm utterly frazzled."

Shayna took a closer look at her friend. Smudges of mascara rimmed Allison's eyes and her normally sleek platinum hairdo looked like it had been attacked by a malevolent dryer. "Have I come at a bad time?"

"There's no such thing as a good time right now. My contact in New York sent me a shipment last week, and with the country club Founder's Day dinner dance coming up, the women from The Highlands are literally clawing each other over the goodies. I've had a dozen customers already this morning and two more just called to say they're on the way."

Allison tucked her cerise-colored silk shirt into her black leather miniskirt and ran a comb through her hair. Her restless gaze darted to the gilt-framed mirror on the opposite wall. "Good God," she exclaimed, "I could drive a sex-starved raccoon to violence." She pulled a tissue from her pocket and scrubbed off her smudged mascara, then touched up her lipstick.

"There, I'm decent again," she said, smiling at

Shayna. "So, sweetie, what's new in the Flats? I hate to admit it, but I miss the old place."

"Like you miss the measles or a case of flu."

Allison chuckled. Like Shayna, she had been born in Titusville Flats—the only child of German immigrants. But nowadays no one equated the ultrathin, ultrasophisticated Allison Cartwright with plump little Alice Kunkel.

Best friends since first grade, the vast differences in their personalities had only cemented the absolute loyalty Alice and Shayna had always felt for each other. Shayna had married the boy next door and settled down to a life much like her mother's. Alice had worked two years in the New York garment district and married a fast-talking lingerie salesman named Harry Cartwright.

The marriage was a disaster, and Alice finally bought a train ticket back to Titusville. Within a month of her return, she'd talked Edgar Schermerhorn into loaning her the money to open her boutique and had established herself as Allison Cartwright, fashion guru to the style-starved ladies of Titusville Highlands.

Kicking off her pumps, Allison tucked her long legs beneath her and studied Shayna with faintly troubled eyes. "I get the feeling something's bothering you, and it must be serious to lure you to this part of town on a Saturday."

"You always could read my mind," Shayna said, clasping her hands tightly in her lap. "I feel a little silly. Compared to the problems you've seen me through in the past few years, this one is pretty trivial." She hesitated. "I think I have an image problem."

Allison laughed. "No kidding. I seem to remember mentioning that very fact a few times over the years."

"Yes, well, I guess I didn't think much about it until yesterday when this thing about the scholarship came up."

"Scholarship?"

"It seems Ronnie's been badgering the new head of the foundry to set up a college scholarship for Megan as some sort of compensation for Tim's death."

Allison's skillfully penciled eyebrows arched their way

up her flawless forehead. "Another of Ronnie's get-rich-quick schemes, I take it. If he has a hand in it, it's bound to end in disaster." She frowned thoughtfully. "On the other hand, I've always thought you got a raw deal from Kyle Eddington, so maybe that devious brother of yours has finally come up with something that makes sense."

"I'm not asking for advice on the scholarship. I've already told Mr. Eddington I want no part of it. What I need is advice on how to change this 'helpless widow' image everyone seems to have of me."

"You've met Joshua Eddington?"

"Yes. I've met him." Shayna cleared her throat self-consciously. "That's part of my problem."

"You call that a problem?" Allison rolled her eyes. "I know at least a dozen women who'd kill for that particular problem. From what I hear, the gorgeous hunk spends all his time holed up in that blasted foundry."

Shayna could see mentioning meeting Josh had been a mistake. Allison had immediately latched onto that and forgotten everything else.

"There's no justice in this world," Allison fumed. "The most eligible bachelor to hit town in years lives right here in the hotel and I haven't even been able to wangle an introduction to him. You never poke your nose out of The Flats, and he falls in your lap."

"Joshua Eddington lives here?" Shayna glanced nervously at the crowded lobby. "I assumed he lived at White Oaks."

"I guess the hotel is more convenient to the foundry." Allison shrugged. "What the heck, it's all in the family. The Eddingtons own the hotel, too. Titus built it around the turn of the century to entertain steel-industry magnates."

Allison flicked a piece of lint from the back of the loveseat. "Joshua's a mystery. Obviously nothing like his rakehell father and brother. At least, he never looks twice at the bevy of beauties who hang around the lobby waiting for him to show. Quoting one of my customers, 'He's polite as a preacher but slippery as a bar of French soap.' '' Allison yawned widely. "I guess I shouldn't complain. Most of the females who stalk him take out their frustration in the boutique, which is darned good for business."

She studied Shayna's face. "So, how did he strike you?"

Shayna was still trying to decide how to safely answer that question when Allison whispered, "Speak of the devil. There he is now." Her eyes widened. "Oh my God, he's heading for the boutique."

Startled, Shayna glanced up to find Josh striding purposefully toward her. He was dressed in jeans and a short-sleeved white T-shirt and his hair was obviously still damp from his shower. Shayna blinked. He was even more handsome in these casual clothes than he had been in the expensive suit he'd worn the previous evening.

"Shayna? I thought that was you." His rich voice carried above the noise of the lobby. "I was just thinking about you, and you materialized before my very eyes."

"Hello, Josh." Shayna had risen at the sight of his advancing figure, but her knees seemed determined to buckle under her. She braced herself against the couch. Out of the corner of her eye, she saw Allison's mouth drop open.

"What are you doing here?" Josh asked. "Buying a dress? Blue, I hope, to match your eyes." He had that look on his face—the one that had scrambled her insides last evening. She felt an attack of the same malady coming on again.

Shayna swallowed hard. "I'm visiting a friend." She turned to face a goggle-eyed Allison. "I don't believe you've met Mr. Eddington."

"No, I haven't, but I've been looking forward to the pleasure," Allison purred, taking on the sleek, satisfied look of a tabby cat with a plump mouse in its sights.

Shayna glanced surreptitiously at Josh, embarrassed by her friend's less than subtle come-on. The look of bland amusement on his face told her he found nothing odd about Allison's demeanor. Apparently this sort of thing was commonplace at the more sophisticated levels of society.

Within minutes, Allison had drawn Josh into a lively discussion of restaurants they'd both patronized and plays they'd both seen in Washington and New York. Shayna listened silently. She'd been to Washington once on a high school field trip, and Tim and she had spent their honeymoon in New York. The chief thing she remembered about both trips was how glad she was to get home again.

Allison chattered on and on, and Shayna found herself more amazed by the minute. Meeting Josh had certainly brought out the best in her friend. She'd never seen her so animated or so witty. Josh didn't say much, but Shayna could tell he was impressed. Allison was, after all, the kind of woman a man like Josh would enjoy. Shayna found their conversation boring . . . and unaccountably depressing.

"I hate to break this up," Josh said finally, "but I have an appointment at one-thirty." The warmth of the smile he bestowed on Allison could have turned the North Pole into a pile of slush. "I've really enjoyed meeting you."

With a twinge of satisfaction, Shayna watched her sophisticated friend blush like a schoolgirl. Apparently she wasn't the only one bowled over by Josh's smile.

He turned to Shayna. "Have you had lunch? How about joining me? I'm on my way to the dining room for a quick bite, although I can't believe I'm hungry again after that great dinner you cooked last night."

She heard Allison gasp.

The magnetic smile spread across Josh's face again. "If it's all right with you, Allison, I'd like to steal Shayna for an hour or so. We have a lot to talk about."

"Don't ask me," she said stiffly. "Shayna's a big girl now—bigger than I'd realized actually." She directed a meaningful gaze at Shayna. "But do stop back here, sweetie. We never did have that discussion you wanted."

Shayna stared helplessly at her friend. She couldn't imagine why Josh hadn't included Alison in his luncheon invitation. The two of them had gotten along so famously. She was still puzzling over his rude behavior when she found herself being propelled through the crowd of gaping spectators milling about the hotel lobby.

"Josh, you have to stop doing these things," she managed breathlessly.

He looked surprised. "What things?"

"This lunch, for one." She tried to wriggle out of his grasp. "It's more like a kidnapping than an invitation."

He chuckled but retained his firm hold on her arm.

"And the plumber. I'm sure you meant well, but I thought I'd made it clear I don't want charity of any kind. I insist on paying for his services."

Josh stopped dead in the middle of the lobby. "You're joking," he said, managing to sound both innocent and offended. "I usually send flowers to my hostesses, but you made such a point of your practicality, I thought something more sensible seemed appropriate. I see I was wrong. You'd rather have had the flowers, wouldn't you?"

Shayna gave him what she hoped was a chilling look. "You're purposely ignoring my point," she accused, glancing furtively around the suddenly silent lobby. "I want to know what I owe you. I'll send you a check."

"Make it thirty-five dollars, if you feel you must," he grumbled, "but why make such a big thing of it?"

"Have you considered what people will think when they hear you're arranging for my plumbing repairs?" Shayna whispered hoarsely.

"Who's going to know besides you, me, and the plumber?"

"This is Titusville, Josh, not New York or Washington. When someone in the south end of town sneezes, a dozen people in the north end pull out their handkerchiefs."

Josh surveyed the lobby with a look that said he'd just realized they had an interested audience. "I'm properly chastised,'' he said in a booming whisper which ricocheted off the beams above their heads. Grasping Shayna's elbow, he strode toward the dining room. "From now on, I'll be so discreet, even your famous Father O'Toole will approve.''

They stopped in the doorway. Every eye was on them; every fork suspended. The silence hurt Shayna's ears.

Josh placed a possessive hand on Shayna's back. "Hello, Joanne," he said to the hostess. "I certainly hope the chef is at his best today, because I'm having lunch with a very special lady.''

Josh had lingered longer at lunch than he should have. He checked his watch as he drove out of the hotel parking lot and headed for the foundry. He'd be twenty minutes late for his appointment with Angus McTavish, and the dour old Scotsman struck him as a meticulously punctual man.

He'd enjoyed his luncheon with Shayna. She was so honest and upfront. Nothing like that chichi friend of hers, who reminded him of an ad agency executive he'd dated briefly his first year in Washington.

He shouldn't have teased her, but she was such a serious little thing, he couldn't resist it. He chuckled, remembering how she'd lectured him on his lack of social awareness. Much, he suspected, like she lectured Megan when she was in need of reprimand.

He was used to women flirting with him; he'd even had his share of interesting propositions. Shayna was the first to lecture him. He loved it. A frustrated mother complex, he decided. Certainly the woman who'd given birth to him had been anything but motherly. In the last twenty-seven years, Josh had seen so little of his mother, he scarcely remembered what she looked like.

He'd been seven and a half and Kyle six when they were parted from their nanny and introduced to the harsh realities of St. Andrew's Military Academy. Josh had been big for his age and exceptionally strong; Kyle had been small and frail, the victim of every upperclassman bully. By the time his eighth birthday rolled around, Josh had been bloodied a dozen times defending his little brother. The habit was hard to break. At thirty-four, he was still bailing Kyle out of trouble. He only hoped he could persuade Angus McTavish to help him salvage what was left of the family business after this latest fiasco of his irresponsible sibling.

Angus was waiting for him in his office, settled in the leather armchair opposite his desk. His hair was snow white and the deep hollows beneath his cheekbones gave his face a strangely cadaverous look. He was so thin, his flannel shirt and cord trousers hung tentlike on his gaunt frame. Only his eyes retained the same piercing intensity Josh remembered from the days when the crusty old Scotsman had been Hiram Eddington's production manager.

"So, Joshua, you came prepared to work." Angus's hooded gaze traveled the length of Josh's jean-clad figure, and his handlebar mustache twitched with approval. "I haven't seen an Eddington in dungarees since your grandfather died."

Josh doubted Calvin Klein would be thrilled with Angus's description of his designer jeans, but he was glad he'd taken Megan's words to heart. Silk suits and Italian shoes obviously didn't make it as work clothes in Titusville.

He studied the old man anxiously. If Angus accepted his employment offer, Josh's plan to restore the foundry to a condition where he could put it on the market had a chance of succeeding. If not, he hadn't the slightest idea where to go about finding another competent production manager.

"I've given serious thought to your offer," Angus said. "Production manager of a foundry this size is an exacting job. You need a younger man."

Josh's heart sank into his Reeboks.

"But I'll help you put it back in working order, on one condition."

Josh leaned forward eagerly. "I'll agree to anything that's reasonable . . . probably anything mildly unreasonable. You're the only man I know who can do the job."

"My condition doesn't seem unreasonable to me. It may to you." A nerve twitched at the corner of Angus's mouth. "I'll come back, Joshua, if you agree to learn the working end of the foundry business."

Dumbfounded, Josh stared at the man facing him across the desk. "You can't be serious!"

"I can and I am."

"But why? I was perfectly frank with you when we spoke the other day. I want to get the place in shape to put it up for sale. What would I accomplish by learning the foundry trade, except waste your time and mine?"

Angus surveyed Josh through hooded eyes. "Once you get involved, you may decide to keep it and run it yourself."

"Be reasonable, Angus. Why would I do that? I have no aptitude for nor interest in foundry work. I majored in political science, and I've built a successful career as an industrial lobbyist. I like what I do, and I'm damned good at it. I have no intention of changing professions."

"You should have been a foundryman." Angus's mouth had a stubborn set. "It's what your grandfather wanted for you. You were a babe in diapers the first time he brought you to the forge. On your third birthday, we tapped the blast furnace and your young eyes glowed watching that metal flow. 'An ironmaster's eyes,' David called them . . . and with such pride. It was only after he died, those fool parents of yours dared send you off to that stupid military school."

"My grandfather died when I was seven. I barely remember him."

Angus continued as if he hadn't heard a word Josh said. "I apprenticed under your great-grandfather and worked side by side with your grandfather. Two finer ironmasters never lived. It's in your blood, Joshua. You're an Eddington. Don't deny your heritage."

Josh couldn't believe what he was hearing. "Need I remind you it was an Eddington who brought the company to the verge of bankruptcy," he said grimly. "Actually, two Eddingtons. The records show my father was not much better at the job than Kyle."

"Those two weren't Eddingtons. They just had the name," Angus said contemptuously. "You can call a jackass a lion; when push comes to shove, it'll still act like a jackass. The last real Eddington was David, and you're the spitting image of him."

"I may resemble by grandfather physically," Josh admitted, remembering the portrait hanging at White Oaks. "There the similarity ends."

Angus's eyes narrowed. "What about your responsibility to the town your family built? If the foundry fails, Titusville will become a ghost town. There are a lot of fine people living here, Joshua, and you're the only hope they have."

"Damn it, Angus. Don't pull that noblesse oblige stuff on me. I have no ties to this town or the people in it. I've only spent a handful of days here since I was seven—most of them miserable. The fact that Titusville depends on the foundry for survival doesn't automatically cast me in the role of savior. I'll do everything I can to protect the interests of the employees when I sell the place. That's all I can promise."

Angus looked grim. "Isaacson Steel, one of the oldest companies in the Pacific Northwest, was sold to the Koreans," he said. "Loaded the whole plant on barges and shipped it off. A lot of good men lost their jobs. Seattle was big enough to absorb them; Titusville isn't."

"For God's sake, Angus, the chances of someone buying a foundry in Indiana and shipping it to the Orient are pretty slim."

"It could happen."

Choked with frustration at the old man's illogical attitude, Josh rose abruptly and walked to the window. The yard below was cluttered with stacks of rusting iron and broken pallets, and beyond it rose the smoke-blackened building that housed the old forge. Josh couldn't see how any man could become emotionally attached to such a place. Yet, Angus showed the same passion for it that another man might for a beautiful woman.

The old man's sincerity touched Josh deeply. He wished he could be entirely honest with him, but he couldn't bring himself to divulge the extent of the Eddingtons' financial problems to anyone. The ugly truth was, even if he wanted to, he couldn't afford to keep the foundry. His father had wiped out the cash reserves and Kyle had compounded the disaster by taking out loans he had no hope of repaying. White Oaks was mortgaged to the hilt and the bank held a lien on the foundry. He was counting on the sale of both to ensure a sufficient income for his grandmother to live out her days in comfort. He'd already decided both his mother and Kyle would have to fend for themselves from now on.

He squared his shoulders and turned to face Angus. "I have to sell the foundry," he said tersely. "Take my word for it. I have no choice."

"A man always has a choice, Joshua. You've heard my terms. You can choose to accept them or reject them."

With obvious effort, he heaved himself from the chair. "Walk with me through the foundry before you make your decision," he pleaded. "Look at it through my eyes. She's a grand old girl with a proud history. She turned on your father and that fool brother of yours because they treated her like a whore. Treat her like a lady and she'll give you more satisfaction than you've ever dreamed of."

Josh couldn't bring himself to refuse the old man. "I'll walk with you," he said wearily, "but nothing you can show me will change the fact that I have to sell the place."

He faced Angus squarely. "And as for my learning the foundry trade, I'm afraid that's impossible. I've arranged for a six months' leave from my work. That's all the time I can spare and you can hardly expect to turn me into a foundryman in that length of time."

"Six months!" Angus's eyes burned fiercely in his weathered old face. His mouth twisted in a brief, sardonic smile. "On the contrary, Joshua. It just so happens that is the exact amount of time I had in mind."

FIVE

A lonely sliver of moon hovered in the sky above Loblolly Street and the first tentative stars dappled the black fabric of evening. The day had been unusually warm, more like July than May, and the night was fragrant with the scents of summer.

Shayna slumped onto the pillows of the old porch swing and wriggled her bare toes against the dusty, heat-soaked wood beneath her feet. She inhaled deeply, savoring the earthy aroma of the geraniums lining the porch railing and the sweet fragrance of the ancient honeysuckle rambling up the corner post.

Usually these familiar scents were comforting; tonight they simply intensified the restless longing clawing at her heart. She'd neither seen nor heard from Josh in the week since their luncheon date. Not that she'd really expected to. Her black mood had nothing to do with him . . . she told herself.

From the humid darkness around her rose a symphony of night sounds—the chirring of crickets, the raspy croak of a frog beneath a neighbor's sprinkler, the tap, tap, tap of old Mr. Abernathy's cane as he passed on his evening walk.

A clamor of voices next door told her the Brenegans'

Saturday-night poker game was in full swing. Somewhere a car door slammed, a gate clicked—and weaving through it all, the insistent memory of Josh's parting words: "I want to see you again, Shayna. It's time you rejoined the living. You've dwelt too long with death."

She knew he was right. She'd reached the same conclusion on her own some time ago. Still, she hadn't been ready for her disturbing reaction to his challenge. Remembering it, her body throbbed in ways she'd thought it had long forgotten . . . and her conscience nagged her. Taking up living again was one thing; forsaking the memory of Tim's beloved face to daydream about a stranger who'd paid her a little attention was another thing entirely. She shivered, repelled by the thought there might have been a grain of truth in Ronnie's disgusting claim she'd simply been without a man too long.

Whatever the reason, Josh had indelibly stamped his image on her mind in the few hours she'd spent with him. Time and again during the past week, she'd imagined she'd seen him crossing a street or entering a shop in a part of town he'd have no reason to visit. It was all so silly and pointless . . . and her eyes were playing tricks on her again. She could swear he was walking up the steps onto her porch.

"Hi!"

Shayna bolted upright, staring in disbelief at the jean-clad figure in the pool of light beneath her porch lamp. "You're real! I thought I was imagining you."

"I'm sorry. I didn't mean to startle you." He sounded hesitant—even apologetic. This was a completely different Josh from her devilish luncheon companion.

He grinned sheepishly. It had been exactly one week since he'd seen Shayna, and he'd spent a good portion of his waking hours thinking about her. Lately, she'd even begun invading his dreams.

The last time he'd acted this foolish about a woman, he'd been sixteen and too young and inexperienced to know better. He could claim neither at thirty-four, and between this emotional insanity that gripped him and the fact that, against his better judgment, he'd finally agreed to Angus's asinine proposition, it had been a hellish long week.

A dozen times he'd picked up the phone to call Shayna, then talked himself out of it. He'd even dialed her number tonight before leaving the foundry. But, remembering her look of dismay when he'd said he wanted to see her again, he'd slammed down the receiver and headed for home.

He'd made it as far as the entrance to the hotel, but before the doorman could open his car door, the Mercedes had taken off on its own, executed an illegal U-turn in the middle of Main Street and headed for The Flats.

"I remembered those flowers I didn't send you," he said, thrusting a bouquet of droopy yellow tulips at her, "but the florist was closed. I found these at a supermarket. I'm afraid they're somewhat the worse for wear."

Shayna swallowed the massive lump in her throat. The last time a man had given her flowers had been her wedding anniversary, a week before Tim was killed. She stared at the dilapidated bouquet and her eyes filled with foolish tears. She could have survived the sterile perfection of flawless blooms. These sorry tulips undid her. They looked as lonely as she felt, and so did the man who held them.

"Thank you." Her voice sounded strange and scratchy, as if it belonged to someone else.

Josh pulled a miniature Raggedy Ann doll from his pocket and handed it to Shayna. "I suppose Megan's asleep. It's a little late to come calling."

"I'm glad you did. I was lonely." Shayna heard the words. She couldn't believe she'd actually said them.

Josh's mouth twisted in a brief, crooked smile. "It's that moon. It's the loneliest damn moon I've ever seen." He frowned. "I received your check for the plumbing work. I wish you hadn't felt it necessary, but I suppose you had your reasons." His gaze fell on the porch swing, and he abruptly changed the subject. "I've always wanted to sit in one of those things. Until I saw yours, I didn't know they still existed.''

"This one has existed over fifty years. It belonged to my grandmother,'' Shayna said, happy to drop the embarrassing subject of her plumbing. She touched the faded canvas lovingly. ''I've spent many a summer evening in this swing listening to her stories about the old country.''

Shayna watched Josh settle his tall frame into the worn cushions. ''Megan will love the doll,'' she said softly. ''Raggedy Ann is one of her favorite story-book characters.''

The lump had risen again, and she swallowed self-consciously. Murmuring something about putting the flowers in water, she fled into the house. She needed a minute to recover from the shock of facing the man who had dominated her thoughts for the past seven days. She was treading dangerous water here. If she had an ounce of sense, she'd politely send him on his way. But tonight her good sense was a casualty of the crescent moon and the loneliness she shared with the man who waited on her porch.

She found a vase and set the flowers on the television next to her wedding picture, pulled her white cotton shift on over her shorts, and poured two glasses of lemonade.

Josh smiled as his fingers closed around the frosty glass. ''This isn't real, you know,'' he said, sliding over to give her room to sit down.

She sank onto the seat beside him. ''It's real. I hate frozen lemonade. I always start from scratch.''

His grin widened. ''I wasn't referring to the drink. I meant this.'' His glance roamed the porch. ''This looks like the set of an old Judy Garland movie. Real people stopped drinking lemonade in porch swings fifty years ago.''

''Maybe in Washington, D.C. It's still a favorite summer pastime in Titusville.'' She paused. ''Titusville Flats, that is. I doubt there are many porch swings in The Highlands.''

Josh stretched his long legs and sighed contentedly.

"They don't know what they're missing." He took a sip of lemonade and stared thoughtfully out at the darkened street. "I've been meaning to ask, where are the pine trees?"

"Pine trees?"

"Loblolly Street. It's an unusual name. I assumed it was named for the Loblolly pine."

Shayna laughed. "You mean like White Oaks is named for the trees on your estate? Nothing so grand as that. We're a practical lot here on The Flats."

He looked puzzled. "The word 'practical' crops up in our conversations frequently, but I can't imagine how it relates to this one."

"Have you ever looked up 'loblolly' in the dictionary?"

"No."

"There are two definitions. The first is a southern pine tree; the second a mudhole."

Josh chuckled. "Mudhole Street? You're kidding."

"No, I'm not. That was the original name. With good reason, too. It's blacktopped now and there's a sidewalk, but fifty years ago it was dirt, and every spring, when Titusville Creek overflowed, it turned into a sea of mud.

"Your grandfather, David Eddington, was stuck with a lot of houses no one would buy, so my grandfather, Sean Brenegan, talked him into deeding him this house and the one next door if he could solve the drainage problem. It took Grandpa a year of figuring and three more of digging every minute he wasn't working at the foundry, but he did the job, and the Shanty Irish Brenegans became property owners."

"Your grandfather must have been quite a man."

"That he was," Shayna agreed. "But then, I've heard the same said about your grandfather more than once."

Josh nodded, remembering Angus's praise of David Eddington. "And how did Mudhole get changed to Loblolly?"

Shayna smiled. "That was my grandmother's doing. She saw the word in a crossword puzzle and decided it sounded more refined than Mudhole. Everyone in The Flats signed her petition, but the City Council wouldn't approve the name change, so Grandma tore down the street sign and put up her own. The city finally gave in. There wasn't much point in holding out against a woman as stubborn as Eileen Brenegan.''

Josh's laugh was deep and rich. ''Somehow I find that easy to believe, having met her granddaughter.''

A companionable silence enveloped them. Shayna waited for Josh to speak. She'd been chattering long enough about her Irish ancestors.

''That was a wonderful story, Shayna. Our families go back a long way, don't they?''

''Most of the families in The Flats go back three or four generations,'' Shayna said, ''And they all depend on the Eddington Foundry for a living.''

''Except the fiercely independent Shayna O'Malley.''

Shayna shook her head. ''If things went bad at the foundry, Titusville would become a ghost town and all the families would have to move away. That would put an end to my dream of teaching here. One way or another, what happens to the foundry happens to us all.''

Josh felt a chill travel his spine. It was uncanny how closely Shayna's words echoed what Angus had said. ''You're the second person to point that out to me,'' he said uneasily. ''It's a little unnerving.'' He drained the last of his lemonade. ''I'm beginning to realize how little I know about this town and the people who live in it.''

''Didn't you grow up at White Oaks?''

''Kyle and I were born there and I vaguely remember living there when my grandfather was alive.''

Josh toyed with his empty glass, then set it on the wicker table beside the swing. ''I was sent to military school when I was seven, from there to prep school and college.'' He stared into the darkness. ''By then, I had no emotional ties to White Oaks, or any other place for that matter. Since I had no interest in the family business, there was no point in coming back here.''

"But now you're back."

"Now I'm back." He almost added "for six months," but common sense warned him to keep his plan to sell the foundry a secret for as long as possible. He was used to keeping secrets; they were his stock in trade. Why keeping this particular secret from this particular lady should bother his conscience was something he didn't care to examine. He quickly changed the subject. "I think you're very lucky to have grown up in a family like the Brenegans."

There was nothing in Josh's tone of voice that asked for sympathy. Yet, remembering her own happy, love-filled childhood, Shayna found herself wondering what kind of parents would send their two small sons away from home to be raised by strangers.

She studied Josh's strong profile. The light from the window played across his chiseled features and turned his hair a deep burnished gold. Just for a moment, she caught a glimpse of the lonely little towhead this sophisticated man must once have been. She clasped her hands tightly in her lap, stifling the urge to brush her fingers through his thick thatch of hair.

Josh turned to look at the young woman sitting beside him. The light behind them shimmered in her silky black hair and cast shadows along the delicate curve of her cheek. She was incredibly lovely. Not even the most vivid picture he'd conjured up during their week apart could compare with the real Shayna.

He breathed in her unique fragrance. The women he knew wore Joy or Poison. Shayna smelled like fresh-baked bread and lemonade. The mixture was unbelievably exciting, and the look in those intriguing eyes of hers . . . tender. She was looking at him with the same tenderness he'd glimpsed when she'd cradled her sleepy child in her arms.

There was a magic about this woman that soothed his jaded soul and melted some of the chunks of ice he'd carried deep inside him for so long.

He wanted to kiss her. Sweetly. Chastely. A-girl-in-a-white-dress kind of kiss. He wanted to taste the magic. He'd never really believed in it before.

Josh slid his arm along the back of the swing, and his skin tingled where it touched her bare shoulder. The longing to feel her in his arms was so acute, it shocked him. He'd had his share of relationships, most of them pleasant, but he'd long ago quit kidding himself they were based on anything more than the mutual needs of two people thrown together by chance. Lately, he'd grown so bored with the whole dating process, he'd all but given it up. Some of his friends had even accused him of being old beyond his years. This small-town woman made him feel young again . . . brand-new and hopeful.

Shayna turned her head and stared directly into the face of the man sitting beside her. The solitary little boy she'd glimpsed a moment before had disappeared. The eyes that looked into hers were those of a lonely man, and the hunger she saw there was the same hunger she felt gnawing at her own soul.

Josh's arm settled around her shoulder and tiny electrical shocks ricocheted down her spine, purging every thought from her mind. Guilt, caution, the innate shyness of her nature were swept aside like flecks of dust before an advancing broom.

She wanted him to kiss her.

For three interminable years she'd lived with grief and death, and the sensuous mouth poised above hers pulsed with life. If only for a moment, she wanted to lose herself in the sweet, mindless passion of that life.

She felt his hand cup her face—watched his mouth descend toward hers until she could bear to watch no longer. Eyes closed, she waited.

His kiss surprised her. She'd expected it to be aggressive and demanding. The lips that brushed hers were feather-light, indescribably gentle. Like his sorry flowers, Josh's tenderness shattered her heart.

Slowly, tentatively he deepened the kiss, until her lips parted in wonder at the sensations coursing through her.

He responded instantly to her unconscious invitation. With an expertise that left her gasping for breath, he launched a sensual exploration of her lips, her tongue, all the secret, sensitive places in her mouth she hadn't even known existed until he discovered them. She'd never imagined a kiss could offer so much—or ask so much in return.

Finally, just when she was certain her thundering heart would burst through her rib cage, he raised his lips from hers and planted a fleeting kiss on each of her closed eyelids.

"Open your eyes, Shayna. Look at me. Tell me I didn't imagine what just happened between us."

She couldn't look at him. She was way out of her depth with a man like Josh. His kiss had proved that. If he looked into her eyes, he'd see the devastation he'd wrought.

For the first time in her life, she was painfully aware of how inexperienced she was concerning the physical relationship between men and women. Tim and she had taught each other everything they knew about lovemaking, mostly by shy experimentation as they grew up together. She remembered kisses as sweet and fun and pleasantly exciting. No one had ever told her a man's lips could send such currents of desire racing through her, she'd feel her skin melting off her bones.

"Say something, Shayna." Josh's voice sliced through her jumbled thoughts like a rapier. His fingers tightened on her arms.

Her bewildered eyes opened and stared into his.

Then she heard it. The tap, tap, tap. Mr. Abernathy returning from his walk. She yanked free of Josh's hands and pressed herself into her corner of the swing.

"Evening, Shayna."

"Good evening, Mr. Abernathy."

"Fine spring evening. Warm for May."

"Yes, sir."

"Who's that with you? Can't see as well as I used to."

Shayna hesitated, staring at Josh's taut face. "This is Josh, Mr. Abernathy."

"Josh?" He sounded puzzled. "Do I know him?"

"I don't think so."

"How do, young fellow. That's a fine young woman you're sitting with on that swing."

"I know that, sir." Josh's eyes searched her face.

"That your fancy car parked out front?"

"Yes, sir."

"Paid for, I hope."

"Yes, sir."

"Humphhh! Got a 1932 Packard myself. Been close to twenty years since I've driven it, but it's still in tiptop shape. You want to see a fine car, you get Shayna to bring you over some time."

"I'd like that, sir."

"Humphhh! Be on my way then."

An uneasy silence descended on the porch as the rhythmic tapping receded along the sidewalk. Finally Josh spoke. "Why didn't you tell him who I was?"

"I did." The lie caught in her throat.

"My name is Eddington, Shayna. Is there some reason why you couldn't tell him that?"

"No . . . yes. I didn't know how to explain you to Mr. Abernathy. He wouldn't expect someone like you to be sitting on my front porch."

"Someone like me?"

"An Eddington. For heaven's sake, Josh, Eddingtons don't make social calls on Loblolly Street."

An angry frown formed between Josh's eyebrows. "Your Victorian social strictures are a little out-of-date. For God's sake, this is the late twentieth century."

"Maybe elsewhere; not in Titusville. We're that holdover from the last century called a company town . . . and the Eddington Foundry is the company." The blood throbbed in her temples and her mouth felt dry, but she had to say it. "The Eddington men have a reputation for playing around on The Flats, and I . . ." The words twisted around her tongue.

"Is that what you think I'm doing, 'playing around on The Flats,' as you so quaintly put it?"

"Right at this moment, I don't know what I think."

He searched her face. "Then go with what you feel."

What she felt was naive and vulnerable and painfully confused. She didn't know how to be coy. Her only defense was her honesty. "I think you know a lot more about this sort of thing than I do," she said. "At least, I've certainly never been kissed like that before." She gulped. "I think where you're concerned, Josh Eddington, 'going with my feelings' would be only slightly less dangerous than putting a gun to my head."

She startled him. He wasn't used to such honesty. The women he dated in Washington dealt in the amusing half-truths of accomplished flirts. Shayna's simple directness disarmed him, left him feeling fiercely protective, yet strangely vulnerable. He wasn't sure he liked the combination.

Josh rose abruptly. His racing pulse warned him it was time to beat a quick retreat. Shayna slid from the swing to stand beside him. He gazed down at her upturned face, conscious of the heavy tightening of his body, of the sweet, lingering taste of her still tantalizing his senses. If she thought her emotions were in a turmoil, she should try coping with the mess inside his head.

Play it cool, he told himself. *Keep it light and get out of here while the getting's good.*

"Your virtue is safe, Shayna," he murmured, tracing a teasing finger down the bridge of her nose. "How could I possibly have wicked designs on a woman whose head barely reaches my shoulder? I'd have to stand you on a box whenever I wanted to kiss you."

He leaned over, planted a quick kiss on her forehead, and strode down the steps to the powerful car parked beyond the neat picket fence . . . before the bewildering emotions she stirred in him shattered what little willpower he had left.

Shayna stared in confusion at Josh's retreating figure. He was the most bewildering person she'd ever encountered. One minute he was kissing her silly; the next he was tweaking her nose and practically calling her a midget.

Her temper flared. Everything about the man infuriated her. He was impossibly moody, he was arrogant, and he apparently thought that because he was one of the exalted Eddingtons, he could tear through her life like a rampant tornado whenever he took the notion.

Well, enough was enough. She'd had it with his embarrassing luncheons and his faucets and his ridiculous flowers. In the future, Mr. Joshua Eddington was going to have to find another way to amuse himself, because Mrs. Shayna O'Malley was definitely declaring herself off-limits.

SIX

Shayna crumpled her napkin, placed it beside her plate, and stared defiantly at the group of people assembled around the Brenegans' Sunday-afternoon dinner table. She'd suspected something was up the minute she'd recognized Grandma Brenegan's ironstone plates and the silverware Maggie had collected with Betty Crocker coupons. Such finery was usually reserved for Thanksgiving and Christmas. When she'd spied the place set for Father O'Toole, she'd grown even more uneasy, and the miserable half hour she'd just endured had proved her suspicions well founded.

Her mother had no sooner cleared the dessert plates from the table and sent Megan out to play than she'd launched into a dramatic recitation of her version of the "scholarship affair" for Father O'Toole's edification—ending with a tearful plea to the good father to "pound some sense into her pride-poor daughter's stubborn head."

"The decision is mine to make." Shayna's quiet words broke the silence that had followed her mother's theatrical tirade.

Father O'Toole leaned forward on his elbows, his fingers laced together pyramid-style. "I understand how you feel, Shayna, but I also see your mother's point." His brows drew together in a frown. "We have discussed this matter of your pride before, my child. Perhaps you are indeed letting it blind you to the practical advantages Megan and you would enjoy from the Eddingtons' financial assistance."

"Aha!" Maggie pointed an accusing finger at Shayna.

"Control yourself, Maggie. Shayna's right. It's her decision to make." John Brenegan's troubled eyes sought his daughter's. "Just make certain you think this thing through carefully, sweetheart, before you burn all your bridges."

"I wouldn't worry about Shayna burning any bridges, Pa. She has bigger fish to fry than a measly scholarship." A nasty smile spread across Ronnie Brenegan's handsome face. "You surprise me, little sister. I never figured a prude like you to make a play for a guy like Eddington."

"What's that supposed to mean?" John Brenegan leveled his gaze first on Ronnie, then Shayna. All eyes in the room followed suit.

Shayna winced. "I don't know what he's talking about."

All eyes shifted back to her brother.

"To begin with, Eddington's Mercedes was parked at Shayna's house for six hours last Friday night."

Maggie scowled at her youngest son. "You know very well he came to talk about the scholarship." She transferred her black look to Shayna. "Not that any good came of it."

"That must have been some talk," Ronnie muttered. "Eddington got Joe Feeney out of bed the next morning to put a new set of faucets on Shayna's kitchen sink. I didn't say anything; I've just been waiting for the fur to fly when Ma saw them." He scowled at his mother. "What happened, Ma? You usually don't miss such things."

"I haven't been in Shayna's kitchen. With the nice weather we've been having, she's carried our coffee outside each morning." Maggie's eyes widened with dawning comprehension. "Shayna . . .?"

"My plumbing exploded when Josh was sitting in my kitchen," Shayna stammered, and watched Father O'Toole's eyebrows shoot skyward. "I reimbursed him for the plumber's services," she added quickly.

"Are you also planning to reimburse him for that fine lunch he bought you?" Ronnie's voice was heavy with sarcasm. "Or was he paying you back for the dinner you cooked him?"

"Lunch? What lunch?" Maggie shrieked. "Nobody told me anything about a lunch."

Ronnie tipped back his chair and cast a smug look around the table. "Guido Santini's sister slings hash in the hotel dining room, and she told him the two of them waltzed in, sweet as you please, last Saturday for a cozy lunch at Eddington's private table."

"God in heaven!" Maggie's horrified whisper punctuated the stunned silence following Ronnie's recitation.

Shayna flushed hotly. "I can explain that. I was in Allison's boutique and he came in . . . ." Her voice trailed off as she read the skepticism on the faces turned toward her.

"I don't believe I'm hearing this." Maggie clasped a hand to her heaving bosom.

"Believe it, Ma, and I can't wait to hear Shayna explain why Eddington's car was parked at her curb until all hours again last night." Ronnie stared sullenly at Shayna. "I know what you're thinking, little sister, but I wasn't spying on you. I just stepped outside for a smoke when we had a break in the poker game. A car like that is hard to miss on Lobolly Street."

Shayna heard a collective gasp round the table.

"We were talking," she stammered, "about . . . things."

"Talking? You could have fooled me. Sure looked like a clinch from where I was standing."

Dumbfounded, Shayna stared into her brother's knowing eyes. Ronnie and she rarely agreed on anything, but he was family, and she'd never questioned her love for him. At that moment, she was close to despising him.

She drew a painful breath. She'd tossed and turned into the wee morning hours remembering that wondrous kiss of Josh's and she'd promised herself such a thing would never happen again, but not once had the idea entered her head that there had been anything cheap or degrading about the experience as Ronnie's ugly words implied.

Her cheeks burned with anger and humiliation. She wanted desperately to turn and run, but she gritted her teeth and held her ground, unwilling to give Ronnie the satisfaction of seeing how deeply he'd hurt her.

Maggie Brenegan slammed the flat of her hand on the table, sending the teaspoon by her plate spinning to the floor. "What do you have to say for yourself, miss? Carrying on like that . . . and poor Tim scarcely cold in the ground." Her voice sank to a horrified whisper. "What are you thinking of? The man will never marry you. People like the Eddingtons don't marry iron workers' daughters."

Martin Brenegan pushed back his chair. "Judas, Ma, Tim's been dead three years, and nobody's talking about marrying anyone."

"Marty's right. I'm sorry I brought it up." Ronnie raised his hands in a conciliatory gesture. "What the hell, Sis. I guess I can't blame you for going for the main chance. Everyone knows Kyle's romps in the hay have cost the Eddingtons a bundle, and it's no secret old Hiram set Hilda Kleghorn up for life before he died. The Eddingtons are all fools where women are concerned. If you play this one close to the chest, you could come out with a lot better deal than I'd planned to get you."

"So help me, Ronnie, if you say one more word, I'll cram it down your throat." Martin Brenegan's usually placid face was suffused with angry color. He raised his massive fist and glared menacingly at his brother. "Have you gone completely loony? Suggesting such a thing! And in front of our priest, too."

A flush spread across Ronnie's face. "Don't get your tail in a knot, Marty." He shrugged. "What's everybody looking at me for? I'm not the one playing patty-cake with Joshua Eddington."

For one moment, everyone remained frozen in shocked silence. Then they all started talking at once.

"What will the neighbors say when this gets around?"

"Damn it, Sis. You have enough sense to know a guy like Eddington only comes down to The Flats for one reason."

"He'll bring you nothing but unhappiness, sweetheart, and God knows you've had enough of that."

"My child, the man isn't even a Catholic. The Eddingtons never are."

Shayna choked back an angry sob. When her Irish was up, she could match the rest of her family shout for shout, but she gritted her teeth and remained silent. Her feeling of betrayal was so profound, she knew if she let herself utter one word, she would say things far too vicious to retract.

She forced herself to calmly rise to her feet, turn her back on the chattering group, and walk through the door Megan had left standing open. The shocked silence behind her told her she'd chosen the right method of bridling the volatile Brenegans, but nausea coiled in the pit of her stomach. For the first time in her life, she felt like a stranger in the midst of her own family.

Pushing through the gap in the hedge, Shayna made her way to the blessed sanctuary of her own kitchen. Like the arms of a loving friend, its shabby familiarity closed about her, soothing the ache in her battered heart.

A shaft of sunlight glinted off her shiny new faucets, and shadows played over the chair where Josh had sat on his first visit to Loblolly Street. She remembered the passion with which he'd discussed the books he loved and the music that stirred him. She remembered his beautiful manners and his quick humor and his fascinating stories of the kind of world she'd never see. In the short time she'd known him, Josh Eddington had stretched her horizons beyond the narrow limits of her mundane, everyday life. For that alone, she would always be grateful to him.

Still, she wouldn't see him again. In the unlikely event he kept his promise to call her, she'd politely but firmly put an end to this improbable friendship of theirs. Because, of course, everything her family had said about the dangers of becoming involved with a man like Josh Eddington was all too true.

She closed her eyes, allowing herself one last tantalizing memory of his kiss. The very thought of it turned her knees to water. It had been like nothing she'd ever before experienced; she doubted she'd ever encounter anything even remotely like it again.

Ronnie and his ugly insinuations be damned. She would never regret that kiss.

The sound of the doorbell jarred her from her ruminations. She was tempted to ignore it, but she suspected it was Father O'Toole, and she couldn't bring herself to be rude to the man who had always been there for her in the terrible months after Tim's death.

To her surprise, she opened the door to an elderly neighbor she knew to be a security guard at the foundry.

"How do, Shayna," he said, staggering under the weight of the large wooden box he was carrying.

He set the unwieldy object down just inside the door. "Makes no sense to me," he remarked, "but Mr. Eddington said you'd know what this fool thing is for." He adjusted his glasses on the bridge of his nose and peered downward, a befuddled expression on his face. "Looks empty to me."

Shayna's gaze followed his, and her heart nearly stopped beating when she remembered Josh's remark about having to stand her on a box to kiss her.

"It isn't," she murmured, tracing a nervous finger across the varnished wood and circling one of the brass screws that locked its sturdy sides in place. "It's full of trouble."

* * *

Ten minutes after he'd dispatched the guard with that stupid box, Josh had sorely regretted his foolish idea. He was still regretting it Monday morning as he parked his car on Main Street and walked toward Mueller's Mercantile. Such horseplay might seem amusing to his friends in Washington, but God only knew what Shayna would think of it.

If he were one of Father O'Toole's flock, he'd be tempted to light a candle or whatever it was they did to pour oil on troubled waters. For, sometime during the sleepless night he'd just put in, he'd come to realize he cared very much what Shayna thought. The realization was a sobering one. Almost as sobering as the knowledge that the kind of feelings she triggered in him could drive a perfectly sane man to do irrational things.

That kiss they'd shared was what had pushed him over the brink. It had literally knocked him senseless, and he'd be damned if he knew why. He was certainly no novice when it came to kissing . . . and he'd kissed women who knew a lot more about the technique than Shayna. But never before had the mere touch of a woman's lips sent such a torrent of emotions ripping through him that he'd lost a night's sleep.

Just exactly what he could or would do about these newfound emotions, he wasn't yet sure. The only thing he was sure of was that, one way or another, he was going to see a great deal more of Shayna O'Malley before he left Titusville.

He found himself smiling at the pleasant possibilities that idea conjured up . . . until he came to a stop in front of Mueller's Mercantile and remembered the reason for his early-morning shopping trip.

Levis, flannel shirts, and steel-toed boots were not items he'd planned to add to his wardrobe, and he seriously doubted wearing them was going to fool anyone into thinking he knew his way around the working end of a foundry. Yet, here he was shopping for those very things, thanks to a bargain he'd been forced to make because a stubborn old Scotsman had him pinned to the wall.

Josh cast a disgruntled look at the grime-encrusted two-story brick building which housed the mercantile. It had probably been an elegant addition to Main Street in its day. Now, like most everything else in Titusville, the elaborate cornices and leaded-glass revolving door were merely sad reminders of times past.

The cluttered window fronting the store was filled with a hodgepodge of bed linens, pots and pans, terry-cloth towels, and a foot-high stack of mustard-colored books entitled *Fanny Farmer's Cookbook*. Two mannequins in faded cotton dresses stood at the back of the display. One was minus an arm and the wig on the other was askew. In the center of the window, on a small gate-legged table, sat a framed photograph of a smiling young soldier in battle fatigues. A thin film of powdery dust covered the whole sad collection.

Josh took a deep breath, pushed his way through the revolving door, and stepped straight into early twentieth-century Americana. The worn plank floor, the hurricane lamp chandeliers, the copper cylinder that zoomed along an overhead wire to the cashier's cage were all 1920's vintage or older—and the massive comptometer clanking away on the open balcony looked like one he'd seen in the Smithsonian.

He stopped just inside the entrance, intrigued in spite of himself by this holdout from the age of high tech. There was something about the place . . . He had an eerie feeling this was not the first time he'd stood in this spot.

Resolutely ignoring the prickling sensation traveling his spine, Josh studied the layout of the first floor to get his bearings before plunging into the jumble of merchandise. Except for the shoe department, which was defined by a circle of wooden chairs and stacks of shoe boxes, the entire floor was covered with row upon row of gray marble counters, all piled high with every kind of drygoods known to man.

The only customers in the store were a group of young mothers with small children congregated in the shoe department. No clerk was in sight. The mothers appeared to be fitting the shoes on their own children, and they were all chattering happily until one of them spotted Josh and passed the word.

The uncomfortable silence that followed made him quickly avert his gaze. During the past week, he'd become increasingly aware that he had this same effect on people everywhere he went in Titusville. He swore softly to himself, remembering Shayna's claim that the local citizens were all Eddington-watchers.

He started up the nearest aisle to search for a clerk, and almost tripped over him. The old man was on his hands and knees, stuffing bundles of white cloth under one of the counters.

He peered up at Josh over the tops of his glasses. "Mr. Eddington!" Shock drained his wrinkled face of every drop of color. He struggled to rise, and Josh automatically reached to help him up. At his full height, his snowy head came to the middle of Josh's chest.

Josh released his hold on the frail, sweater-clad arm. "Mr. Mueller?" he asked, remembering the sign on the front of the store.

"*Ja*, the same." Mr. Mueller adjusted his glasses and studied Josh's face. "Of course; the grandson who has come home," he said in a heavy German accent.

Josh felt the prickling sensation start up again.

The old man's face cracked into a smile. "I think I see a ghost, so like your grandfather you are." He extended a trembling, blue-veined hand, and Josh clasped it gingerly, afraid he'd crush the fragile fingers.

"Diapers," Mr. Mueller said.

"Sir?"

Mr. Mueller pointed to the bundles of cloth. "Every year a new crop of babies. Sixty-two years I cover the bottoms of Titusville. What do you think of that?"

Josh stammered something inane and quickly changed

the subject. "I need work clothes, Mr. Mueller, and steel-toed boots suitable for working in the foundry."

Mr. Mueller nodded. "*Ja,* the pants and shirts I got ready for you. The boots you got to try on."

"Sir?"

"Three pants and three shirts your grandfather ordered the week before he died. Always he wants the same kind so I got to special order. You don't remember?"

"My grandfather died when I was very young. I don't remember much about him." Josh glanced furtively around the store for someone else who could wait on him. He was getting nowhere fast with the owner. The poor old fellow was obviously playing with a short deck.

Mr. Mueller shook his head sadly. "Of course, how could you remember? Only this high you were." He held his hand waist-high. "Now you are the same size as Mr. David, I think."

Crooking his finger for Josh to follow, he headed toward the rear of the store. "Wait till I tell the wife of my son." He cocked his head toward the brown-haired young woman operating the comptometer. "An old fool I am, she says. But always I know you will come back." He stopped before a row of open bins bearing printed letters of the alphabet. Searching through the "D-E-F" bin, he produced a brown paper package.

"Mr. David said someday his grandson would buy pants and shirts from Mueller's." To Josh's acute embarrassment, the old man's eyes filled with tears. "So many years, and still I can't believe . . ." He handed Josh the package. "Wear these with pride. Your grandfather was a man of honor."

Mr. Mueller produced a handkerchief from his pocket and wiped his eyes. Suddenly, he was all business. "So, now we find the boots. Forty-two dollars and ninety-five cents they cost. A terrible price. But what can I do? The world has gone crazy." He shuffled up the aisle ahead of Josh—a fragile, dried leaf of a man who looked as if the smallest gust of wind would blow him away.

This brush with the past had started a host of long-forgotten memories rattling around Josh's head, and his nerves felt as raw as an open wound. With dread, he viewed the group of curious onlookers awaiting them in the shoe department. "Maybe I should come back when you're not so busy," he protested.

"*Ach,* all day there will be mamas and children. Always the first day of summer holiday they come for the sandals. They will wait." Mr. Mueller shrugged. "Where can they go but Mueller's?"

With Megan in tow, Shayna hurried along Main Street toward Mueller's Mercantile. She'd spent another restless night after her confrontation with her family, and she'd gotten a late start. Always a serious mistake on the first Monday of summer vacation. By this time of morning, the store would be crowded with mothers purchasing the multistrapped brown sandals that every child in The Flats had worn from June till September for as long as anyone could remember. Sandal day was a Titusville tradition, and the best part for the children was Mr. Mueller's shiny brass token redeemable for a banana split at the drugstore soda fountain across the street.

She sent Megan through the revolving door ahead of her. It was always safer than having the rambunctious youngster pushing from behind. Halfway through the revolution, she saw the tall man loaded down with parcels who was revolving outward.

Megan spotted him at the same time. 'Joss!'' she shrieked, and pushed with all her might, sending both Shayna and herself full circle to spill out onto the sidewalk. Shayna groaned. Despite all her soul-searching and the promises she'd made herself, she was completely unprepared to face Josh Eddington, especially early in the morning in the middle of Main Street.

"Megan . . . Shayna." Josh stepped back as the force of the door drove them toward him. "What are you two doing here? No, wait. Let me guess. Sandals."

Megan hopped up and down excitedly. "And ice cream with chocolate and strawberries and bananas. It's Mr. Mueller's surprise, but everybody knows already."

"It seems Mr. Mueller is full of surprises. I've just been treated to one myself." Josh had a peculiar, dazed expression on his face that made him look shockingly vulnerable.

Shayna instantly forgot her embarrassment at seeing him again. All her firm resolutions to terminate their budding friendship toppled like dominos before the bewilderment she read in his eyes. "Is something wrong, Josh?" she asked gently. "You look like you've seen a ghost."

"I think I have." He glanced up and down the street. "Is there someplace around here where we could get a cup of coffee? I really need one."

SEVEN

There were more than a dozen customers in The Bluebell Cafe. Every one of them looked up when Josh and Shayna entered. Shayna pasted a smile on her face and headed for the nearest empty booth. She'd known what she was letting herself in for when she'd agreed to have coffee with Josh, but the unspoken appeal in his eyes had been irresistible. Without a second thought, she'd asked Laura Fitzpatrick, the mother of Megan's best friend, to keep Megan with her while she shopped in Mueller's, and led Josh the two blocks to The Bluebell.

The sole waitress, a lady of indeterminate age and generous proportions, was trading jokes across the counter with the butter and egg delivery man. With each laugh, her cheeks grew rosier and her ample bosom expanded inside her starched pink uniform like a batch of rising bread dough.

Grabbing two menus, she lumbered toward the booth Shayna had chosen. "Well, I'll be . . ." She gave Josh a hard stare. "Been a lot of years since I've waited on an Eddington. I heard you'd come home, and doggoned if you aren't the spittin' image of your grandpa." She wagged her head from side to side, sending wisps of blue-gray hair fluttering about her broad, cheerful face. "I wasn't old enough to drink legal first time I poured that man his mornin' coffee.''

She turned to Shayna. ''And you're Maggie Brenegan's girl. Your ma and me started working at The Bluebell the very same day. Of course, Maggie didn't last long. Married Johnny Brenegan and broke the heart of every girl in The Flats—including mine. Your pa was a handsome devil when he was young, and that younger brother of yours looks a lot like him. Not near as sweet-natured, though.''

A toothy grin spread across her face. ''It's good to see you. You haven't been in here since . . .'' She hesitated, obviously embarrassed. ''Must be more'n three years.''

Her gaze swept from Shayna to Josh and back to Shayna. ''Well, ain't this a day for the books!'' She took a pencil from behind her right ear and an order pad from her pocket. ''What'll you have?''

''Just coffee for me.'' Shayna could feel the heat creeping up her neck and across her cheeks. The dark look on Josh's face told her he was as uncomfortable as she with their sudden notoriety. She smiled weakly at him. ''They serve a great breakfast here, if you're interested.''

His expression darkened even more as he took a quick appraisal of his surroundings, and Shayna found herself looking at The Bluebell through his eyes. It was spotlessly clean, but seventy odd years of wear and tear had taken their toll. Tufts of cotton batting protruded from the tears in the vinyl-upholstered booths and the plastic table covers had been scrubbed so many times, the checkered pattern was all but obliterated. Behind the counter, the ornate mirror that had once been the owner's pride and joy was now mottled and cracked. The Bluebell had definitely seen better days. But then, except for the posh Highlands district, so had most of Titusville.

Suddenly she felt terribly defensive about the old town, and more than a little resentful of the man whose disdainful gaze made her see all its flaws.

''I am hungry,'' Josh said, handing his copy of the menu to the waitress. ''What do you suggest?''

"The special. It's the best deal in town."

"The special it is then."

"Good choice, sonny. If you're anything like your grandpa, you've got a hollow leg." She headed back to the counter, calling out her order as she went. "Shoot the works, Charlie, and pile it on."

Shayna kept her gaze riveted on the table while the waitress returned to pour their coffee. She doubted she could keep a straight face if she looked "Sonny" in the eye.

"I'm beginning to understand why you don't want to be seen with me," Josh said grimly. "I feel like some odd new species of bird at an Audubon Society meeting."

Shayna smiled, feeling more at ease. Shabby though it might be, this was her turf; Josh was the one playing by a new set of rules. "Give us time. We'll get used to you. It's been a long time since we've had an Eddington to ogle. Your father and brother rarely left The Highlands."

She leaned forward. "What happened at Mueller's that upset you?"

Josh produced a flat, brown-paper package. "Read this." He pointed to the invoice stapled to one corner.

The spidery handwriting was difficult to decipher. "It looks like three pairs of Levis and three flannel shirts."

"Look at the date."

"April 24 . . ." Shayna gasped. "That's almost thirty years ago."

"Right. Apparently my grandfather ordered them the week before he died. I walked into the store this morning to buy some work clothes and Mr. Mueller handed me this package and said he'd been waiting for me to claim it. I felt like I'd dropped into a late-night rerun of *The Twilight Zone*. The crazy old guy wouldn't even let me pay for it."

Shayna looked at the invoice again. "It says 'special order.' Your grandfather must have paid for it in advance. You always have to if it's a special order."

"Oh, well, that explains it. Come on, Shayna. You

must admit this scenario is a little off-the-wall even for Titusville.''

Even for Titusville. Shayna gritted her teeth and took a tight rein on her temper. "I'm sure I'd find it very strange if some men I know were that conscientious in their business dealings," she said coolly, pausing to let the inference sink in. "It's exactly what I'd expect Mr. Mueller to do. One reason why he's managed to stay in business so long in Titusville is that he would never consider putting a time limit on honesty.''

Josh's face went blank. He pushed his coffee cup aside and rested the palms of both hands on the table in front of him. For one horrified second, Shayna was afraid he was going to come over the top of the table at her. But, as suddenly as he'd tensed, he relaxed against the upholstered back of the booth. "Now, why didn't that simple explanation occur to me?" he asked conversationally. "With six weeks in this remarkable town of yours under my belt, you'd think some of these fine old-fashioned principles would have rubbed off on me.'' The flinty look in his eyes sent chills down Shayna's back. Too late, she remembered who he was and the power he wielded over her family.

She lowered her eyes. She wouldn't provoke him further, but she'd be darned if she'd apologize to the arrogant so-and-so. He'd asked for everything he got.

A strained silence stretched between them, multiplying Shayna's misgivings by the minute. She was so glad to see the waitress arrive with Josh's breakfast, she almost kissed the woman.

Without a word, he tucked into the oversize platter of ham and eggs, country fried potatoes, and toast like a man who hadn't eaten for a week. Just watching him started Shayna's stomach roiling, but it was apparent their brief set-to hadn't bothered his digestive system in the least.

He finished the last bite, sat back, and smiled as if nothing unusual had transpired between them. "Thanks for the tip. I'll keep this place in mind. The food here makes the pap they serve at the hotel look like a joke."

"The hotel is for tourists. The Bluebell wouldn't last a week if they served that kind of food to foundry workers." Shayna's breath caught in her throat. She hadn't meant to say that. It had just slipped out.

"Another dig at the city slicker? Shame on you, Shayna. What would Father O'Toole say about such un-Christian behavior?" A full stomach had obviously improved Josh's disposition. His eyes glinted with amusement. "So, tell me what triggered that famous temper of yours this time. Did you imagine I was criticizing your precious town?"

Shayna glared at him. "I wasn't imagining anything," she said sharply. "And that's the second time you've referred to it as *my* town. It's yours, too, Josh. Maybe even more than it's mine. Your great-grandfather built it and your family has controlled its destiny ever since. Now, everyone knows the future of the town is in your hands. Do you wonder why I get upset when you poke fun at it?"

He sobered instantly. "I wasn't ridiculing Titusville or its citizens. If I'm guilty of anything, it's of letting my frustration get the best of me. Two months ago I was a happy man—living where I wanted to live and making damned good money doing what I knew best. Now, here I am, the designated savior of an outdated business I know nothing about and a town that's turned its back on time. I seriously doubt either can be saved, and I doubt even more that I'm the one to do it."

Shayna looked into Josh's troubled eyes and the flood of compassion that overwhelmed her instantly diluted her anger. She'd been so mesmerized by his air of self-assurance, she'd failed to see that charm and arrogance were the masks he wore to hide the same kinds of doubts that plagued everyone else. Impulsively, she reached across the table and put her hand in his. Every eye in the place was on them and for once, she didn't care.

"Maybe neither the foundry nor Titusville can be saved, Josh, but you're the only one in a position to try. Nobody expects you to perform miracles. Just do the best you can."

Josh grinned lopsidedly. "Well, that much I can promise . . . for what it's worth."

His fingers tightened around hers. "But enough about the foundry and its troubles. I have a much more immediate problem." He dropped his voice to a whisper. "You. I'm starting to stay awake nights just thinking about kissing you again." He grinned. "Which reminds me, what did you do with that kissing box I sent you?"

Shayna felt her cheeks flame. "It's on my back porch, next to the washing machine."

"You're keeping your laundry in it? Honest to God, Shayna, there's such a thing as being too practical." He shook his head sadly. "No wonder I'm losing sleep. I'm crazy out of my mind over a stubborn, opinionated woman with a wicked temper and no romance in her soul."

"Stop your foolishness, Josh. I'm not into playing silly games."

"What games? I'm deadly serious, and since we've just survived our first fight—a milestone in any relationship— maybe it's time we did a little serious talking about where we're heading."

Alarm bells clanged in Shayna's head. She yanked her hand from his. "There's nothing to talk about. We don't have a relationship."

"Maybe not yet, in the strictest sense of the word. But we will. And that, my lovely Irish spitfire, is a promise."

For a man who rarely made promises of any kind, Josh had certainly made more than his share lately. He already bitterly regretted the one he'd made Angus McTavish. Partly because he felt like an absolute fool posing as a foundryman in jeans and steel-toed boots, and partly because he knew there was no way he could fast-talk his way through an apprenticeship under the tough old Scotsman, as he sometimes did in sticky situations that came up in Washington.

"Morning, Mr. Eddington."

"Howdy, Mr. Eddington."

"Fine spring day, Mr. Eddington."

Every man he passed greeted him, which was amazing. He'd encountered absolute silence on his previous visits to the forge. He couldn't believe a change of clothes would make him instantly acceptable.

He shook the outstretched hand of the quality control manager, a spare, gray-haired man who squinted at him through thick bifocals. "Happy to see you, sir. When Angus told us you'd decided to learn the foundry business from the ground up, it was the shot in the arm we all needed."

Josh groaned. That devious old codger had set him up. Shayna might claim nobody expected him to perform miracles; the hopeful faces of these men told him a different story.

He found Angus in the pattern shop talking to a wiry, ruddy-complexioned man whose bald pate barely reached the older man's shoulder.

"Good morning, Joshua. Meet Horace Abernathy, our master patternmaker. He trained under his father and his grandfather—two of the best patternmakers ever worked in the trade. Horace can teach you all you need to know about this end of the business."

Josh held out his hand. "Abernathy? I think I may have met your father. Does he have a 1932 Packard?"

Horace grinned. "Sure does. Pride of his life. Where'd you meet Dad?"

"I was visiting a friend and he came by on his evening walk. We talked cars for a few minutes."

"The old man must have loved that. Since Ma died, his main pleasure in life is that old Packard of his."

Angus regarded Josh quizzically. "You have a friend in The Flats?"

Too late, Josh realized his mistake. Between that suggestive box he'd sent Shayna and his presumptuous statement about their "relationship," he already had enough to answer for. Adding grist to the Titusville gossip mill would be another strike against him.

Josh hesitated, picking his words carefully. "I was at Mrs. O'Malley's house—discussing the foundry's financial liability in her husband's death."

"Humphh. That must have been interesting." Angus pinned Josh with a "we'll talk about this later" look, and Horace made a serious study of the toe of his right boot. Josh got the impression neither man bought his explanation.

"Enough of this. Let's get to work," Angus said abruptly. "It all begins here in the pattern department, with prototypes, in wood or plastic, of the castings to be poured. The trick is to allow enough tolerance in the pattern to compensate for metal shrinkage and machining. A patternmaster can make or break a foundry. Luckily, Horace can figure specs closer than a gnat's eyebrow."

With Josh and Horace close behind, Angus next toured the molding department, where John Brenegan was foreman. The stocky Irishman's vivid blue eyes looked so much like Shayna's, Josh knew instantly he was her father. Brenegan's grudging acceptance of the hand Josh offered left no doubt about the animosity he felt toward the new head of the foundry. A family trait, Josh concluded, remembering Shayna's initial reaction to him.

After an embarrassing moment of stunned silence, Angus continued his lecture. "Once the pattern's set," he explained, "the men in this department pack sand around it to create the mold cavity, set up the gates, and pour the metal. Sounds simple, doesn't it? Well, it isn't."

He turned to Horace. "You old enough to remember that cannon order we struggled with back in 1942?"

Horace's laugh started deep in his belly. "I was the kid David Eddington sent out looking for horse manure. Spent the whole month of January scraping snow off horse droppings and drying the muck on the shop furnace."

"Sure. Now I remember." Angus smiled reminiscently. "The War Department was champing at the bit for the cannons and every one we cast was so full of gas holes, anyone crazy enough to fire one would have been blown to kingdom come. We laced the core sand with every binder on the market. Nothing worked. We were just about to forfeit the contract when David came up with the idea of mixing dried manure into the sand. The hot metal burned away the straw in the manure so the gasses could escape, and we poured the sweetest-looking cannon you ever saw." He chuckled. "And the history books claim the horse wasn't used in World War II."

The rest of the day was more of the same. In every department they visited, the men told stories of David Eddington and his prowess as a foundryman. David had the "eye." He could look at hot metal and judge to the second when to pour. David had the "feel"—that sixth sense that told him when to slip a scrap of aluminum into molten brass to make it flow like cream—whether to use a green sand mold or the lost wax process to produce a superior casting.

Josh squirmed uncomfortably in the clothes he'd inherited. His grandfather had been dead twenty-eight years and the men who'd worked for him still missed him. Josh found himself wondering if anyone would even remember his name if he stayed away from Washington more than six months.

When the five o'clock whistle blew, he was more than ready for a hot shower and a stiff drink. It had been one of the most frustrating days of his life. Nearly every foreman and lead man Angus introduced him to held the same job as his father and grandfather before him, which left Josh feeling like a poker player who'd been dealt a blind hand in a game where everyone else had seen the cards. At the same time, he found himself strangely moved by the idea of generations of Titusville men training their sons to take their place in the Eddington Foundry. The combination was a disconcerting one to a man who had no strong family ties and made his home in a city of political transients.

"What's the trouble between you and Brenegan?" Angus asked as Josh and he walked to the parking lot. "I've known John forty years. Never seen him act like that before. Only thing I know would rile him is a threat to his family."

Josh scowled. "I can't say I cared much for Ronnie Brenegan, but I didn't threaten him."

"John wouldn't waste time worrying about Ronnie. The lad's a born troublemaker. I'd lay odds it's his daughter that's fretting him. Good God, Joshua. You haven't been sparking Shayna O'Malley, have you?"

"If sparking means what I think it does, the answer is no—not that it's any of your business." Josh struggled to control his rising temper. "Let's get one thing straight, Angus. I let you blackmail me into this apprenticeship because I couldn't see any other way out. That doesn't give you the right to interfere in my personal life."

"Maybe not, but I'm going to have my say anyhow. Shayna is too fine a young woman to be tarred with the same brush as Hilda Kleghorn or the floozies Kyle cavorted with, but she will be if you chase after her. Things are a lot different here than in a city the size of Washington, D.C."

"So help me," Josh exploded, "if I hear that 'this is Titusville' garbage one more time . . ."

Now, on top of all his other frustrations, Angus was forcing him to take an honest look at his intentions toward Shayna O'Malley. She was the one bright spot in this provincial little hamlet he'd committed himself to for the next six months, but he certainly didn't want to hurt her. It was becoming increasingly obvious he could do just that by merely being seen with her.

Much as he hated to admit it, Angus had a point. This was not the place to carry on a casual affair. Unless he had some sort of commitment in mind, he had no business promoting a relationship with the lovely widow.

It was certainly something to think about.

And who the hell was Hilda Kleghorn?

Shayna ransacked her refrigerator for something quick and easy to fix for Friday-night supper. She was too antsy to think of cooking. After five days of nearly jumping out of her skin each time the phone rang, she'd finally come to the conclusion Josh had had second thoughts about pursuing their "relationship." Oddly enough, the idea left her feeling more upset than ever.

To add to her dilemma, her relationship with her family was strained to the breaking point. Word had gotten around The Flats about her breakfast with Josh. Her mother had learned about it at her Holy Rosary Altar Society meeting and stormed home breathing fire. Shayna had done a little fire-breathing of her own, and her mother had stayed strictly to her side of the hedge ever since.

Ronnie and Martin picked up the news at Grogan's Tavern. They still hadn't spoken to each other since their Sunday quarrel, but they both found a lot to say to Shayna.

Father O'Toole heard it from his housekeeper, who'd heard it from the butter and egg man. Shayna was still smarting from his lecture on the duty of a Christian mother to set a good example for her daughter, and there was a strong possibility she might, at her next confession, have to admit to having murderous thoughts about her own priest.

Her father was the only one who'd resisted upbraiding her, and the heavy footsteps on her back porch warned her that omission was about to be rectified. Her spirits sank to a new low. Criticism from Pop could shatter her as none other.

He stepped through the door and set his lunch pail on the kitchen table—the same dear, dust-covered figure she'd run to meet each night as a child. "Stopped on my way from work," he said. "Guess I should have washed up first."

His blue eyes, so like her own, looked bleak. "Been

thinking of how we lit into you Sunday like a pack of wolves cornering a deer. I'm mighty sorry for my part in it."

"Oh, Pop." Shayna flung herself into her father's arms, her heart nearly bursting with love.

"Careful, sweetheart. You'll be getting that nice clean blouse of yours covered with black dust and iron shavings."

"I don't care."

He chuckled. "Remember how mad your ma used to get when I hugged you dirty? Poor woman had to bathe you and change your dress every night before you could eat your supper. I always felt guilty about the extra work I made her. Not guilty enough to miss my hug, though."

His calloused fingers traced a gentle line on Shayna's cheek. "Your ma told me the latest gossip."

Shayna tensed.

"I met him," John Brenegan said quietly. "Angus brought him round."

"Josh? You didn't say anything, did you, about . . ."

"Nope. Felt like it, but I held my tongue. Foundry work's all I know, and the Eddingtons put the bread on our table. Think of the ruckus your ma would raise if I showed up some Friday night without a paycheck."

"I've done nothing to be ashamed of, Pop."

"Never figured you had." He frowned. "Anyways, after working all week with Joshua, I'm kind of getting used to him."

Shayna looked up sharply. "Josh is working out in the foundry? So that's why he was buying work clothes."

"Yep. Angus says he plans to spend a month in each department. Kind of a crash course in the foundry business, I guess. Right now he's in the pattern department, and Horace Abernathy says he never trained a faster learner."

Shayna could believe that. It was the idea of the fastidious Josh Eddington working in the grimy old foundry that boggled her imagination.

"The men like him, and that's sure a change from the way they felt about Hiram or Kyle. They respect him, too. Green as he is, he's got his share of grit. Angus rides him harder'n all the rest of us put together, and Joshua never says a word." A slow smile spread across John Brenegan's face. "Once in a while he gets a little white around the mouth, but there's not a one of us hasn't itched to tell old Angus to go to hell from time to time."

He removed the battered railroad cap he always wore to work and scratched his head. A deep groove creased his forehead where the cap, or one like it, had sat for forty years. "One thing's sure. Joshua's not afraid to get his hands dirty. First time I've seen an Eddington do a day's work since his grandpa died. Fact is, he reminds me a lot of David. All the old-timers have remarked on it."

Absentmindedly, he twirled the cap on one finger. "You like him a lot, don't you?"

"I guess I do," Shayna admitted, "but that doesn't mean I understand him."

"That figures. Likable or not, he's still an Eddington. He may show up every day, like the rest of us, in a hardhat and levis and one of those ugly shirts of Zig Mueller's, but somehow he still looks . . ."

"Elegant," Shayna said, remembering how intimidated she'd felt the first time she'd seen Josh.

"That's the word. He's a different breed of cat, sweetheart, and my gut feeling is you're asking for trouble if you take up with him."

"Clouds and butterfly nets," Shayna said softly.

"Huh?"

"Grandma Brenegan used to say, 'The quickest way to get your heart broken is to chase after clouds with a butterfly net.' " Shayna smiled. "Don't worry, Pop. My butterfly net is safely under lock and key. I don't regret the time I've spent with Josh, but I'm not foolish enough to think we could ever be any more than casual friends. I have a daughter to raise and a teaching career to pursue, and Josh has a foundry to get back on its feet. I doubt we'll be seeing much of each other in the future. Once he finds time to do a little socializing, he'll meet someone more his type. Maybe he already has. He halfway promised to call, but I haven't heard from him all week.''

''Poor fellow's probably too worn out to pick up the phone. Angus keeps him hopping all day, and the night guard says Joshua's still working in the foundry office every night when he comes on at midnight. But he'll call you. Mark my words.'' He sighed. ''For your sake, I wish he wouldn't, but he's not stupid. He can see you're just about the smartest and prettiest woman God ever put on this earth.''

''Oh, Pop. You always make me feel so special.'' Shayna gave her father a bear hug and sent dust flying in every direction. ''Do you have any idea how much I love you?''

''Well now, that's the very thing I came here to say to you. All this talk and I never did say it. You always were better with words than all the rest of us put together.''

He planted a kiss on Shayna's forehead. ''Best get home. Your ma's cooking corned beef and cabbage.'' His eyes twinkled. ''She's trying to get on my good side. Today's payday.''

EIGHT

One week dragged into two and two into four. Because the love the Brenegans shared was so strong, they soon forgot their differences and returned to their normal daily routines. At first everyone was so carefully polite, Shayna felt ill at ease. But caution was not a natural part of the Brenegans' makeup; before long they were back to their usual boisterous give and take.

Josh never did call. After the first two weeks, Shayna quit expecting him to. She wasn't really surprised he'd lost interest in her; she'd just expected him to show a little more class in terminating their friendship. How typical of an Eddington to make a lot of frivolous declarations and then ride blithely off into the sunset without even a backward glance. The more she thought about his sorry behavior, the more furious she became.

What did surprise her was how dull her days had suddenly become without Josh to liven them up. Still, it was for the best. It saved her the embarrassment of explaining to him why a "relationship" between them was out of the question.

On the surface, her life was exactly as it had been before Josh walked into it. At a deeper level, she'd made one significant change. She'd finally made a firm decision to bury the past and look to the future. "It isn't that I've stopped loving you," she'd whispered as she disconnected Tim's little cuckoo. "I'll never do that. But you don't need me anymore, and I must get on with my life."

That same day she'd hauled Josh's "kissing box" across the lawn and through the vegetable garden and stacked it beside the garbage can—a thing she should have done the minute it arrived. It was Thursday, and the trash wouldn't be picked up until the following Wednesday, but she needed to get the ridiculous thing out of her sight.

Then she cleaned her house from top to bottom, pulled every last weed out of her garden, and washed and polished her dilapidated old Ford. She slept like a baby that night. Stripping one's life to the bone proved very therapeutic.

When the letter arrived two days later from the Titusville school board announcing an opening for a permanent teaching position, she felt as if fate had placed a stamp of approval on her efforts. She instantly dialed the number listed and made an appointment for an interview, sent Megan next door, and headed for Allison's boutique.

"Sweetie, where in the world have you been?" Allison exclaimed. "It must be three months since I've seen you."

"Only one, actually." Shayna studied her friend's face anxiously. She hadn't been sure how Allison would receive her. She'd been decidedly cool when Shayna had stopped back by the boutique after that unfortunate luncheon with Josh.

Allison's smile looked genuine; apparently she was over her hurt feelings. Shayna breathed a sigh of relief. It would have been too ironic to bear if someone as false as Josh Eddington had caused a rift in the true friendship Allison and she had shared for so many years.

"I'm glad you stopped by," Allison said. "I've been meaning to call you, but I've been so busy." She cleared a place for Shayna on the couch. "What brings you to this part of town?"

"Two things. First this." Shayna removed a sheaf of papers from her purse. "Everything you ever wanted to know about Alexander Hamilton."

Allison clutched the manuscript to her breast. "Oh, my God. I'd forgotten all about it, and the meeting's next Thursday. Thank you, thank you, thank you. Once again you've saved my life." She placed the report on the table flanking the loveseat. "Now, what's your second reason for coming to see me?

"Believe it or not, I'm here as a customer. Ordinarily your prices are much too high for me, but I need a miracle dress for a very special occasion."

Allison chuckled. "I'm not sure how many miracles I have in stock, but if you can find one on the rack, it's yours free of charge."

"I can pay for it."

Allison shrugged. "You already have. Think what I'd have to pay a speech writer to come up with the drivel I feed the local intellectuals." She raised a suggestive eyebrow. "Got a big date with Mr. Wonderful?"

"If you're referring to Josh Eddington, the answer is no. I've neither seen him nor heard from him in over a month." *Thirty-four days, to be exact.*

"You're kidding, and after all those soulful looks he cast your way that Saturday morning." Allison's eyes flashed sudden fire. "I'm glad you're not sitting around moping over the jerk. No man is worth it—especially an Eddington. Kyle gave me a brief rush when I first came back from New York and I fell like a ton of bricks. Then one day he quit calling—no explanation, not even a 'good-bye' or a 'see you around.' I found out later he'd dumped me for some bimbo from Kokomo with an I.Q. around thirty-five. Apparently he liked his blondes dumb, which, considering Kyle, wasn't too surprising."

Dumbfounded, Shayna gaped at her friend. "You and Kyle? I can't believe it."

"I never said anything. I was embarrassed to admit I'd been such a fool, especially over someone I knew you hated." Allison sighed. "For your sake, I was hoping Joshua really was as different as he seemed. I should have known better. They're all cast from the same mold. So . . . the only smart thing to do with an Eddington is forget him."

"Amen to that," Shayna declared vehemently.

Allison leaned forward eagerly. "So, if not Joshua Eddington, who is this lucky guy you're dating?"

"I'm not dating anyone. I'm interviewing with the school board for a teaching position at South Titusville High School, and I need to make a good impression."

Allison shook her head in amazement. "Are you serious? Haven't you heard what a nightmare it is to ride herd on a bunch of teenagers nowadays?"

"It's what I've always wanted to do." Shayna toyed nervously with the straps of her purse. "It's so perfect, I'm almost afraid to think about it. With what it pays and my widow's pension, Megan and I could live very nicely—even put a little aside each month."

"Well, if it's what you want, go for it. I'd rather kill myself, but we never did see eye to eye on what made the world go round." Allison frowned. "If it's so perfect, why do you look like someone just ran over your dog?"

"I'm scared." Shayna set her purse aside and anchored her hands between her knees to keep from fidgeting. "I want it so much and I know I'll have stiff competition. I'll have to look spectacular and act brilliant to even be considered."

"You can handle the 'brilliant' with your hands tied behind your back," Allison declared, "and I'm the resident genius at 'spectacular.' " She jumped to her feet. "It's you and me against the world, sweetie, and that's a killer combination."

The light of battle gleamed in her hazel eyes. "We have to plan our strategy. The first thing we have to do is find out who's on the board so we know who to impress."

"I asked when I requested the interview." Shayna opened her purse and extracted the notes she'd taken.

"There's Mr. Bancroft, superintendent of schools, and Mrs. Carter, the lawyer's wife . . ."

"Ugh!" Allison shivered. "Two devout members of the Historical Society. He's a straitlaced bore and she's the town's worst gossip."

"And Mrs. Colville, the mayor's wife," Shayna continued, "and Mr. Schermerhorn, the president of the Merchant's Bank." She glanced up at Allison. "Isn't he your friend?"

"Right," Allison grinned. "Schermy's a pussycat. He'll vote for you. He's always saying how impressed he is with those speeches you write for me. And Bonnie Colville is a good old girl—used to be a Sullivan before she married into money. Coming from The Flats herself, she'll figure you'll do a better job of teaching the kids from that area. Which leaves the first two. Now, what would make those two pillars of society sit up and take notice?"

She riffled through a rack of dresses. "Definitely something in blue. Too bad it's summer. A sheer wool would be perfect." She picked out a silk print in periwinkle blue. "What do you think of this Laura Ashley number?"

Allison held the dress up to Shayna. The silk felt heavenly on her bare arms, and a glance in the mirror told her the color turned her eyes a fathomless blue. "It's perfect," she breathed, "but how do you know it will fit?"

"It's a size six. As I remember, that's your size." She eyed Shayna speculatively. "You'll need a teddy and a half-slip, and we may have to make some alterations. You look like you've lost weight recently."

Shayna shrugged. "I haven't had much appetite."

Allison pinned Shayna with a piercing gaze. "I hope you haven't done something stupid . . . like fall for a certain good-for-nothing son-of-a—"

"Don't be silly," Shayna said a little too sharply. "Give me credit for some sense."

"Sweetie, when it comes to a man like Josh Eddington, no woman on earth has good sense." She gave Shayna a quick hug. "Just remember, I'm always here if you need me."

She slipped the dress off the hanger. "When is this earth-shaking interview of yours taking place, just in case we have to make alterations?

"Tomorrow morning at ten o'clock."

"Oh, my God!"

Josh nodded good morning to his secretary and pushed open the door of his office just as his great-grandfather's pendulum clock struck eight A.M. Normally, he arrived at seven, which gave him an hour for paperwork before starting his day in the foundry, but he hadn't been able to drag his aching body out of bed. There were limits to how long a man could survive on five hours of sleep a night, but he'd drop in his tracks before he admitted that to Angus McTavish. He swore softly to himself. That crusty old buzzard had him acting like a schoolboy terrified of his headmaster.

He leafed through the letters and memos waiting for him on his desk, tossing all but the most urgent pieces into the basket marked Pending. As usual, there were a dozen or so notices of meetings and social events, which his secretary separated from the rest of his mail. A wasted effort, since he never attended any of them.

About to drop the entire batch in the wastebasket, he spied a familiar name on one of Mrs. Warren's handwritten messages. *"School board meeting, nine A.M. Wednesday at Carter & Mulvaney Law Offices. Purpose: applicant interviews for teaching position. Shayna O'Malley, Rodney Sanford, Mary Alice Ingraham."* Josh read the message a second time, and pressed the intercom. "Why did you put this school board notice on my desk, Mrs. Warren?"

"The foundry manager is a permanent member of the board, and is always notified of the meetings."

"I see." Josh flipped off the intercom. He traced his finger over the name heading the list of candidates.

"Shayna." He spoke her name aloud, savoring the musical sound of it. It had been a month since he'd seen her. *Thirty-four days, to be exact.* He'd lost count of the number of times he'd picked up the phone to call her, then, remembering Angus's warning, had put it down again. He'd grown so used to the empty ache inside him, he'd almost convinced himself it was the natural way to feel.

So, Shayna was reaching out for that dream she'd told him about. Good for her. Scowling, he suddenly remembered that unless a miracle happened, her dream would be short-lived—as short-lived as Titusville itself unless a well-heeled buyer was found for the foundry. So far, every industrial realtor he'd contacted had told him it was a hopeless cause.

The foundry manager is a permanent member of the board. The words played over and over through his brain, like a tune with a one-line libretto. *Don't even think about it.* He crumpled the piece of paper and held it over the circular file beside his desk.

On the other hand, the foundry owes Shayna. A teaching position in Titusville—even a short-lived one—would ensure her a reference if she had to look for work in another town.

It was the worst kind of rationalization. He was beyond caring.

He pressed the intercom again. "Mrs. Warren, please inform Mr. McTavish I have a meeting this morning and will not be in the foundry until after lunch."

"You are not expected to attend the school board meeting, Mr. Eddington. Your membership on the board is merely honorary."

"I choose to, Mrs. Warren. The education of Titusville children is of great interest to me."

"Your father never attended a school board meeting in the twenty years I worked for him, nor did your brother."

"Just call Angus, please," Josh said, striving to keep the frustration out of his voice. Mrs. Warren never missed a chance to voice her disapproval of him. If it weren't for her many years of service to the company, she'd be out the door in a minute.

Of course, she wouldn't be the only one to oppose this move. Angus would heartily disapprove if he knew about it. With only the slightest twinge of guilt, Josh consigned both opinions to the same judgmental trash bin. After thirty-four days of misery, he was desperate enough to snatch at any excuse to see Shayna again, even if only across a conference table in a room full of people.

He stared down at the piece of paper he clutched in his work-roughened fingers—fingers he scarcely recognized as his own, wondering just when and how Shayna had worked her witchcraft on him. He was acting like a sixteen-year-old kid in the throes of his first crush.

A crush on the teacher, no less.

Shayna entered the Carter & Mulvaney Law Office just as a clean-cut, bespectacled young man in a navy pinstriped suit exited. "Hi, Mrs. O'Malley."

Startled, she stared closely at his face. "Good heavens. I didn't recognize you. You've cut your hair." When he'd sat beside her in her biology class, his hair had hung below his shoulders and he'd worn a T-shirt with a frankly erotic slogan emblazoned across it.

He grinned. "It seemed the thing to do."

Shayna couldn't remember his name. Right at the moment, she was having trouble remembering her own. She took another look at him. "I've never seen you wear glasses before," she said. "Are they something new?"

"Window glass. I thought they made a nice touch." His grin widened. "Speaking of nice touches . . . that's a great dress. The exact color of your eyes."

Self-consciously, Shayna smoothed the basted darts Allison had insisted accented her small waist. "Thank you."

His face sobered. "Good luck on your interview. You'll need it. That bunch of barracudas really sharpened their teeth on me, and four of them are my neighbors. You'd think they were interviewing for a brain surgeon."

Shayna perched on the edge of a straight-backed chair and watched the receptionist apply a coat of polish to her nails. "It shouldn't be long." she purred. "They're evaluating Mr. Sanford's qualifications."

Shayna smiled thinly, certain he'd made a good impression. He obviously didn't suffer from the kind of shyness that was knotting her stomach.

The buzzing of the speaker on the receptionist's desk sounded like a bomb exploding. "You can go in now, Mrs. O'Malley," she said with a toss of her long blond hair. Her smile was friendly, if a bit practiced. "Don't be nervous. You'll knock 'em dead. That's a terrific dress."

Shayna stepped through the door, and her knees went weak from shock. Five people faced her across the expanse of conference table instead of the four she'd expected, and the additional man on the far left was Josh Eddington.

"Please sit down, Mrs. O'Malley." Mr. Bancroft indicated the lone chair on her side of the table. Shayna dropped onto it and Mr. Bancroft introduced the other members of the board. She managed a tight smile as she met the gaze of each member. Mr. Schermerhorn was the only one who smiled back.

The next few minutes were a blur. Josh's unexpected presence had knocked Shayna completely off balance. She answered the questions fired at her, trusting to blind faith the words coming out of her mouth made some kind of sense. With five pairs of eyes trained on her, she felt more like a criminal facing a jury than a job applicant.

The first three board members completed their questioning and turned the interview over to Mr. Bancroft. He shuffled through the sheaf of papers in front of him while Shayna squirmed uncomfortably.

"Your scholastic record is remarkable, Mrs. O'Malley, considering the five-year interruption in your studies, apparently due to your marriage." Mr. Bancroft's tone of voice implied this had been a serious error on her part.

He scrutinized her through his tortoiseshell-rimmed

glasses. "Since the integrity of the teachers to whom we trust the education of Titusville children is of the utmost importance, there are certain personal questions that I feel obliged to ask."

Shayna nodded mutely, and Mr. Bancroft launched into a series of questions about her family, her friends, her social life, her intellectual interests, even the babysitting arrangements she would make for Megan should she be awarded the teaching contract.

Josh remained silent throughout the interrogation, his scowl growing blacker by the minute. "If you've finished your inquisition," he said when Mr. Bancroft paused, "I have only one question for Mrs. O'Malley."

Spots of angry color flared in the superintendent's sallow cheeks. "Certainly, Mr. Eddington. Since you are the first representative of the foundry to attend a board meeting, I assumed you were simply monitoring the proceedings."

Josh ignored him. He turned to Shayna, and her knees started to tremble. It was difficult to believe this impersonal stranger had once brought her a bouquet of wilted flowers and kissed her silly on a warm Saturday evening.

"Tell me, Mrs. O'Malley," he said in a dispassionate tone of voice, "why do you think you can make a significant difference in the lives of the youngsters you teach?"

Shayna gripped the edge of the table. Josh was asking her to tell these strangers the dream she'd confided in him in a weak moment that first night in her little kitchen.

Paralyzed with shyness, she haltingly explained her ambition to share the world of literature with the children of The Flats and free their young minds to explore beyond the social and economic limitations their parents had accepted as a way of life.

She finished speaking and studied her white-knuckled fingers. Even to her own ears, she'd sounded impossibly pompous and idealistic. The nausea churning in her stomach rushed into her throat. Whatever his reasons for betraying her confidence, Josh had set her up to make a fool of herself when she desperately needed to make a good impression, and she would never forgive him for it.

The next applicant arrived just as Shayna was leaving. Shayna remembered her well. They'd shared three classes in Shayna's senior year at college. Mary Alice Ingraham was the daughter of the manager of the Titusville Highlands Country Club. She was twenty-two years old and every gorgeous five-foot-eight inch of her exuded supreme self-confidence. She bestowed radiant smiles on both Shayna and the receptionist and settled gracefully onto a chair to await her turn with the board.

Shayna's already shaky ego plummeted. There'd be no frantic gripping of the table for Mary Alice.

Allison was waiting at the boutique to hear about the interview. She studied Shayna's face with sympathetic eyes. "It's not the end of the world," she murmured, giving Shayna a comforting hug.

"Maybe not, but it certainly feels like it." Shayna made a brave attempt at a smile. "Josh was on the board. Don't ask me why—but seeing him there wiped me out. I made a fool of myself. I can't remember how I answered most of the questions and I'm trying to forget how I answered the rest."

"Joshua Eddington was on the board? Why wasn't his name on the list of members you were given?"

"Mr. Bancroft said it was the first time anyone from the foundry had attended a meeting. Wouldn't you know this would be the one he'd pick."

"The first time, you say?" A puzzled frown wrinkled Allison's brow. "Well, isn't that an interesting development. I wonder what that snake is up to now."

NINE

Mr. Bancroft had promised he would notify all applicants of the board's decision before the day was out. Growing more anxious by the minute, Shayna waited through the long afternoon for the phone to ring. The call finally came at five o'clock when she was cooking supper.

He wasted no time on preliminaries. "The board has completed its review of the qualifications of the three applicants for the teaching position and found them to be surprisingly similar. However, since you are a resident of the area where the school is located, certain members of the board felt you had a slight edge." His tone of voice left no doubt he had not been one of those members. "I am authorized to offer you the position subject to a three-month probationary period. Please report to South Titusville High School at eight o'clock the morning of August twenty-fifth for the teachers' preliminary planning session for the fall term."

The click of the receiver sent Shayna slumping onto the nearest chair, weak with elation . . . and shock. Elation that the job she wanted so badly was hers and shock at Mr. Bancroft's unmistakable antipathy toward her. The only reason she could think of for his attitude was that Josh had gone into another of his noblesse oblige acts toward the small-town widow and shoved her down the board's throat.

She dialed Allison's number and listened with mounting frustration to the recorded message saying her friend couldn't answer the phone at the moment. "Call me when you get in," Shayna said. "Or stop by if you're anywhere near here. I really need to talk to you."

Somehow, despite her agitation, she managed to get supper on the table, bathe Megan, and read her a story before her eight o'clock bedtime. She was drying the last of the dishes when the front doorbell rang. She ran to the door, plate in hand, and threw it open. "Thank God you're here," she exclaimed, then gasped as a tall figure stepped out of the shadows.

"I'd have come sooner if I'd known I'd get this kind of reception."

"Josh! What do *you* want?"

"I came to congratulate you on your teaching appointment. I know you'll do a fine job."

Shayna stood firm, blocking his way as he stepped forward to enter the house. "Why were you at the meeting, Josh? I gathered you were as much a surprise to them as to me. And how much did you have to do with my appointment? Was this another of your charity crusades? Mr. Bancroft made it clear he didn't want me. I'm surprised he didn't accuse me of being another Hilda Kleghorn."

"Whoa. Slow down." Josh leaned against the doorjamb with one foot thrust purposefully across the threshold. "I don't know what Bancroft intimated, but I never even entered the discussion. It's true Bancroft favored the Ingraham girl—I got the impression the Bancrofts and Ingrahams were close friends—but Schermerhorn insisted your knowledge of The Flats made you the superior candidate; and the two women fell into line. Shoot me if you wish; I did vote with the majority." He paused. "Who is Hilda Kleghorn?"

Shayna ignored his question, but his calm statement of facts had taken the wind out of her sails. She offered no resistance as he moved past her into the living room and gazed about him with the satisfied air of a wanderer returning to his homeland.

He favored her with one of his heart-warming smiles. "So, are we friends again?"

"We are not and never have been friends," Shayna snapped, coming within inches of throwing the plate at his head. "Friends don't wander into a person's life and . . ."

"Kiss them like I kissed you, make a lot of promises, and then disappear for thirty-four days," Josh said. "All right. I admit I owe you an apology . . . and an explanation."

"Why, you . . . you conceited jerk!"

"Temper, Shayna, temper. And such unimaginative language. *Jerk?* Hardly the standard of eloquence we expect from the educators of our children."

Shayna glared at him, certain she detected laughter in his voice.

"Aren't you going to ask me to sit down?" Josh asked after a moment of uncomfortable silence. "I'd like to tell you why I've stayed away."

For the briefest moment, Shayna hesitated. "I'm afraid not," she said finally. "I really don't care to hear it. I've learned a couple of valuable lessons this past month—the first one being, friendship with you has more ups and downs than a roller-coaster ride; the second, I have no interest in emotional thrill-seeking."

"I know you're angry at me, and I can't blame you, but we really do need to talk about this, Shayna."

"Talking about it won't change anything. The truth of the matter is I can think of at least a dozen reasons why we shouldn't be friends and not even one why we should."

"I can't dispute your logic," Josh admitted. "God knows, I've run through the same wretched list often enough myself this past month, trying to convince myself I'd be doing you a favor by staying away from you. The minute you walked into that conference room this morning, my noble intentions went up in smoke. I need to see you, Shayna, and talk with you and touch you—and the look I saw in those lovely eyes of yours made me think you just might feel the same way about me. All the logic in the world can't stand up against that simple truth.''

Josh's words rammed through Shayna's already battered defenses. She could feel her heart thundering painfully against her rib cage. "Don't do this to me," she cried. "It isn't fair, and it hurts too much."

His swift intake of breath told her she'd admitted much more than she'd meant to with her outburst.

"I knew it. This past month has been every bit as miserable for you as it has for me." Josh sounded triumphant. "Well, I say to hell with logic and to hell with nosy people and their helpful advice. Something this good may never happen again for either of us. If we lose it, we'll both regret it bitterly."

"I'd regret a brief affair even more," Shayna declared, steeling herself against the seductive magic Josh was so good at weaving.

"For God's sake, Shayna, don't you think I know that? One of the things I admire most about you is your set of unshakable values. Believe me, my fantasies about you are definitely the long-lived kind."

His voice mellowed, almost as if he were talking to himself instead of her. "I promise we'll take things slowly, get to know each other one step at a time. Like the song says, 'make all the stops along the way.' For my sake as much as yours. This is a first for me, and at the ripe old age of thirty-four, that's pretty awesome. I have no intention of missing a single bit of the whole miraculous process."

Shayna searched his face. "Fantasies. Miracles. For heaven's sake, Josh, stop talking in riddles. What exactly are you trying to say?"

He laughed softly, a provocative kind of laugh that sent ripples of awareness coursing through her. "To put it as plainly and simply as possible, my dear Mrs. O'Malley,

I think . . . no, I'm sure . . . I'm falling in love with you, and I plan to do everything in my power to make you fall in love with me."

Too keyed up to think of sleep, Josh drove back to the foundry after leaving Shayna's house. He'd given her a chaste good-night kiss and left her to think over his declaration, hoping with all his heart she would give him a chance to redeem himself. If anyone had prophesied two months ago he'd tell a woman he'd seen only five times and kissed twice that he was falling in love with her, he'd have said they were out of their minds.

He was probably out of his. There was no logic to the way he felt about Shayna. From his first glimpse of her, he had sensed she embodied all the elements he had searched for and never found in any of the other women who had passed through his life. Yet, the very things about her that intrigued him most—her honesty, her deep sense of family, her loyalty to a hopelessly reactionary small town—were the chief obstacles in the way of planning a future with her after he shook the dust of Titusville from his feet.

With a weary shrug, he consigned his fate to the gods and forced himself to return to his seemingly endless perusal of the dusty ledgers recording the disastrous business decisions that had led the foundry to the brink of bankruptcy. He had another meeting with the bank officers coming up, and he wanted no surprises sprung on him.

He'd already worked his way though the five years of Kyle's administration, picking up item after item of unnecessary expense, including a ten-thousand-dollar cement floor to "give the foundry a modern appearance." Josh had groaned aloud when Angus ordered it covered with a four-inch layer of sand. "The best ladle operator spills now and then," he'd explained. "Molten metal sinks into sand; it flows across a cement floor and combines with the moisture to spit and fly. The men have suffered serious burns since that stupid floor was installed."

The ledger covering his father's last year heading the foundry was next in line. He was leafing through it, planning to take a closer look later on, when a large debit amount caught his eye. It was listed as "Trust Fund H. K. per A. McT." His brain kicked into overdrive. The initials A. McT. were self-explanatory and a sick feeling in the pit of his stomach told him what H. K. stood for.

He sorted through the card file on his desk, reached for the phone, and dialed a number.

"McTavish here."

"Angus. It's Josh. I know it's late, but I have something I need to talk over with you that I can't discuss on the phone. Is it all right if I drive out to your house?"

"Of course, Joshua. Do you know how to find it?"

"I'll manage."

"Very well then. I'll look forward to seeing you."

Twenty minutes later, Josh drove slowly down the wide, tree-lined street of one of Titusville's solid, middle-class suburbs and pulled into the driveway of the house at the corner of Barton and Fenwick. The neat numbers on the front door were clearly visible under the brass porch lamp, but even before he'd checked the address, he felt certain the two-story brick house belonged to Angus McTavish. It looked like Angus. Solid, no nonesense, built to last forever.

Josh stood for a moment beside his car, massaging the throbbing cords in the back of his neck and contemplating what he would say when he faced the old Scotsman.

Until he'd run across that suspicious item in the ledger, Josh hadn't realized how much admiration he'd developed for Angus during their month of working together. He was anything but naive where human frailty was concerned. His years in Washington had inured him to the shock of discovering unexpected weaknesses in the men he knew. But the idea that Angus could have been involved in anything the least bit underhanded while he was the production manager left Josh feeling both sickened and betrayed.

He picked up the telltale ledger and started toward the house. No use putting off the unpleasant task any longer.

Angus answered the first ring of the doorbell and ushered Josh into an oak-paneled entrance hall. "Welcome to my home, Joshua."

"Thank you. I appreciate your seeing me on such short notice." Josh looked around appreciatively. "It's a great house and, for some reason, it looks oddly familiar."

"You came here often with your grandfather when you were a wee lad." Angus nodded toward the staircase. "You wore holes in your britches sliding down that bannister. Like to gave David and me heart attacks the first time you shot off the end onto this stone floor, but you never shed a tear. Just picked yourself up, climbed the stairs on those stumpy little legs of yours, and tried it again."

Angus smiled apologetically. "Don't let me get started reminiscing. I never know when to stop. At my age, the past often seems more real than the present."

He led the way into the living room. It was a man's room, warm and inviting, but without a single feminine touch. Chestnut-colored leather couches flanked a huge stone fireplace, and antique brass lamps stood on sturdy slate-topped tables. One entire wall was floor-to-ceiling books; another a series of leaded-glass windows that looked out on a walled garden. Gleaming oak plank flooring framed a richly colored Persian carpet.

Josh sat down on one of the couches. "I must have happy memories of this house stored somewhere in my mind," he remarked, making small talk to postpone the moment when he had to face Angus with his discovery. "I feel strangely at home here."

"I'm sure you have. We had some good times here before David died." Angus regarded Josh thoughtfully. "But you didn't come here to talk over old times. What's bothering you, Joshua?"

"I've been going through some old ledgers and I came across a questionable entry for which I'd like an explanation." He looked Angus squarely in the eye. "Do the initials H. K. mean anything to you?

"H. K.?" Angus sounded puzzled. "I'd have to think on that one."

"Would the name Hilda Kleghorn shed any light on the subject? As I recall, you mentioned it yourself once."

"Oh, that H. K. Of course. I should have known you'd come across that item eventually." Angus regarded Josh with a hooded gaze. "Leave it alone, Joshua. I hired one of the best lawyers in Indianapolis to set up that trust fund. You can't touch it, and the interest makes the monthly payments. None of the current working capital of the foundry is involved."

"I want an explanation, Angus, for my own peace of mind, if nothing else."

Angus remained silent.

Josh patted the heavy ledger on his lap. "I take it Hilda Kleghorn was a particular friend of yours."

Angus looked startled. "Of course not." An expression of dawning realization crossed his face. "Is that why you came hightailing it out here?" He brushed a gnarled hand across his eyes. "God Almighty, Joshua, I thought you knew me better than that. I only got involved because your father begged me to. He was dying and he was obsessed with the idea of taking care of Hilda. It was probably the only truly decent thing the man ever did." He shrugged. "I can't say I liked the woman; she had a vulgar way of talking that didn't sit well. But then, Hiram was as coarse as they come himself. They'd 'carried on' for over twenty years. I suspect he kept Hilda dangling with promises of marriage. He'd never have gone through with it, of course. Hiram was a natural-born snob—not the kind to marry a woman with a blue-collar background. All of which is an old story not worth telling. I did what he asked because I figured Hilda had earned every cent he left her. Your father wasn't an easy man to get along with."

"Where is she now?"

"Still lives in The Flats, far as I know."

"Are there any other family secrets waiting for me in the archives?" Josh asked drily.

"No more trust funds, if that's what you mean, but I'm afraid you'll find that Kyle put some rather large legal costs on the foundry books."

Josh remembered the items well. He'd wondered what they represented when he came across them. "Why did Kyle need legal advice?"

"It seems he made promises to some local ladies which he had no intention of keeping, and they called him on them."

Josh sighed. He'd devoted most of his adult life to extricating Kyle from the disastrous aftermath of unkept promises. It was only logical his reckless brother would be in trouble in Titusville as well. A leopard doesn't change its spots because it prowls a different jungle.

Angus reached for the pipe and humidor on the table at his elbow. "The truth is, every Eddington from Titus on down to Kyle has played around on The Flats at one time or another. Even David, who was the pick of the lot, had his moments. I'm hoping you see fit to break the mold."

Played around on The Flats. That disgusting term again. Josh cringed. No wonder Shayna was wary of being seen with him.

He stood up, thanked Angus for the information he'd imparted, and quickly took his leave. He had a feeling the old man had been working up to another lecture on the dangers of getting involved with an employee's daughter, and Josh had no intention of defending his feelings for Shayna to anyone—including Angus McTavish.

In the brief time Josh had been in Angus's house, an army of sooty clouds had marched across the moon. The wind that whipped through the open window of his car had a smell of rain in it and over the purr of the engine, he heard a distant belch of thunder.

He cursed softly to himself, his mood as black as the summer storm gathering above him. Nothing came easily for him in this stupid little town. Winning the love of a woman with Shayna's lofty principles was tough enough. He didn't need the added problem of living down the sordid reputations of every Eddington who'd used Titusville Flats as his personal playground.

The first drops of tepid rain made dusty splatters on the hood of the Mercedes as he drove into his slot in the hotel parking lot. Grabbing his briefcase, he ran for cover. It had turned into a rotten night . . . in more ways than one.

Shayna awoke with a start and sat up in bed. She'd been in the midst of a lovely dream about Josh, when something bright and menacing had flashed through her drowsy fantasy. She glanced at the lighted hands on her bedside clock. Only eleven o'clock. It seemed much later.

The room was masked in darkness and the air felt sticky and oppressive. A shaft of lightning split the night sky and moments later, thunder rumbled overhead like a heavy truck rattling down a cobblestone street.

Rubbing her eyes, she slipped out of bed to close the window. Titusville was caught in a summer storm, one of those freakish choreographies of nature that sometimes danced across the Midwest, leaving everything in its wake drenched and steaming.

She climbed back into bed and, stretching out beneath the thin sheet that covered her, let her mind wander with delicious abandon over Josh's unexpected visit. She didn't dare let herself believe anything could come of this relationship he was promoting; still, she'd succumbed to temptation and agreed to have dinner with him on Friday evening.

Allison had phoned shortly after Josh had left, and Shayna felt swamped with guilt at the lies of omission she'd fobbed off on her caring friend. She'd simply been unable to talk about Josh's unbelievable declaration.

Lightning zigzagged across the sky again, startling Shayna with its brilliance. A gust of wind sent rain pelting against the window and a maple leaf, torn from the tree in her backyard, spread its webbed fingers across the dripping pane.

She stared blindly through the stormy darkness toward the spot where she knew Josh's "kissing box" sat next to the trash bin. It would be soaked by now and probably collecting windblown debris. The thought was unbearably depressing. Josh had told her he was falling in love with her and she'd consigned him—at least figuratively—to the trash pile.

Something clattered against the side of the house—probably an empty flower pot she'd left at the edge of the garden when she'd potted some seedling tomatoes. The wind was growing more fierce by the minute, and the more she thought about the box, the worse she felt.

She sighed and reached for the flashlight she kept next to her bed. By the time she found her boots and rain slicker, the wind had calmed a bit and the spate of rain had subsided. She stepped off her back porch and trained her flashlight on the ground ahead of her. Finding her way across the lawn was relatively easy, but the farther she progressed through the vegetable garden, the blacker the shadows became.

The pungent odor of wet loam took her breath away, and she remembered Pop had given her garden a heavy dose of horse manure earlier in the week. Rivulets of the smelly stuff were oozing over the toes of her boots.

"Why am I doing this?" she moaned. Less than two months before, she'd congratulated herself on getting her life back on track. From the first moment she'd met Josh, everything, including her sanity, had been hopelessly derailed.

The narrow beam of light picked out the box propped against the fence. Shayna reached for it and, too late, spied the two almond-shaped amber lights glowing in its depths. A streak of fur and fury catapulted toward her, sending her careening backward into the soft, wet soil of the garden.

"Dear God," she shrieked, and above the hammering

of her heart, she heard a sound like a defective buzz saw close to her left ear. Cautiously turning her head, she came eye to eye with the neighbor's ancient tomcat.

"Herman!" Shayna struggled to a sitting position, but not before Herman had sloshed his sandpaper tongue across her cheek. "Ugh," she said, dislodging two muddy paws from her chest and wiping her face with the back of her hand.

The flashlight was hung up in a clump of rhubarb, its beam spotlighting Herman's bristly black coat and the splotch of white on his chest. A recent fight had cut a notch in one ear and the whiskers were missing from the left side of his face. Everything about Herman looked off kilter. Shayna giggled. More than anything else, he resembled a tipsy old rake in a scruffy tuxedo.

The idea of a randy tom taking up residence in Josh Eddington's kissing box struck her funny. She leaned back on her elbows, roaring with laughter. Herman took this as a sign of camaraderie on her part and flung himself across her in a frenzy of slavish devotion.

At his best, Herman had a unique odor. Tonight something new had been added. "Phew, Herman. You smell like wet horse manure," Shayna declared, then caught a whiff of herself and realized the problem wasn't all Herman's.

Only Josh's box had survived intact. Soaking wet but pristine as the day he'd had it built, it reposed on the only clump of grass left in this section of the garden. "Wouldn't you know," Shayna remarked, and dissolved into another fit of giggles.

The return trip to the house was a nightmare. The rain started again with a vengeance, the battered flashlight gave up the ghost, and the box grew heavier with each step she took. Past cabbages and bush beans, carrots and cucumbers she trudged, with her mud-soaked nightgown clinging to her legs. Twice she stumbled over Herman, who seemed determined to walk between her feet.

Finally reaching the porch door, she jostled the box

through it and back to its place beside the washing machine. She pulled off her rain slicker and muddy boots, turned off the light, and slipped out of her filthy nightgown.

Herman hovered on the bottom step, his engine running full bore. "Beat it, Herman," Shayna said. "Toadying up to me will get you nowhere."

She felt a swipe of silky fur against her ankle and realized Herman's toadying was aimed not at her, but at Parsley. The dainty female arched her sleek back, and Herman's purr shifted into high gear.

Shayna blinked. For just a moment, the Cheshire grin on the old tom's face looked startlingly similar to the one she'd seen on Josh's face the day he'd taken her to lunch at the Victorian Hotel.

"I know what you have in mind, Herman. Forget it," Shayna hissed. "Parsley has too much sense to fall for your dubious charms."

The words were scarcely out of her mouth when a ball of orange-and-gray fur flew through the open screen door and down the steps toward the loitering tom.

"Come back here, Parsley," Shayna groaned. "He's not for you. You're only going to get your heart broken."

Her warning fell on deaf ears. Head high, tail waving and purring like a miniature motorboat, Parsley trotted down the garden path side by side with the raunchy old tom.

With a sigh of resignation, Shayna turned back into the darkened house and made her way to the bathroom for her second shower of the evening.

Good sense had definitely taken a beating on all fronts tonight.

TEN

The minute she answered the door on Friday evening, Shayna knew she was in trouble. Josh was in a crazy mood. Without so much as a "by-your-leave," he greeted her with a kiss that left her as limp and wobbly as a noodle.

Megan loved it. "You kissed my mama," she squealed, hopping up and down and clapping her hands. Josh swooped her up in a giant arc above his head. "This is my night for kissing pretty girls," he proclaimed, giving her a peck on her cheek and a playful whack on her bottom as he set her back on her feet.

"How come Mama and you are going someplace without me?" Megan asked, clinging possessively to his long legs.

"Because tonight we're going to do grown-up things." Josh ruffled her mop of silky curls. "Maybe Sunday, if your mother says it's okay, we can go out for pizza."

Two pairs of eyes turned toward Shayna. "We'll see," she murmured, casting a "behave yourself" look at Josh.

"We can, we can, we can." Megan twirled round and round until she fell to the floor in a dizzy heap. "Mama always says 'we'll see' when she means 'yes.'"

Josh cast a Simon Legree leer in Shayna's direction. "Thanks for the tip," he growled. "I'll keep that in mind."

Shayna groaned. He was in a mood all right. She was growing more apprehensive by the minute over this date of theirs.

"Put your nightie on and collect the toys you're taking to Grandma's," she ordered Megan, and watched her daughter scoot down the hall to her bedroom. She turned to Josh. "I'm not sure this date is such a good idea."

Josh seemed genuinely surprised. "Is the idea of spending an evening with me really so terrifying?"

"It isn't just you." Shayna smoothed an imaginary wrinkle from the skirt of her blue silk dress. "I'd probably feel like a fish out of water dating anyone. I've never really done this sort of thing, except with Tim, and I'd known him all my life. There were no surprises with him. With you, I never know what to expect."

"Expect to be happy, Shayna," he said, cupping her face in his hand and planting a brief kiss on the tip of her nose. "Despite our differences, I think we have a great potential for happiness if we just give ourselves a chance. There probably will be surprises ahead . . . for both of us, but that's what keeps life interesting. Trust me, honey. The one thing I'll never do is hurt you."

Josh stepped back as Megan, in her best nightie and bunny slippers, came trudging down the hall with a box of coloring books and crayons. "I'll go with you," he said. "I want to talk to your grandfather before we leave."

Shayna gulped. "You're going to my parents' house?"

"Is there some reason why I shouldn't?" He scowled. "Didn't you tell them you were going out with me?"

"I just said I was going out to dinner. I think they assumed I was going with my friend, Mirabelle."

"An assumption you encouraged, no doubt." He glanced toward Megan. "How did you expect to keep it a secret?"

"I didn't. I just thought it would be easier to explain tomorrow after . . ."

"After the dirty deed was done." Josh shook his head. "No way, Shayna. I want everything open and above-board. If that embarrasses you, I'm sorry, but it's your problem—not mine." He took Megan's hand. "Let's go, punkin."

Shayna watched the two of them troop out the back door. On a sudden impulse, she hurried to catch up with them. With a few curt words, Josh had managed to reduce her to the status of a small child reprimanded for some thoughtless deed, and she didn't like the feeling one bit.

The look he'd given her when he'd passed the kissing box on her back porch hadn't helped. She wasn't sure if it was a promise or a threat, but she breathed a sigh of relief that she'd retrieved the box before the trash man had carried it off.

"Hi, Grandma," Megan chirped as she threw open the Brenegans' back door and trotted through the kitchen to the living room.

Maggie Brenegan was standing at the kitchen sink peeling potatoes. She looked up, saw Josh, and dropped everything—peeler, potato, and her mouth. "Sweet Mother of God." She crossed herself fervently. "Come here this minute, Johnny," she yelled. "It's Mr. Eddington, himself, come visiting."

Shayna's father appeared in the doorway, the evening paper in one hand and a can of beer in the other. He blinked in astonishment. "Evening, Joshua," he croaked, dropping the paper and his beer onto the kitchen table. "What brings you here?"

"I wanted your opinion on the casting we poured today."

John Brenegan scratched his head, a puzzled look on his face. "I thought we hashed that out this afternoon. The sorry thing looked like it was shrinking faster than a piece of fatback in a hot skillet. I told Angus I'd meet him at eleven when the swing shift boys cut her loose, but I know in my bones we've got another piece of junk on our hands.''

"This is our third try at casting this one," Josh said gravely. "If we don't get it right pretty soon, we'll have to forfeit the order, and Angus says they're talking about a run in the thousands. I don't have to tell you, it's one we can't afford to lose.''

John Brenegan nodded. "Nope. You sure didn't have to come all the way out to The Flats just to tell me that.'' He pushed his glasses down the bridge of his nose and peered over the top of them at Josh and Shayna. "So, you got anything else on your mind, Joshua?''

"As a matter of fact, I have.'' Josh draped his fingers across the back of Shayna's neck in a gesture so blatantly possessive, she felt her ears grow hot with embarrassment. "I wanted to let you know I'm taking Shayna out to dinner.''

She heard her mother's startled intake of breath, and attempted to move out of Josh's grasp. His hand slid down to her shoulder, holding her to him. Shayna managed a sick smile. This situation was growing more ridiculous by the minute. What was Josh trying to prove?

Her father looked momentarily taken aback. "So, Joshua, you're taking my girl out to dinner," he echoed.

"Yes, sir, I am. I intend to see a lot of her from now on. I hope you have no objections.''

John Brenegan scowled thoughtfully. "None I can think of right off, so long as you mind your P's and Q's and treat her with the respect she deserves.'' He cleared his throat. "But Mother and I appreciate your asking.''

"I thought you would.''

Shayna looked with dismay at the two men towering over her. "For heaven's sake," she said sharply, "I'm a twenty-six-year-old widow with a daughter—not some wide-eyed teenager. You don't have to ask my father's permission to take me out to dinner.''

Neither man acknowledged her comment, and the look

they exchanged hinted at some unspoken agreement to which she wasn't privy. Her temper flared. She opened her mouth to tell them what she thought of their high-handed tactics, but her father interrupted her before she could get a word out. "That's a mighty pretty dress, sweetheart. Is it new?"

"Yes. It's from Allison's shop," she replied, and watched the disapproving frown on her mother's face grow even blacker. Maggie Brenegan had remarked more than once that only a fool would pay the kind of prices Allison Cartwright charged.

John Brenegan's gaze shifted back to Josh. A foolish grin spread across his lined face. "So, you're taking my girl out to dinner, Joshua," he said again.

Josh's grin looked equally foolish. "Yes, sir," he said, then, quickly changing the subject, he extended a hand to Shayna's mother. "I don't believe I've had the pleasure of meeting you, Mrs. Brenegan."

Maggie Brenegan blushed like a schoolgirl. She wiped her hands on the towel hanging at the end of the counter and shook Josh's hand gingerly. Shayna turned away to hide her smile. If nothing else, Josh had accomplished one miracle with this impromptu visit of his. This was the first time she'd ever seen her mother at a loss for words.

The smile was a little harder to manage a few minutes later when the Mercedes pulled away from the curb and headed up Loblolly Street. It was suppertime, and the street should have been deserted. Today, it seemed as if every occupant of every house had found an excuse to be outdoors. One and all, they craned their necks as she passed.

The ride was a silent one. Josh concentrated on his driving, and Shayna was still mulling over the amazing scene in her parents' kitchen. Out of the corner of her eye, she studied the determined thrust of Josh's chin. He looked more like a man on a mission than someone embarking on a social engagement.

They left The Flats, drove through the center of town, and climbed the hill to The Highlands. There was only one place in this district where they could have dinner—The Highlands Country Club. She certainly hadn't expected him to take her there. Everyone in town knew both the golf course and the clubhouse were restricted to Highlands residents. She should have known Josh would be a member. White Oaks was the largest and most elegant of all the old homes in the district.

She tensed. With her luck, the whole school board would be dining at the club tonight. Seeing Josh and her together might arouse ugly suspicions. She felt more uneasy than ever about this so-called date she'd let herself be talked into.

Josh reached over and patted her hand. "Stop worrying. Everything's going to be just fine."

Great! Now he was reading her mind. She scrunched down in her seat and blanked out every thought in her head for the remainder of the ride.

The parking attendant at the club was a boy from her neighborhood. The automatic smile on his freckled face froze when he opened her door. He gaped at the Mercedes, Josh, and her, in that order. "Gee whiz, Mrs. O'Malley," he stammered. "I sure never expected to see you here."

Josh's scowl silenced him instantly, but Shayna couldn't help but laugh at the boy's open-mouthed astonishment. For the first time since the evening began, she felt herself relax. This whole crazy situation was so unreal, there was simply no point in taking it seriously. She took the arm Josh offered her, winked broadly at the red-faced attendant, and walked up the stairs to the imposing entrance.

To her surprise, the interior of the clubhouse looked more somber and depressing than elegant, as she'd expected. A brass plaque in the entrance hall stated it had been built in 1932, and from the looks of things, the rather dismal ambiance of The Great Depression Era had been faithfully preserved ever since. None of the bright, cheerful colors modern decorators used were in evidence here. Dark wood paneling covered the walls of both foyer and dining room, and the uniforms of the waiters were the same somber dark brown as the upholstery.

More than half the tables in the dining area were occupied, but the room was strangely quiet. Everyone seemed to be talking in the hushed tones people used in church or doctors' waiting rooms. Even the muffled clink of silver on china sounded subdued.

Every eye assessed them as the maître d' led them to their table, and Shayna instinctively straightened her back and lifted her chin. Taking her seat, she glanced surreptitiously at the diners around her. If this was the way the rich had fun, give her a blue-collar night on the town anytime.

Josh looked up from the ornate menu the waiter had placed in his hands and surveyed the dining room with distaste. His secretary had assured him this was the in place to go for great food and entertainment. He sincerely hoped both were livelier than the decor. He took a sip of his martini and acknowledged that the bartender, at least, knew his business. Maybe there was hope for the chef.

He met Shayna's wide-eyed gaze and felt a surge of tenderness sweep through him. She looked a bit overwhelmed by the heavy atmosphere. "Funereal, isn't it?" he murmured. "I keep expecting the ghosts of diners past to materialize."

"Do you come here often?"

"Good God, no. I was desperate for a nice place to take you and I'm sick to death of the hotel dining room. Mrs. Warren recommended the club. I didn't even know my family had a membership until she pointed it out to me. If you'd rather go someplace else, we can leave."

"No, of course not. It's really quite nice . . . in a gloomy sort of way." She smiled hesitantly. "The menu's all in French, which is fun. After four years of classes, I'll finally get to use some of what I've learned."

Josh watched a frown form between her finely arched brows as she studied the menu. She looked up. "There are no prices," she whispered.

"There are on my copy," he whispered back, and chuckled at her look of confusion.

"Well, I never." Shayna sounded highly indignant. "That's the most impractical idea I've ever heard of. How would a person know if she were ordering something terribly expensive?"

"How indeed?"

She studied his face closely. "Are you laughing at me?"

"Never, honey," Josh assured her. "If I'm laughing, it's because being with you makes me feel so good." God, how he wished he could skip all this courting foolishness and take this sweet, unpretentious woman home to that lonely bed of his and awaken the simmering passion he'd glimpsed when he'd kissed her earlier. It took all his willpower to concentrate on the menu, when the voracious appetite he'd developed had nothing whatsoever to do with food.

Two hours and six courses later, he had to admit he'd thoroughly enjoyed his dinner. Mrs. Warren was right; the food served at The Highlands Country Club was outstanding, and watching Shayna enjoy it was half the fun. Her pleasure in each new taste sensation was so intense, he found himself wondering if she made love with the same fierce joy with which she attacked a serving of Boeuf Bourguignon.

He lifted the champagne bottle from the ice bucket beside the table and refilled her glass. He had never cared for the stuff, but it had seemed the sort of thing Shayna would like. The dreamy, sensuous look in her eyes told him he'd guessed right. "I'm going to have to ply you with champagne more often, Mrs. O'Malley," he teased. "It makes you look very sexy."

Shayna smiled. "I feel all soft and fuzzy, like I'm sort of slithering around inside my skin." She took a healthy drink of the amber liquid. "And it tickles my nose." She set her glass down. "But I think I've had enough; I have this overwhelming desire to giggle."

Josh took a closer look at her. Two bright circles of color dotted her cheeks, much like the painted cheeks of the Raggedy Ann doll he'd bought for Megan. He laughed. Everything about Shayna was unique, even the way she looked when she was slightly tipsy. He returned the champagne to the ice and signaled for coffee.

Shayna sat quietly until the waiter had finished, then leaned across the table and smiled conspiratorially. "Do you really think I look sexy, Josh?"

"Honey, if you looked any more sexy than you do right this minute, I'd probably go into cardiac arrest."

"What a lovely thing to say. Thank you very much." Shayna hiccupped. "Oops!" She covered her mouth with her hand to suppress a giggle. "Did you know that no one in my entire life has ever called me sexy before? Tim thought I was sweet." She toyed with her coffee cup. "Usually I get called dull things like dependable and lady-like and wholesome." She grimaced. "Can you imagine what 'wholesome' does to a woman's ego?"

Josh raised his right hand. "I swear the word will never cross my lips."

Resting her chin on her tented hands, Shayna regarded him solemnly. "You look sexy, too, Josh . . . even in that tie."

He glanced down at his sober gray tie with a minute navy fleck, which he'd originally purchased to impress an ultraconservative senator he was lobbying. He'd hoped it would convey a "solid citizen" look to Shayna and her family. Perhaps he was guilty of overkill. "You don't like my tie?" he asked innocently.

"Not really. It reminds me of this room." She gestured expansively. "Terribly expensive but sort of stuffy." She glanced furtively around her at the nearby diners. "Do you know when you look the sexiest?" she whispered.

He fought the urge to laugh aloud. She was staring so intently at him, her eyes were beginning to cross. "Give me a clue so I can dress accordingly when I get around to seducing you," he whispered back.

Shayna gave him a squelching look. "You really look sexy in your T-shirt and jeans." She hiccupped daintily. "Allison's eyes nearly popped out of her head that day at the hotel."

Josh reached over to trace a finger along the back of her hand, and her shiver of awareness echoed deep inside his own body. "Allison's opinion isn't the one that counts," he said, closing his fingers around her slender wrist. "What I want to hear is how you feel about me."

For a long moment, her gaze locked with his. "If you haven't figured out how I feel by now, you're certainly not as smart as you look." She chewed thoughtfully on her lower lip. "You've probably noticed I go reeling off into space every time you touch me. It's a little bewildering. I'm not sure I like being so . . . so out of control."

Josh nodded. "I know exactly how you feel. It scares the hell out of me, too. It's like sailing into uncharted waters without a compass. I guess we'll just have to trust our instincts, and mine tell me we can handle anything so long as we do it together."

Her eyes clouded with sudden panic. "You're going too fast for me, Josh. I need time to think about this."

Time was the one thing he didn't have. Somehow he had to convince her to put her future and Megan's in his hands before he had to tell her that future didn't include this small town she was so attached to. "Take all the time you need, honey. I'm a patient man," he said, cursing the circumstances that forced him to be less than truthful to the most honest woman he'd ever known.

Somewhere in the background, he heard musicians warming up and he breathed a sigh of relief. This conversation was skirting a little too close to the edge for his taste.

He glanced up to see four white-haired old men in ancient tuxedos assembled on the raised platform next to the dance floor. Like everything else in the place, they looked a bit musty and timeworn, but the first bars of Cole Porter's "Night and Day" told him they were no slouches when it came to playing the great dance music of the thirties.

He sighed contentedly. Somehow the future would take care of itself. Right now, life was looking good. He took a sip of the excellent brandy with which he'd topped off his dinner. Sweet music, great food, and the woman he loved. It didn't get any better than that. Even this dreary old club was beginning to look mellow and nostalgic.

He rose and held out his hand. "Dance with me, Shayna."

"I'd better have some coffee first. Everything looks a bit hazy. And I'm out of practice. I haven't danced since before Tim died."

Josh felt a twinge of frustration. That was the second time she'd mentioned her husband's name in the past few minutes. He wondered how long these echoes of Shayna's past would haunt them. "A little exercise is exactly what you need right now," he said tersely. "Just relax and follow my lead." Pulling her to her feet, he led her onto the dance floor. Once she quit protesting, she fit into his arms like she'd been designed for that very purpose.

Her instant response to the music told him she liked to dance every bit as much as he did. By the time they'd circled the floor once, she was fitting her body rhythm to his as surely as if they'd been dancing together for years. Instinctively, he knew it would be like this when they made love—that perfect blending of bodies and minds that only happens when two people are linked by an indefinable magic.

The musicians slid effortlessly into a lilting version of Gershwin's "Always," and Josh waltzed them through the gathering crowd of dancers toward the center of the floor.

The wine had loosened Shayna's inhibitions. She closed her eyes, nestled her head against his shoulder, and pressed her pliant body so close to his, Josh finally had to force himself to pull away from her. "I love the feel of you against me, honey," he said, managing a half-hearted grin, "but if we dance like this much longer, I'm going to embarrass us both."

Shayna's lips tilted in a mischievous, knowing smile. Wine was a wonderful thing, Josh decided. It unearthed a deliciously naughty streak in his prim and proper lady that conjured up all kinds of interesting possibilities. He was just deciding what do to about the fascinating situation when he felt a tap on his shoulder.

"Good evening, Mr. Eddington." Josh turned his head and found himself staring into the eyes of Roger Bancroft, the superintendent of schools. Bancroft's gaze slid to Shayna. "And Mrs. O'Malley. I didn't realize Mr. Eddington and you were acquainted."

Josh felt Shayna tense, and tightened his arm around her waist. Bancroft's tone of voice set his teeth on edge, and he didn't much care for the appraising look he gave Shayna, but he managed a polite smile.

Bancroft's answering smile was equally polite. "I'm the program chairman for our annual Founder's Day dinner dance, and since your grandfather was one of the club's charter members, the committee feels you're the logical choice for banquet speaker. It would be the first time since your father died that a member of your family attended."

A glacial anger descended on Josh, chilling him to the core. Bancroft's pointed exclusion of Shayna from his invitation was insulting, and the grim set of her mouth told him she'd instantly picked up on the slight.

"Thank you for asking. I'm afraid I don't have time to work up a speech, but I might be able to take in the event. I'll have to talk it over with my lady before I give you a definite answer." He smiled down at Shayna. "How do you feel about it, darling? We probably should consider it out of respect to my grandfather, if nothing else."

Mr. Bancroft smiled thinly at Shayna. "We hope you'll agree, Mrs. O'Malley. Naturally, any friend of Mr. Eddington's is welcome." His emphasis on the word "friend" was unmistakable.

Josh didn't give Shayna a chance to answer. He pulled her to him and whirled back into the crush of dancing couples. They finished the waltz in silence and swung into the following fox trot before Shayna had time to catch her breath. Josh's lead was as strong as ever, but the lovely, fluid sensation was gone. The tightly coiled feel to his body and rigid set of his mouth told Shayna he was still seething over their encounter with Mr. Bancroft.

"It isn't important enough to get angry over," she said quietly.

"It is to me. I've never cared a damn what anybody thought about me before, but I find I care very much how this town looks at our relationship."

Perplexed, Shayna leaned back to study his face. "That makes no sense whatsoever. I can't imagine why you'd care what people around here think."

"Why do you say that?"

"Come on, Josh. I know how you feel about Titusville."

"And I know how *you* feel about it."

Shayna stared in amazement at the handsome man in whose arms she was dancing. "Good Lord, is that what this evening's all about? Some kind of public statement that's supposed to protect my reputation?"

A faint flush showed through the remnants of Josh's tan. "Like I said, I want everything out in the open so no one has any doubts about how I feel about you."

"And you think taking me to dinner at the country club and calling me 'darling' will silence the gossip?"

"I think it will help."

Shayna smiled into his anxious eyes. "Thank you for caring," she said simply.

She couldn't remember when anything had touched her

as deeply as this foolish campaign Josh had embarked upon. He was probably an expert in public relations when it came to national politics; she didn't have the heart to tell him how little he knew about life in small towns.

ELEVEN

The house on Loblolly Street was dark when Josh and Shayna returned to it. "You must remember to leave a light on when you go out in the evening so it looks like someone's at home," Josh chided her. "A woman living alone has to be very careful these days." He insisted on inspecting every room to make certain no one had entered the house while they were gone.

Shayna had a hard time keeping a straight face when she contemplated how desperate a thief would have to be to consider robbing her house, but she kept her counsel. Josh seemed serious about his role of protector. She was just grateful she'd remembered to lock the door. More often than not, she forgot.

"I'll make coffee while you finish your sleuthing, Detective Eddington," she promised.

"Thanks. I could use a cup." Josh checked his watch. "It's five minutes after ten. Don't let me forget I have to meet your father and Angus at the foundry at eleven."

Shayna nodded, relieved their time together was so limited. Without Megan's noisy chatter, the house seemed uncomfortably small and intimate . . . and Josh was in a funny mood tonight.

He'd been very quiet on their return ride from the country club. But at every stoplight they'd come to, he'd pulled her to him and kissed her—and each kiss had been progressively more passionate than the last. Just thinking about it sent Shayna's heart slamming against her rib cage. Thank God Main Street only had four signals. She should never have drunk that treacherous wine. Champagne and kisses were a lethal combination when the kisses were as hungry and demanding as Josh's were tonight.

She nearly jumped out of her shoes when he suddenly loomed in the doorway. "Everything in the house looks okay." He regarded her solemnly. "I think we should have a little talk before I leave and settle things between us."

Shayna's heart took another startled lurch. Ever since she'd met Josh, she'd clung to the belief that because his world and hers could never mix, she was somehow insulated from his devastating charm. Tonight had changed all that. Everything he'd said and done since he'd walked into her parents' house had shown he expected to become a serious part of her life. Now he wanted to *get things settled between them*. The idea was intriguing . . . but a little frightening.

"I'm not sure this is the night for a serious discussion," she protested. "I'm still dizzy from all that wine." It was a lame excuse, but it was all she could come up with on such short notice.

Josh shrugged. "You'll be fine once you have a cup of coffee. I'll wait for you in the living room."

Shayna returned to her coffeemaking with grave misgivings. She should have known nothing she said would deter Josh. The man was like a bulldog with a bone once he got an idea in his head. *And he called her stubborn!*

Josh hadn't planned to wait in the living room. He'd rather have sat in the kitchen watching Shayna work as he had that first day. The sight of her wedding picture on the television had changed his mind. It never hurt to know your competition, and Tim O'Malley's name came up too often to pretend he was no longer a rival for her love.

He picked up the framed photograph and stared in disbelief at the slender, black-haired boy standing beside a girlish version of Shayna. Whenever he'd tried to picture Tim O'Malley, Josh had imagined someone resembling the three burly Brenegan men. The boy in this picture was slender as a reed and only a couple of inches taller than his diminutive bride. The rest of the wedding party towered so far above them, the two central figures in the picture looked more like the dolls atop the wedding cake than the actual bride and groom.

Disgruntled, Josh put the photograph back in its place. He'd never lacked self-confidence when it came to competing with other men for the women he'd found attractive. Now, in the most important competition he would ever face, none of the usual axioms applied. *How could any man compete with a ghost who would remain a sweet-faced boy forever?* For the first time in his life, he found himself wrestling with jealousy. It was an ugly adversary.

"Coffee's ready." Shayna carried the tray to the coffee table. One look at Josh and her smile froze. He had a strange, tight-lipped look about him that hadn't been there a few moments before. "Is something wrong, Josh?"

He settled onto the couch and stretched out his long legs. "Not wrong . . . just more complicated than I'd like it." He removed his jacket and loosened his tie. "I've been looking at your wedding picture. It's hard to believe you're the same person as that pretty child."

"I'm not," she said. "Life saw to that." She searched his face, wondering what her wedding picture had to do with the complications bothering him.

She handed him a cup of coffee, poured one for herself, and sat down in the room's one easy chair.

Josh's left eyebrow quirked upward. "Why are you sitting way over there?"

"You said you wanted to talk."

"I also want to hold you in my arms. Is there something wrong with that?" Josh's brows drew together in an angry frown. "What the hell is the matter with you, Shayna?

An hour ago you were a warm, sensous woman; now you're perched on the edge of that chair like some Victorian maiden ready to fight for her virtue. Have I said or done something that led you to believe I planned to have my wicked way with you the minute I got you alone?''

"Don't be silly. The thought never entered my mind."

"Thanks a lot. That remark ranks right up there with 'wholesome.' '' Josh's scowl darkened. "The truth, Shayna. What is the problem . . . and don't tell me there is none, because I'm fine-tuned to the vibes you send out."

Shayna's grip tightened on the arms of the chair. No one had ever pried into her private thoughts and feelings like this man—not even her husband. The few times she'd tried to express herself to Tim, she'd simply confused him. Now it was her turn to be confused. Josh's demands left her feeling naked and vulnerable.

She took a deep, steadying breath. "If you're serious about this talk you think we should have, you'll have to keep your distance," she declared flatly. "I simply cannot think when you touch me. You seem charged with some kind of electrical energy that shortcircuits every brain cell I own. It's the most distracting sensation I've ever experienced. Take your pick, Josh—talk or touch. You can't have both."

His laugh infuriated her. "Just what is so funny?"

Josh stood up. "You are, honey. You're the funniest thing that's ever happened to me." He laughed again. "Is it any wonder I'm in love with you?" With one swift move, he covered the space between them, swept her into his arms, and returned to the couch.

Shayna flailed the air ineffectively. "What do you think you're doing?" she squealed.

"You gave me a choice. I made it." He settled her on his lap. "Touching beats talking hands down." Lowering his head, he teased her lips apart in a fiery kiss.

His tongue delved deep into the throbbing softness of her mouth and the heady taste of brandy permeated her senses. She gasped, struggling for control, but the groan that rumbled in his throat scattered her last particles of restraint like grains of sand whipped by the wind. Her fingers slid into his hair, and she tugged him closer. He groaned again, deepening his demanding kiss, until her tongue matched his, thrust for thrust, in a fierce and tender mating ritual.

His hands were everywhere—along her back and the swell of her hip, across her belly to the sensitive peaks of her breasts. One by one the tiny pearl buttons on her dress yielded to his exploring fingers, until he slipped it and the lacy straps of her teddy off her shoulders and cupped her aching fullness in his hand. The feel of his calloused fingers on her breast sent such waves of desire spiraling through her, she clung to him and whimpered with delight.

Her small, sexy cry nearly drove Josh over the brink. With a ragged groan, he dragged his lips from hers and stared down at her. The glazed look in her eyes told him she was his to take, and God knew he'd never felt such raw passion as she kindled in him with her uninhibited response.

He drew a shallow, painful breath, as reason warred with the carnal needs raging within him. With any other woman, the choice would have been simple. He'd been celibate much too long, and the temptation to lose himself in the sweet, mindless pleasure of lovemaking here and now was almost overpowering. But his need for Shayna wouldn't end with "here and now" and his heart told him he'd live to regret the passion he'd kindled in his sweet little puritan tonight if he saw remorse in her lovely eyes tomorrow.

Groaning softly, he buried his face in her tousled hair and willed his thundering heart to return to normal. The pulse racing through his arteries sounded like the erratic throbbing of a faulty engine. With closed eyes, he waited for the sound to abate. It grew louder.

He raised his head. Good God. It was an engine. The startled look in Shayna's eyes said she'd heard it, too. For a second, they stared at each other. Then her lips formed a silent "Pop" at the same instant he said "John."

"That's his old truck. He's leaving for the foundry. I was supposed to remind you." Her voice sounded heavy with guilt—too heavy for the small sin of forgetfulness.

She pushed against his chest, trying to sit upright, but Josh tightened his arms around her. More than anything else, he wanted to hold her and comfort her and make her understand the depth of his feeling for her. The stunned look in her eyes warned him this was not the time to make his amorous declaration.

Gently, he slid her lacy straps back onto her shoulders and buttoned her dress. "I love you," he murmured, burying his nose one last time in the silk of her hair. He waited hopefully for Shayna's answering pledge, but she turned her face into his shoulder and said nothing.

"I'll call you tomorrow about Megan's pizza party," he said quietly. "Maybe we can have that talk on Sunday. I promise I'll keep my distance. I think we've just proved your theory that touch and talk don't mix for us."

She was still sitting on the couch when he let himself out the door.

All the way to the foundry, he berated himself. He'd promised Shayna they'd take things "slow and easy." Hell. A runaway freight train showed more control than he'd displayed tonight. It would be a miracle if she ever trusted him again. He suspected her uninhibited response to his lovemaking had been as much a surprise to her as it had been to him. Once the haze of passion cleared, she'd probably start having serious regrets.

Her ominous silence when he'd told her he loved her was unnerving. Gripping the steering wheel, he stared with unseeing eyes at the dismal little town passing by his window. *Could it be possible he'd been flying so high with these newfound feelings of his, he'd failed to realize he was on a solo flight?*

*   *   *

Shayna watched the door close behind Josh. Just like that, as if nothing of any consequence had happened, he'd called a halt to their lovemaking and gone off to inspect a casting. And if he hadn't had an appointment with her father, what then? Would he have carried their passionate episode to its natural conclusion? Probably so. He certainly hadn't encountered any resistance from her.

She felt drowned in humiliation, remembering her wanton response to Josh's lovemaking. If this was his idea of "slow and easy," God help her if he ever got up to speed.

He'd declared he loved her. Yet, he'd obviously been in complete control of his emotions, while she'd gone up in flames the instant he'd touched her. Everything about this situation with Josh was topsy-turvy. Whenever Tim and she had made love, he'd been the one to go off the deep end. She'd assumed that was the natural way with men and women. For months after he'd died, she'd been haunted by his plaintive whisper their last night together. "Just once, I wish I could make you love me the way I love you."

She knew now what he'd meant. In one brief interlude on her living-room couch, she'd given more of herself to Josh than she'd given to Tim in the five years they were married. The knowledge broke her heart . . . and left her feeling hopelessly vulnerable. Loving a man was one thing; relinquishing her soul to him every time he took her in his arms was another thing entirely.

With a weary sigh, she placed the cups of cold coffee neither Josh nor she had drunk on the tray and carried them to the kitchen. She'd just poured herself another cup when she heard the knock on her back door. She groaned. Not Ronnie again. She couldn't handle any more tonight.

She opened the door to tell him to go home and found herself facing her mother. "Mom! What in the world brings you out this time of night?"

"Megan's asleep on the couch and Ronnie's tinkering with car parts at the kitchen table. There was no place for me to go but bed, and I can't sleep with Pop gone. Your light was on, so I thought I'd visit a minute.''

Shayna stepped aside to let her mother's bulky, robe-clad figure through the door. ''How about a cup of coffee?''

Maggie shrugged. ''Why not? I've a notion I'll be awake all night anyway.'' She settled onto a kitchen chair. ''That was a bit of a surprise you gave us this evening, my girl.''

''It was a surprise to me, too, Mom. I don't know why Josh thought he needed Pop's permission to take me out.''

'Twas a nice gesture. One I wouldn't have expected from an Eddington.'' She sniffed. ''Pop was pleased as punch. Said it showed Joshua was dead serious about you. Of course, we both know your pa sees good in everyone.''

''But you don't.'' Shayna sensed where this conversation was leading. She didn't need it. Josh had confused her enough for one night, and the wine had worn off, leaving her headachy and depressed.

''The man's besotted for sure. 'Twas plain to see he couldn't keep his hands off you. That doesn't mean he won't break your heart if you let him.'' Maggie's eyes searched Shayna's. ''How do you feel about him?''

Shayna's first inclination was to tell her mother to stay out of her affairs. One look at her anxious eyes and she knew she couldn't do it. This wasn't just idle curiosity on Maggie's part; she was genuinely worried.

''I guess I feel more bewildered than anything else right now. I certainly don't feel the same way about him I did about Tim. But when he kisses me . . .''

''It's like Fourth of July and Christmas and New Year's Eve all rolled up together. Lord Almighty, Shayna, don't think I don't understand. I wasn't always a fat old lady.''

''You're not that now, Mom.''

''Yes, I am, but that's neither here nor there.'' Two grim white lines formed at the corners of Maggie's mouth. ''I don't suppose Joshua Eddington's said anything about wanting to marry you.''

"Of course not. Tonight was the first time he's taken me out, for heaven's sake."

"Humph. From the way he was looking at you, I'd wager he's told you he loves you. Seems like such words come easier to fellows like him than they do to your pa's kind."

The barb struck home. Shayna had wondered herself at the suddenness of Josh's surprising declaration.

Maggie concentrated on rolling the paper napkin Shayna had set by her cup into a tight cylinder. When she'd unrolled it and pressed it flat again, she looked up. "It may not always look like it, the way I act, but more than anything else in this world, I want you to be happy."

"I know that, Mom."

"Which is why I'm going to say something to you I always hoped I'd never have to say."

Shayna sighed in exasperation. Her mother's lectures were painful at any time. As vulnerable as she was feeling right now, the idea was almost too much to contemplate.

Maggie cleared her throat. "When I was young and not half bad to look at, I fell head over heels in love with a boy from The Highlands."

Shayna gaped at her mother. "I thought Pop and you were high school sweethearts."

"We were, but one look at that fellow and I forgot about John and my friends, even my family. It was a hot summer that year, and I guess the prairie sun must have fried my brain. Leastwise, I sure acted like I didn't have an ounce of sense for a few months there."

With nervous fingers, Maggie twisted the napkin into a tight little knot. "It wasn't all one-sided, either. He fell just as hard as I did. I thought because he told me he loved me, that was all that mattered. I should have known better. There's a lot more than just miles separating The Flats from The Highlands. His folks weren't as rich as the Eddingtons, but his pa drove a fancy Cadillac. Mine drove a forklift at the foundry."

"Those things aren't as important nowadays," Shayna

protested, echoing the sentiments Josh had expressed so vehemently that night on her front porch.

"They didn't seem important then, either. But when summer ended, he went off to Harvard and I went to work at The Bluebell. He wrote every day for the first few weeks; then the letters dwindled off and stopped, except for the registered letter telling me he was sorry to have to hurt me but he'd gotten himself engaged to some senator's daughter from New York. By then I was in the worst kind of trouble a girl could be in, and I didn't know what to do about it. Except I knew I loved him too much to try to make him marry me when he didn't want me anymore."

"Oh, Mom . . . !"

"John guessed right off. That dear, foolish man never said a word of blame; just told me I had to pick up the pieces and go on. Before I could draw a breath, he'd talked to the priest and set a date. I was still in a daze the day of our wedding Mass. It wasn't until after Martin was born, I realized how lucky I was to have a fine man who wanted to give my child a name."

Shock ripped through Shayna. "Marty isn't Pop's son? Then that's why he looks so different from the rest of us." She pressed her hand to her trembling lips. "Oh, Mom, does he know?"

"Nope, and I never want him to. It would just plain kill him. You know how he worships Pop."

Shayna's eyes filled with tears. She clasped her mother's hands in hers. "Thank you for caring enough to be so honest with me, Mom. I love you for it, but you shouldn't have put yourself through this ordeal. Josh and I aren't . . . that is, we haven't . . ."

Maggie's grip on Shayna's fingers tightened. "That's not my only worry. You're missing my point just like Pop did. All he could say was it didn't matter that Joshua's an Eddington. With your college education and fine way of talking, you'll make those 'swells' on the hill sit up and take notice. Maybe you will. That still won't change the way of things."

"I'm not sure I know what you mean."

Maggie's faded blue eyes swam with tears. "What I'm trying to tell you is there are two kinds of love—the sweet, quiet kind I feel for Pop and the crazy, wonderful kind I felt for the other one. Don't you see, girl. Life's played a dirty trick on you. You've got things all backward. Joshua Eddington should have been your first love, because that kind of love can't last."

A weariness, more despairing than the mere aftermath of wine, gripped Shayna. "You may be right, Mom," she said bleakly. "I'm not sure it matters much. I can't seem to help how I feel about Josh." She managed a sickly smile. "Anyway, every woman should have Fourth of July, Christmas, and New Year's Eve all rolled up together once in her life. If it doesn't work out, I'll just have to learn to live with the pain. I've lived with worse."

"And what about Megan? She's as taken with the man as you are. All that child could talk about after you left this evening was 'Joss did this' and 'Joss said that.' When this great love of yours falls apart, how will you explain to a five-year-old who's already lost one father that she'll just have to learn to live with the pain?"

A string of naked hundred-watt bulbs provided the only light in the molding department. It was more than enough to see the casting was every bit as bad as John Brenegan had predicted. Even Josh, with his untrained eye, had spotted the shrinkage the minute they broke the mold.

He stared at the downcast faces around him, and his spirits plummeted. It looked like the next step was the forfeiture of a potentially lucrative contract and a healthy fine he hadn't the money to pay.

To add to his misery, he'd stopped at his office on the way into the forge and found a message on his telephone recorder from his cousin, who owned the only industrial real estate firm that had shown any interest in searching for a buyer for the foundry. "No luck so far. It seems no one wants to take on a down-at-the-heels foundry.'' Moments like this made Josh realize why.

A gloomy silence pervaded the cluttered shop. Like mourners viewing a body, Angus, John Brenegan, and Josh gathered around the hapless casting.

"Got any suggestions, John?" Angus asked.

"None you'd want to hear." John Brenegan shook his shaggy gray head. "I can't figure this one out. I'd swear we've got the mix right." He kicked at the ledge of metal hemming the body of the casting. "The damn riser looks better than ninety percent of the part."

Riser. Something clicked in Josh's brain. He shifted uneasily from one foot to the other. As the only greenhorn involved, he felt foolish venturing a suggestion when men like Angus McTavish and John Brenegan were stumped.

The silence deepened. The only sound was the faint "ping" of a hammer on metal in some far reach of the forge. One by one the swing shift men who had gathered around them shuffled off to attend to their other duties.

Josh jammed his hands into his pockets. His fingers encountered his tie. He smiled to himself, remembering how Shayna had decreed it stuffy. That was the champagne talking. She'd never have voiced such an opinion stone cold sober. He could use some "fool's courage" himself at the moment; that idea was still rattling around in his head.

Hell! What did he have to lose except his pride.

"I've been reading those books on foundry procedure you loaned me, Angus," he said. "The one on the history of the industry has an interesting account of how the molding process has changed over the years. Apparently in the old days, when quality—not quantity—was their major aim, foundrymen used to build up the risers to absorb the shrinkage. I imagine they wasted a lot of metal, but the writer claimed they made better castings."

Both men stared at him, mouths agape. "By golly, the lad's right," Angus declared, slapping the palm of his hand atop the massive casting in front of him. "In David

Eddington's day, we put near as much metal into risers as we did into the castings for the express purpose of absorbing shrinkage. In some ways it was a wasteful process, but by God, we turned out some real beauties.''

John Brenegan's grin spread from ear to ear. "I was still running the jitney in those days, so I wasn't in on it, but it seems to me I've heard some of the old-timers talk about it. Funny I didn't think of it.''

"I'm thinking the same thing about myself," Angus said ruefully. "What do you say, John? Shall we try it?''

"What do we have to lose? I'll get the boys right on it." John Brenegan beamed at Josh. "You're David's grandson all right. This is the kind of rabbit I've seen that old wizard pull out of his hat time and time again.''

He thumped Angus on the back as he passed. "Looks like we've got us a real Eddington at the helm again. By God, Angus, we're not down for the count yet.''

"He's right," Angus said as Brenegan hurried away. "You've come a long way, Joshua, considering you couldn't tell a crucible from a quenching tank a month ago.''

An acid smile twisted the old man's face. "Yes, sir, lad, you're a smart one all right, and it's a good thing, because you have a tough road ahead of you. I don't envy you the job of telling men like John you're dumping the old place.''

He shrugged. "Maybe Shayna will do it for you. I take it you're planning to break the news to her any day now. Must be getting pretty serious between the two of you if you're willing to pop for one of those fancy dinners at the country club.''

"I see the Titusville toms-toms were busy as usual tonight," Josh remarked sourly.

"People just naturally take an interest in each other's goings-on in a small town. And you're an Eddington. You should have figured out by now that Eddington-watching is Titusville's chief form of entertainment.''

"One which I heartily resent.''

"Maybe so, lad, but if I were you, I'd act accordingly. If you're serious about selling the foundry, I wouldn't count on keeping it a secret much longer." Angus cast a meaningful glance in John Brenegan's direction. "It occurs to me some mighty nice folks are going to have their feelings hurt if they have to learn about it through the grapevine."

TWELVE

Shayna woke Saturday morning resolved to stop thwarting Josh's demands to discuss their future—for Megan's sake if not her own. Her daughter's excitement over the prospect of spending an afternoon with him only confirmed Maggie's contention that Shayna could hurt her daughter deeply if she had a short-lived involvement with Josh. Nothing was worth that risk. When he called to confirm their pizza date for Sunday, she agreed immediately. Sometime, before the evening was over, she'd make sure they had their talk.

Josh sounded surprised at her quick consent. Funny. She'd never thought of herself as an argumentative kind of person. Tim and she had rarely disagreed about anything. Josh and she had done nothing but disagree since the first moment she'd met him. Hardly a propitious omen for considering any kind of future with the man.

Josh hadn't expected Shayna to make an issue of his rash behavior of Friday night; she had, after all, been a willing participant. But knowing her as well as he did, he had expected her to back off once she thought it over. The fact that she hadn't worried him.

He'd mapped out his campaign to win her with the same care he'd have planned an assault on a legislator whose vote he wanted to influence, but things were falling into place too easily. Past experience had taught him whenever that happened, trouble was usually waiting for him down the road. He had a feeling, with Shayna, it was a near certainty.

Somewhat warily, he launched into phase two of his plan. "It's a little early for dinner," he said, as he pulled away from the curb in front of Shayna's house on Sunday afternoon. "I have to pick up some legal papers at White Oaks, and I thought maybe you might enjoy seeing the Eddingtons' white elephant."

"You have an elephant?" Megan squealed from the jump seat behind him. In the rearview mirror, Josh could see her squirming excitedly beneath her seat belt.

"Sorry, punkin. I wish I did. It would be much easier to sell than an old house no one in his right mind would want."

"You're selling White Oaks?" Shayna sounded almost as flabbergasted as Megan. "Why? To whom?"

"The 'why' is easy. My brother took out a loan against it to make the foundry payroll and I don't have the money to pay it back." He could tell from her look of shocked commiseration, she was finding it hard to adjust to the idea that an Eddington could have financial troubles. Good. Much as he hated to divulge his family's problems, he had to make her understand what he was up against before he broke the news that the foundry was also on the block.

"The 'to whom' is a little harder to determine," he continued. "A few of the homes in The Highlands have been bought by professional people willing to commute to and from the city to get a fine old house at a reasonable price. I'm afraid the upkeep alone on White Oaks rules it out of that category."

Shayna's eyes were troubled. "I knew the workload at the foundry had dropped off, but I had no idea things were that bad. Oh, Josh, your family home! I'm so sorry."

Her emotional words startled him. He'd forgotten what

a sentimental little thing she was. He reached over to pat her hand. "Thank you for your sympathy, Shayna, but it's misplaced. My decision to sell White Oaks is simply one of economics. The dreary old place holds nothing but unhappy memories for me, and I'll be vastly relieved if I can find someone crazy enough to buy it."

Shayna turned her head away, to hide her distress. Only someone who'd had as bleak a childhood as Josh would fail to realize his lack of feeling about his family's home was even sadder than if he'd grieved over losing it.

"Does Joss have to sell his house, Mama?" Megan's perplexed voice interrupted her thoughts.

"Yes, dear, he does."

"That's okay, Joss. It doesn't matter. You can come live with us. Can't he, Mama?"

Shayna mouthed a silent "Don't you dare say a word" at Josh and turned to face her young daughter. "Josh lives in the hotel, Megan."

"Oh."

They rode in silence for the next few minutes.

"Joss?"

"Yes, Megan."

"Are you ever going to sell the hotel?" The hopeful note in her voice was impossible to miss. Shayna made a small, strangled sound and heard Josh's rumble of laughter.

"I'm seriously considering it," he quipped as he turned into the gates of White Oaks. Ignoring Shayna's black look, he glanced in the mirror to catch a smile of sly satisfaction on Megan's face. He winked broadly at her and heard her happy giggle. Score one for the home team. At least one of the O'Malley ladies was already on his side.

"Is this your magic place, Joss?" Megan sounded awe-struck, and Josh took a closer look at the canopy of ancient, twisted oaks framing the drive. Leafy shadows danced across the hood of the car, and a ghostly mosaic of shade and sunshine patterned the cobblestone roadway ahead.

"I hadn't thought about it before, but it does look like something out of *Grimm's Fairy Tales*."

"Fairy tales are make-believe," Megan said firmly. "But it could be a dinosaur place."

"Dinosaurs are her favorite thing at the moment," Shayna explained. "Santa Claus brought her a dinosaur book at Christmas, and she's been looking for one ever since. I'm having trouble convincing her they no longer exist."

Josh chuckled. "I'm afraid the dinosaurs who resided at White Oaks aren't the kind in your book, Megan, but one day soon I'll take you to the Smithsonian. That's the place to see dinosaurs. They have a Diplodocus skeleton and a reproduction of a Stegosaurus and a lot of other things that'll blow your mind."

Megan's ecstatic gurgle told Shayna her daughter was taking Josh at his word. Washington was a long way from Titusville, and she couldn't imagine how or when Josh could contrive to keep his rash promise. If he didn't, he would break Megan's heart. This was just the sort of thing her mother had warned her about. "Don't tell me you're a paleontologist," she snapped.

"Hardly. But I had a teacher at St. Andrew's who was. I idolized him, and he let me spend two Christmas vacations with him at his family home in Georgetown."

Josh's mouth curved in a reminiscent smile. "Those were the happiest weeks of my young life. While everyone else was singing 'Jingle Bells' and trimming Christmas trees, we stalked dinosaurs at the Smithsonian. I sometimes think the main reason I gravitated to Washington when I got out of college was that the Smithsonian felt more like home than any other place I knew."

His casual admission clutched at Shayna's heart. If spending Christmas prowling a museum with a teacher qualified as Josh's happiest childhood memory, she hated to think what his unhappiest might be.

"Well, Megan, it looks like you've found a fellow dinosaur lover," she said quickly before her emotions got the better of her.

Josh's grin looked smug. "Which makes two things we agree on, doesn't it, punkin?"

Shayna was still pondering his mysterious comment and Megan's answering giggle when the car rounded a curve and the mansion came in view. She gasped. It looked more like a red-brick fortress than a home. Rows of narrow, leaded windows paraded across the lower level and smaller matching windows stared from the dormers protruding from a gray slate mansard roof. Tall chimneys flanked both ends of the house and two white marble lions crouched on either side of the massive carved entry.

"Homey little place, isn't it?" Josh remarked drily, pulling to a stop in the circular driveway. He opened the car door for Megan and Shayna and led them up the shallow steps. "The caretakers have the day off, so the house is all ours," he said, unlocking the door. "You might enjoy prowling through it. It's kind of interesting from an historical standpoint."

He was right. The next hour was one of the most fascinating Shayna had ever spent. She and Megan wandered through the house on their own while Josh worked in the library. Shayna lost count of the rooms, but they were all an antique lover's dream. She and Megan peeked under dust covers at exquisite period furniture and stared openmouthed at the priceless china and crystal and silver in the china closets and cupboards. There was even a ballroom on the second floor with a crystal chandelier she knew must be worth more than her entire house.

Josh came looking for them in the third-floor nursery. "This is where Kyle and I spent most of our time until my grandfather died and we were sent off to boarding school."

Shayna peered about her in amazement. The room looked more like an expensive toy store than a playroom. Wagons and tricycles and trucks were lined up in perfect order along the walls, and armies of metal soldiers faced each other across a gleaming walnut table. As far as she could see, there wasn't a nick or a scratch on a single toy.

Identical teddy bears reposed on the twin beds at one end of the room, and Shayna found herself comparing their pristine condition to the delapidated bear Megan took to bed with her each night. She shivered. There was something indescribably sad about teddy bears that looked unloved.

"Everything is so . . . tidy," she murmured.

Josh nodded. "Two tidy little boys lived here. Our English nanny subscribed to the 'neatness is next to Godliness' theory." He grimaced. "I swear to God. No child of mine will ever be raised by strangers."

Megan's eyes were round and solemn. "Where did the little boys go?" she asked. "Did they die?"

Josh swept her up in his arms. "No, punkin, but I can understand your confusion. The place does feel like a mausoleum." He ruffled her curls. "The 'little boys' are both alive and well and at least one of them has hopes of living happily ever after." His eyes met Shayna's and the smile he gave her nearly melted her toes.

Josh took them to a pizza parlor the hotel manager had recommended in a neighboring town. The place was crowded and noisy and full of wonderful, spicy smells. Megan obviously thought she'd discovered heaven, and for a short time, Shayna relaxed and put aside both her anxiety over her upcoming talk with Josh and the emotional impact her glimpse of his childhood had had on her.

When they'd polished off two large Canadian bacon and pepperoni pizzas—Josh's pizza-eating capacity bordered on the unbelievable—Megan begged to play in the outdoor playground. Josh and Shayna nursed cups of coffee while Josh watched the little girl make friends with the children of other patrons and Shayna watched him. What was it about this man that set him apart? When the other men she knew wore jeans and T-shirts, they looked like they'd cleaned up after working on their cars; he looked like the cover photo for *Gentlemen's Quarterly*.

She'd seen the admiring glances cast his way when they'd walked through the door. Even now, two bright young things at the next table were doing their level best to gain his attention. Shayna felt a stab of jealousy—something she'd never before experienced. She'd been so sure of Tim, but, as Pop had pointed out, Josh was a different breed of cat.

"What did you think of White Oaks?" Josh asked suddenly.

Shayna abandoned her musings and concentrated on his question. "It was overwhelming. I can see why you might have trouble finding a buyer." She frowned. "What will you do with all the furnishings?"

"A college friend of mine, who's a Chicago antique dealer, is coming next week to advise me how to dispose of them. With so much stuff involved, he may have to arrange an auction. I don't care how he handles it, just so the proceeds from the sale of the furnishings cover the bulk of the loan. Selling the house itself could take a long time."

"It's too bad the State Historical Society can't buy it," Shayna remarked. "I know they're looking for an old home they can turn into the state museum."

"Are you sure of that?"

Shayna nodded. "Allison has mentioned it often." She blinked, suddenly aware of where Josh's thoughts were leading. "That's not your answer. The Society doesn't have the kind of money it would take to purchase White Oaks."

Josh ignored her comment. "How does Allison know the Society's plans?"

"She's the president and her friend Mr. Schermerhorn is the treasurer." Shayna had a sudden thought. "Good heavens! Does Mr. Schermerhorn hold the mortgage on White Oaks?"

"No, thank God. It could constitute a conflict of interest

if Schermerhorn were to negotiate the purchase of a house on which his bank held the mortgage.'' Josh's emerald eyes were brilliant with excitement. ''Honey, you may have come up with the solution to one of my problems. I'll have to do some more research before I'm sure of my facts, but I remember seeing a substantial bequest to the Historical Society in a copy of my grandfather's will. It didn't register as anything important at the time, but if that money has been drawing interest all these years, the Society could be a lot more affluent than one would expect.'' He paused. ''Did Allison say what they expected to pay for this museum of theirs?''

''No . . . but White Oaks? Surely you're talking millions of dollars.''

''Not really. I have to accomplish two things with the sale of the estate—pay off the loan and establish a trust fund so my grandmother can live out her days in comfort. If I clear enough with the furnishings, I can dispose of the house and grounds very reasonably. The main thing I want to do is get out from under the upkeep.'' He laced his fingers through hers. ''Lord, Shayna. This thing just might fly. With the tax break a nonprofit organization like the Society would get, they could afford the upkeep, and the idea of White Oaks as a museum would appeal to my grandmother—give her something to brag about. I've been wracking my brain trying to figure out how to get her to agree to sell the place without telling her about the family's financial troubles.'' He smiled. ''She's a very old lady with a great deal of pride.''

''I had no idea your grandmother was still living,'' Shayna said softly. ''So, you do have someone in your family you're close to after all.''

''Close to? My grandmother?'' Josh laughed. ''No one is close to my grandmother. She made my grandfather's life a living hell and she'd do the same to mine if I'd let her. Once a year I make a duty trip to Martinique where she retired when my grandfather died. Other than that, I never see or hear from the old curmudgeon.''

"But you feel obligated to provide for her?"

"She's the matriarch of my family—such as it is. I owe her my respect."

Shayna stared at him, then burst out laughing.

"What's so funny?"

"You are, Josh. You're the funniest person I've ever known. I certainly never expected to hear such a Victorian piece of sentiment coming out of your mouth."

She sat back in her chair, convulsed with laughter. "When I think of all the times you've intimidated me with your big-city looks and your big-city ways! You're a phony, Josh Eddington. Underneath all that cool urban sophistication, you're harboring the same old-fashioned Titusville values as the rest of us."

Megan slept all the way home, exhausted from her exciting day. Josh lifted her gently and carried her into the house and down the hall to her bedroom, with Shayna following close enough behind to hear her daughter's sleepy, "I love you, Joss."

"I love you, too, punkin." Josh's voice sounded gravelly and his eyes looked suspiciously moist. Only yesterday, the scene would have reinforced Shayna's worry over Megan's attachment to him; now she felt a surge of warm contentment as she watched the two of them together. She'd learned a lot about Josh in the past few hours, and everything she'd learned told her she could trust him with her and Megan's happiness. He was nothing like his callous brother or the irresponsible boy who had hurt her mother. Unbelievable as it might seem, a sensitive, caring man had evolved from the destructive lifestyle of the powerful Eddington clan. Never again would she question Father O'Toole's faith in miracles.

Josh was waiting for her when she returned to the living room after settling Megan for the night. This time, he was sitting in the easy chair. "I won't stay long," he promised. "I want to hit both your friend Allison and Edgar

Schermerhorn with my idea tomorrow morning, which means I'll be up all night planning my strategy."

Shayna sank onto the couch. "Good luck. I hope it works out for you . . . and the foundry. You'll have a lot better chance of getting the old place back on its feet without that loan hanging over your head."

She swallowed the lump in her throat. The expectant look in Josh's eyes said he hadn't stayed around merely to discuss foundry business. The time for that long-delayed discussion of theirs had obviously arrived. She waited for Josh to begin.

He leaned forward, elbows resting on his knees, his gaze riveted on the carpet at his feet. A tuft of pale hair, like a shock of wheat, capped the crown of his head, and she ached to bury her fingers in the thick flaxen mass.

"Damn it, Shayna," he said, looking up. "I've spent so much time thinking about what I want to say to you, I'm suffering from 'paralysis by analysis.'"

"You once told me to go with my feelings. Maybe that's what you should do now."

"I think I already did Friday night." He shook his head emphatically. "No. That's only partially true. There is a lot of healthy lust in what I feel for you, but that's just a small part of it."

He clasped his hands together, rubbing one thumb methodically over the other. "What I'm trying to say is, you . . . and Megan represent everything that's been missing in my life. The concept of home and family was so foreign to me, I didn't even know I needed such things until that day I walked into your kitchen. It took a month away from you to make me realize how empty the rest of my life would be without you."

His eyes darkened with sudden intensity. "I know you said you needed more time; I can understand that. Until you've relinquished the past, you can't make a decision about the future. I promise I won't rush you or make demands you're uncomfortable with, but I have to know how you feel about me because I find I'm beginning to think of you and Megan as a permanent part of my life. If I had to walk away from you today, I might still be able to do so and keep my sanity. I don't think I could six months from now. So, Mrs. O'Malley,'' he said quietly. ''I guess what I'm asking is, do you think there's a chance you'd consider changing your name to Eddington sometime in the near future?''

Shayna felt as if her heart had suddenly suspended its beating. ''Oh Josh!'' she gasped. ''Are you sure you know what you're doing?''

''Honey, I'm as certain of my idea of heaven as your famous Father O'Toole is of his. Only mine's right here on earth with you and Megan.'' Josh raised a quizzical left eyebrow. ''How about it, Shayna? What are my chances of entering the Promised Land?''

For a long moment, Shayna stared at Josh—adjusting to the myriad emotions rippling through her. She dug her fingers into the padded arm of the old couch to keep from leaping over the coffee table to throw herself into his arms the way Megan did each time she saw him. ''You'd better . . .'' Her voice cracked. She cleared her throat and tried again. ''You'd better think this thing through, Josh. I'm not sure I'm the kind of woman you should marry.''

He looked surprised. ''What makes you say that?''

''You're an Eddington . . . a member of the town's leading family. I have neither the desire nor the aptitude to become a pillar of society.''

Josh shrugged. ''The Titusville social register has no bearing on my plans for the future. In fact, if that crowd of deadheads I saw at the country club represents the town's elite, I'll count myself lucky if I manage to avoid them altogether.''

''Then there's the problem of our incompatibility,'' Shayna pointed out quietly.

''You think we're incompatible?'' Josh asked, obviously startled.

"I'm very stubborn, Josh, and so are you. We're bound to lock horns continually."

"That's true."

"And, in case you haven't noticed, I have a terrible temper."

"Believe me, honey, I've noticed. I even have scars to prove it. I have to admit to being a little hotheaded myself at times, so we'll undoubtedly have some knock-down-drag-out battles before we're through." Josh grinned. "But think of the fun we'll have making up."

He stood up and moved to join her on the couch. Sliding his arm along the backrest, he encircled her shoulders and pulled her to him. "Do you have any other thoughts on the subject . . . before I kiss you?"

Shayna held up her hand to ward him off. "Just this, and I don't want you to jump to any conclusions, because I need more time to think about this . . ."

"Yes?"

She drew a deep, steadying breath. "My experience in such matters is limited, so I haven't much to go on . . . but I think there's a chance I may be falling in love with you."

Josh's eyes widened briefly, then narrowed to smoky emerald slits. His lips hovered inches from hers. His breath, spicy with oregano and basil, mingled with her own. "How soon do you think you'll be sure?" he murmured.

"Soon," she promised. "I guarantee you'll be the first to know." With her fingertip, she outlined the sensuous contour of his lower lip. "Now, I have a question for you."

"Anything. Just ask me."

She shifted in his arms. "How is it we always end up on this couch when we have a perfectly good kissing box we've never even christened?"

THIRTEEN

Josh nosed the Mercedes through the gates of the Titus Eddington Memorial Park. From the number of cars in the parking lot, it appeared the Foundrymen's Union annual picnic was in full swing.

He glanced at Shayna, sitting beside him. He could think of better places to spend an afternoon with the woman he loved than a crowded picnic ground. But Angus had urged him to attend and Shayna had been so enthusiastic when he'd called her about it, he'd felt he had little choice.

It had been a full week since he'd kissed her soundly and bid her good night the previous Sunday. They never had gotten around to the kissing box. Their lovemaking had progressed much too rapidly on the old couch to think about changing venue. In fact, things had almost gotten out of hand. Walking out that door had been the hardest thing he'd ever done, but he'd been too close to getting the commitment he wanted from her to let a premature hormone attack destroy the progress he'd made. Josh smiled to himself. His campaign to win Shayna was coming along very nicely.

They'd talked on the phone each evening, but he'd forced himself to stay away from her—devoting every waking minute, when he wasn't working in the foundry, to promoting his idea of White Oaks becoming the State Historical Society Museum. Allison Cartwright and Edgar Schermerhorn had both been wildly enthusiastic and, between the three of them, they had worked up the offer to be presented to the society's board of directors.

His antique dealer friend had stayed over two days at White Oaks to make a detailed inventory of the furnishings and had given him an estimate far exceeding his wildest hopes. Plans for the auction were already under way.

Even his suggestion about enlarging the risers on the problem casting had paid off, and production had started in earnest on the order.

Josh gave a deep sigh of satisfaction. All in all, it had been the most productive week he'd had since he'd come to Titusville. Things were definitely looking up.

"Well, here we are," he said, parking the car in one of the few remaining spaces. "I hope I'm doing the right thing. Mrs. Warren claimed the union only invited me to the picnic out of courtesy, and I'd make everyone so uncomfortable, I'd ruin the day if I showed up. Do you think that's possible?"

Shayna's smile was reassuring. "I think the men will take it as a compliment. Neither your father nor your brother ever attended, but Pop says your grandfather never missed a single picnic when he was head of the foundry."

Josh unloaded the picnic basket from the trunk of his car and locked up. He hoped Shayna was right, but his reason for attending had little to do with establishing a rapport with the men. He was simply making another public statement about his relationship with Shayna.

The looks of blank astonishment they encountered when they entered the picnic grounds unnerved him at first, but very soon he heard, "Hey, Mr. Eddington, glad you came" and "Good to see you, Mr. Eddington" on every side.

"I told you they'd be pleased," Shayna whispered as she led him toward the Brenegans' table. Megan was perched on her grandfather's lap, eagerly scanning the crowd. The minute she saw him, she let out an ear-piercing shriek and launched herself at him. "We've been waiting for you," she cried. "Grandma and me came early and did all the work, and we've got watermelon." Josh smiled, already feeling more at ease. Leave it to his staunch little ally to break the ice.

"Glad you could join us, Joshua." John Brenegan stood up and held out his hand. "You're just in time. They're about to start the games." His eyes twinkled. "The two of you had better get over there if you're going to enter any of the races. Ronnie and Martin are already in line."

"*Games?*" A sinking feeling started in the pit of Josh's stomach. He'd envisioned a picnic as merely a lunch eaten outdoors where he and Shayna could see and be seen. He certainly hadn't planned to get involved in *games*.

The eager look on Shayna's face said she had a different idea. "Hurry up, Josh. I don't want to miss a thing."

"Joss will win every prize," Megan declared firmly.

Josh wished he shared her conviction. With grave misgivings, he followed Shayna to where a crowd had gathered at the edge of an open field. What had he gotten himself into? Too late, he realized he should have listened to his secretary's advice.

Shayna disappeared into the noisy, chattering crowd and a few minutes later pushed her way back out carrying two enormous gunnysacks. She handed one to him. It felt scratchy and smelled a lot like the musty basement of the Cape Cod beach house he'd rented one summer. "What am I supposed to do with this?" he asked.

Shayna smiled up at him. "It's for the potato sack race. Oh, dear, I don't suppose you've ever done anything like this before." Grasping his hand, she led him over to where a dozen or more men were lining up along a wide white line painted on the grass. "You get into the sack and hop. The first one to reach the finish line wins." She pointed to another white line about a hundred yards away. Her smile clouded over. "Don't look like that, Josh. It's really a lot of fun once you get into the spirit of things."

Josh grimaced. It would take a lot more lead time than he'd been given to whip up enthusiasm for hopping around in a smelly sack. He searched for a convenient escape route. There was none. All around him, strong, sober-minded men who made their livings laboring in the heat and grime of the foundry were enveloping themselves in these absurd sacks and jostling into place behind the white line. Horace Abernathy greeted him as he hopped by. "Good luck, Mr. Eddington. You should do great with those long legs of yours."

Josh felt completely out of his element. "I can't believe grown men actually do this sort of thing," he mumbled sourly.

Shayna shrugged. "Well, you can't back out now. You don't want your men to think you're a quitter."

Josh glared at her. He'd been called many things by many people. Quitter wasn't one of them. With a few choice obscenities, he struggled into his sack. He seriously doubted his reputation hinged on hopping around inside a potato sack, but, for some unknown reason, it seemed important to Shayna. Damn. He couldn't believe the things a man would endure in the name of love.

Somehow, he made it to the line and found himself positioned next to Martin Brenegan. "You ever been in a potato sack race before?" the big man asked.

"Good God, no."

"I'll give you a tip. Keep your weight back on your heels or you'll find yourself flat on your face." Before Martin had time to explain further, a shrill whistle pierced the hubbub and everyone fell silent.

The quality control manager stood at the sidelines, megaphone in hand. "The race will commence at the count of three," he shouted. "One . . . two . . . three."

Josh hopped forward. With each step he took, the front of the sack grew shorter until he found himself bent double and clutching frantically at the descending edges. "Weight on your heels," Martin yelled as he hopped by.

Quickly adjusting his balance, Josh started again. Just as he was getting the hang of it, Ronnie Brenegan shot past him like he'd been fired from a cannon. Unnerved, Josh took a gigantic leap forward and plowed into the backside of Horace Abernathy. The next thing he knew, he was sprawled atop Horace at the bottom of a pigpile of fallen racers. By the time the men above him untangled themselves, the race was over, with Ronnie declared the undisputed winner.

Josh felt Horace stir beneath him. Rolling off him, he lay winded and dust-covered beside the stubby little man. "Are you all right, Horace?" he asked.

Horace turned over on his back, shaking with laughter. Blades of grass and globs of dirt were plastered to his perspiring face. He raised up on his elbows and spit a pebble from between his teeth. "I'm fine," he choked, "but Judas Priest, Mr. Eddington, you gotta watch where you're going. I told you those long legs could cover ground."

Josh rubbed his head, waiting for his ears to quit ringing and the two Horaces lying beside him to fuse into one. Struggling out of his sack, he got to his feet. "I'm sorry," he said, reaching to give Horace a hand. He slapped the dirt off his jeans, picked up his sack and Horace's.

Horace accepted his sack with a cheerful grin. "Thanks, Mr. Eddington."

Josh grinned back. "Under the circumstances," he said wryly, "I think it's about time you started calling me Josh." They left the field arm in arm.

Shayna beamed at him as she hurried past to line up for the women's sack race. "Didn't I tell you it was a lot of fun once you got into it?"

If Josh hadn't had his hands full of gunnysack, he'd probably have strangled her.

John Brenegan was waiting at the sidelines. He handed Josh a cold beer and together they watched the women line up. Stretched full out, the sack would have reached to Shayna's chin. Josh saw her roll the top to her waist and clutch it tightly. At the count of three she took off, skimming the ground with the power and grace of a small kangaroo, while the other women stumbled and tripped and crashed behind her. At the finish line, she was twenty feet ahead of her nearest competitor. Josh choked on his beer.

"That daughter of mine is a caution," John remarked casually. "Too darn competitive for her own good. It's a family trait. Shayna used to beat poor Tim at every game they tried. He took it good-naturedly, but I always felt kinda sorry for the little bugger. I guess I'm what the youngsters nowadays call a chauvinist, but I sure wouldn't like my woman to outdo me at every turn."

"You're not talking chauvinism," Josh said grimly. "You're talking self-preservation." For some reason Josh couldn't fathom, John Brenegan's answering smile had a 'pleased with himself' look to it.

"So, Joshua," he said, "how about pitching some horseshoes? Shayna'll be tied up for the next hour or so. She enters all these fool races 'cause she always wins. Ronnie and she are alike in that respect."

"More races?" Josh asked weakly.

"Lord, yes. They'll be carrying eggs on spoons they've stuck between their teeth . . ."

Josh groaned.

"Then there's the three-legged race where two people tie their legs together, and . . ."

"Oh my God!"

"Right. About this time Marty and I usually wander over to the horseshoe pit for a game with Angus McTavish." John scanned the crowd. I wonder where he is. He never misses a picnic, but I sure haven't seen him around today." He smiled. "The sly old devil goes from table to table, tasting a little of each woman's cooking and telling every single one of them she's the finest cook in Titusville."

"He'll probably be along soon. He talked me into coming." Josh swallowed the last of his beer. "Okay, John. Let's pitch some horseshoes. I've never tried it before, but I'd rather make a fool of myself doing that than running around with a spoon between my teeth."

"My sentiments exactly, and you never know, you might turn out to be a natural. You're big enough and strong enough. All you have to do is develop the 'eye.' Marty can give you a few tips. He's won the state tournament three times in the last five years."

Josh stored the information about Martin Brenegan in his mental notebook, along with the other observations he'd made of Shayna's relatives. It was obvious she came from a highly competitive family. Okay. He could handle that. He was pretty competitive himself when the prize was worthwhile. He exhaled slowly. Who was he kidding? He hated to lose at anything—even a stupid potato sack race. Especially when Shayna had made it look so easy. Unlike her husband, Josh knew he'd be anything but good-natured if she beat him at every turn.

One thing was certain; he'd never again be fooled by that proper manner of hers. Beneath her prim exterior lurked a veritable tigress waiting for the right man to set it free. He couldn't remember when he'd been offered a challenge he was more eager to accept.

Martin Brenegan and Horace Abernathy caught up with them just as they reached the horseshoe pit. Martin's gray eyes twinkled, but he refrained from mentioning the disastrous sack race. Josh decided he liked this brother of Shayna's a lot better than Ronnie.

Shayna didn't see Josh again until the family gathered for lunch. She was fixing a plate for Megan when he arrived, flushed and sweaty, in the company of her brother, her father, and Horace Abernathy, who'd stopped by the Brenegan's table for a beer.

Horace chugalugged his beer, dropped the empty bottle into the trash bag, and wiped his hand across his mouth.

"You should have seen the way Josh took to horseshoes,"
he exclaimed. "Two ringers and a double on one of Marty's. We showed him how to take a flip shoe grip, and
whammo, he beat the socks off John and me and came
close to tying Marty. We're trying to talk him into taking
up the game."

Josh grinned. "Beginner's luck."

"No way." John Brenegan shook his head. "Looks to
me like you're a natural, Joshua. What do you think,
Marty?"

Marty nodded. "Best I've ever seen for a first timer."

Megan put down the chicken leg she'd been chewing
on. "I told you Joss would win everything."

Josh reached over to ruffle Megan's curls. "Thanks for
the vote of confidence, punkin."

Martin smiled. "What do you say to a little game of
baseball after lunch, Josh? Horace and I are getting up a
team."

Josh's face lighted up. "Now that's a game I do know
something about. I played a lot of ball in college."

"Great. You're on our team then." Horace clapped
Josh on the shoulder. "Well, I'd better get back to my
table before that brood of mine eats everything in sight."
He grinned at Marty. "See you in an hour or so. I just
hope we can find someone to give us a little competition."

Ronnie had been standing at the end of the table listening to the conversation. He sat down next to Josh. "A
real pro are you, Mr. Eddington?"

"Mind your mouth, Ronnie." Maggie Brenegan lifted
a bowl of potato salad from the ice chest and plopped it
onto the table. Next came a platter of sliced ham. Her
mother had been so quiet, Shayna had almost forgotten
she was hovering in the background.

Ronnie frowned at his mother. "Judas Priest, Ma, you
sure are getting touchy lately. It's getting so a guy can't
even do a little joking around you."

"Humph!" Maggie set a platter of chicken beside the
ham. "Eat up, Mr. Eddington," she said. "There's more

where that came from. Shayna must have thought she was feeding an army, the amount of chicken she fried.''

Shayna smiled to herself. From the way Josh was eyeing the food, she doubted there'd be a scrap left when he'd had his fill. Horseshoe pitching must have sharpened his appetite.

Ronnie loaded four pieces of chicken onto his plate and reached for the potato salad. ''So you're getting up a team, Marty?'' He grinned across the table. ''What do you say, Shayna, should we teach these guys how to play baseball?''

Shayna was tempted. She loved all sports, but baseball was her absolute favorite. However, she didn't really relish the idea of playing against Josh. Tim had never minded when she beat him; she had a feeling Josh would feel differently about winning and losing.

Josh paused, fork in midair over the chicken platter, to stare at Ronnie. ''The game is co-ed? I thought we were talking serious baseball here.''

Martin spluttered into his beer and her father suddenly busied himself making a sandwich. ''I'm dead serious,'' Ronnie declared, ''but knowing how much my little sister likes the game, I can never bring myself to leave her out of things.''

''Don't believe a word of it,'' Marty warned. ''They don't call her Killer O'Malley for nothing.''

Shayna could tell, from the look on Josh's face, he thought Marty was joking. *Serious baseball, indeed.* She'd give him one last chance, which was more than she'd give anyone else who'd made such a blatantly chauvinistic remark.

''I play a pretty good game, Josh.''

''I'm sure you do, honey.''

Shayna clenched her teeth at his patronizing tone of voice. She slapped a piece of ham onto her plate and helped herself to more potato salad than she could possibly eat. ''You're on, Ronnie,'' she said. ''I'll be glad to play on your team.''

She hoped Josh had a good appetite, because she strongly suspected he might have to top off his lunch by eating a few of his words before this afternoon was over.

Josh dug the toe of his Reebok into the sandbag at first base and squinted morosely at the young jitney driver Martin had chosen to pitch for their team. The boy had one pitch. A fast ball. The batters for the other team had easily adjusted to his speed. Even Shayna had hit a single off him in the third inning.

Now, in the fifth inning, with the other team already two runs ahead, he'd allowed a single, a double, and a walk. The bases were loaded, and Shayna was the next batter up. If she got any kind of hit at all, she could bring in another run. Josh groaned. She'd already successfully fielded two hard-hit ground balls and caught a pop fly. He could almost taste the helping of crow she was planning to serve him for his Sunday-night supper.

Josh kicked at the sandbag again. He'd give anything for a crack at that pitcher's mound, but there was no way he could tell his teammates he was a lot better pitcher than the one they had without sounding like a conceited fool.

He watched Shayna step up to the plate, grip the bat, and wriggle her cute little butt. It seemed to be a habit of hers. She'd wriggled it each time she'd addressed the plate. He doubted she even realized she was doing it, but every man on the field, including the young pitcher, seemed mesmerized by the provocative little twitch.

Sure enough, in the next few minutes, the young fool lost what small amount of control he'd had and threw Shayna two wild balls in a row. Josh's blood boiled just thinking about that punk eyeballing his lady.

With great relief, he saw Martin come in from second for a conference on the mound. Josh joined him just as Horace arrived from third, and the three of them confronted the pitcher. "Look, kid," Martin began, "don't let that pint-size sister of mine fool you. She may look little and helpless, but the truth is, she's a lot more dangerous than most of the guys on that team. For Pete's sake, don't give her anything she can swing at."

Horace's advice was a little more specific. "Forget she's a woman, get your mind back on your pitching and wing one in there that'll set her back on her heels."

The kid's lip curled. "Yeah. That's easy for an old duffer like you to say, but from where I stand, that is one pretty lady, and she's got a real cute . . ."

"Hold it!" Josh stepped forward until he was nose-to-nose with the skinny youngster. "In case you hadn't heard, the lady's spoken for, so keep your eyes off her rear end. Understand?"

The boy turned four shades of purple. "Yes, sir, Mr. Eddington," he stammered, wiping frantically at the sweat trickling into his astonished eyes.

With a single accord, the three men returned to their respective bases.

"Play ball," said the quality control manager-cum-umpire.

With a fleeting moment of sympathy for the young pitcher, Shayna lifted her bat. The poor boy looked like a candidate for apoplexy. She made the little adjustment she always made to ready herself for the pitch, and for some unknown reason, this seemed to aggravate him even further. His face turned the color of a ripe plum.

He wound up like he was planning to wing one into the next county and delivered a pitch directly into the fourth row of the stands.

"Ball three," the umpire intoned.

The pitcher's flush turned chalky. Clutching the ball the catcher threw him, he marched to first base and thrust it at Josh. "I can't pitch to Mrs. O'Malley," he stated loud enough for everyone on the field to hear. "You do it."

Josh walked to the pitcher's mound and took a few practice pitches. He looked mighty good. Shayna heard Ronnie groan, "Judas Priest. I think we're in trouble now."

She had a feeling Ronnie was right. The determined

look on Josh's face warned her he took his baseball seriously. Fine. That was exactly how she wanted it.

Shayna gripped the bat and watched Josh take his powerful wind-up. Quickly, she made her stance adjustment, and Josh's face went strangely blank. The pitch was waist-high, a little outside and surprisingly wobbly. Shayna was ready for it. The sharp WOP of her bat striking the ball was the sweetest sound she'd ever heard. The outfielder still hadn't lobbed it back to the catcher when she jogged across home plate and acknowledged the applause from the stands.

It took all her willpower to keep from peeking at Josh's face, but she managed to restrain herself. She was, after all, too much of a lady to rub his nose in it.

As it turned out, she was glad she hadn't gloated. Things went steadily downhill from then on. Once Josh got warmed up, he pitched like a man possessed. Fast ball, knuckle ball, curve ball, slider. He had the whole collection. Shayna's team never scored again and finished two runs down at the end of the game.

Ronnie was fit to be tied, but Shayna didn't care in the least. She'd made her point, and the admiration she read on Josh's face made her feel higher than if her team had won.

She watched him raise his hands in a gesture of surrender as he strode toward her across the field. "What's that for?" she asked. "You won the game."

"But you won the argument."

"We didn't have an argument . . . exactly."

"Sure we did, and I apologize for my bonehead remark. I'm really not a chauvinist. If it had been anything but baseball . . ."

"I know. I get kind of rabid myself where the game's concerned." Shayna smiled grudgingly. "You're a pretty good player."

"You're not too bad yourself."

"I plan to get a lot better. I haven't played much in the last three years, but I'm going to get back into it. Ronnie and I are going to practice every chance we get." Shayna shook her fist. "You won't have it so easy next year."

Next year. By next year's picnic, Josh would be long gone from this funky little town, and if things went the way he planned, Shayna and Megan would be with him. For the first time, he felt a twinge of regret at the thought of leaving Titusville.

Together they walked back toward the picnic area. Every man they passed shook Josh's hand and congratulated him on a great win; every woman hugged Shayna and congratulated her on showing those men a thing or two. It should have been great fun; Josh grew more depressed by the minute. For the first time, he found himself wondering if a woman accustomed to the warmth and affection these people in Titusville showed so openly could ever be happy in an impersonal place like Washington.

He was so engrossed in his worrisome thoughts, he failed to notice the crowd gathered by the Brenegans' picnic table until Shayna called it to his attention. "I wonder what's going on," she said. "That's Elmer Farnsworth, Titusville's chief of police, talking to Pop."

The uniformed officer stepped forward. "Mr. Eddington?"

Startled, Josh stared into his solemn face. "Yes," he said warily.

The man was nearly as tall as Josh and probably weighed sixty pounds more. Perspiration beaded his brow and dripped off his heavy jowls. His cotton twill uniform was wrinkled and sweat-stained, as if he'd spent many long, hot hours in the patrol car now parked at the edge of the picnic area. He removed his visored cap. "I've been looking for you everywhere, sir. The last place I expected to find you was the union picnic."

"You've been looking for me? Why?"

"It's Mr. McTavish, sir. The hospital thought you should know."

Josh heard Shayna's startled gasp, felt his own heart

hammer against his rib cage. For a moment, shock robbed him of his power of speech.

"Are you saying Angus McTavish is in the hospital?" Shayna sounded as stunned as he felt.

"Yes, ma'am. His housekeeper called 911 right about noon." The police chief's blunt fingers twisted at his cap. "It's his heart. I guess he's in a pretty bad way." He stared anxiously at Josh. "He keeps asking for you, sir."

A knot of icy, numbing fear amassed in Josh's chest. He suddenly realized how much the irascible old Scotsman had come to mean to him in the short time he'd known him and worked with him. Without even realizing it, he'd begun to look forward to the lectures and arguments, trials and accomplishments that made up the days they spent together.

He turned to Shayna, registering the compassion in her eyes. "I have to go to the hospital," he said inanely. He felt disoriented and strangely detached, as if the shocking news had somehow anesthetized his brain.

"I'll go with you. Megan can stay overnight with my folks." Shayna mouthed a silent "thank you" to her mother as Maggie put her arm around Megan's shoulders and led her toward the Brenegans' truck.

She reached for Josh's hand. Every drop of color had drained from his face. The pain and fear she saw there confirmed the stories her father had told her of the close relationship he'd seen developing between Josh and Angus, and her heart ached for this man who'd known so little real affection in his life.

As she walked with him to his car, she breathed a silent, fervent prayer. *Please, dear God, don't make Josh face the anguish of losing someone he cares so much about. Not now . . . when he's just beginning to learn how to love.*

FOURTEEN

Saint Ignatius Hospital was five miles out of town on the road to Milidgville. It was small, compared to the hospitals Josh had occasionally visited in New York or Washington, but much larger than he'd expected for a town the size of Titusville. He suspected it had been built to serve all the small towns in the area.

The very look of it sent chills down his spine. Built in the starkly practical style of the thirties, it sat like a gray stone outcropping in the midst of what must once have been a corn field.

The interior was even more depressing. Its endless hallways of white octagonal floor tiles and mustard-colored walls had all the homey charm of a New York subway bathroom. Shayna and he followed the nursing supervisor to a dreary waiting room inside the Coronary Care Unit. Here the walls were white and the threadbare carpet mustard colored.

Josh waited beside the room's one narrow window for the doctor to appear. His stomach churned ominously from worry over Angus and from the strong antiseptic smell permeating the old building. He caught Shayna's smile and his heart swelled with gratitude. Through the storm of fear and confusion engulfing him, her steadfast support was a lifeline to which he clung unashamedly.

The door to the C.C.U. unit opened and an emaciated man in faded jeans and a plaid cotton shirt limped toward Josh. Streaks of gray threaded his shoulder-length brown hair and a gold filigree earring dangled from his left earlobe. A stethoscope hung around his neck and a pair of thin rubber gloves protruded from his back pocket.

Josh's first thought was that he looked strangely familiar; his second was a fervent hope this aging hippie wasn't the doctor entrusted with saving Angus's life.

The man held out his hand. "Mr. Eddington?"

"Yes."

"I'm Siegfried Mueller. Angus has been my patient for the last five years."

Josh tensed, tempted to order the old man removed by ambulance to an Indianapolis hospital. He felt Shayna grip his arm and realized she'd read his mind.

"Ziggy is an excellent doctor. Angus is lucky to have him," she said firmly.

The doctor glanced at Shayna with obvious surprise. "Hi, Shayna. I didn't realize that was you." He frowned. "Where was I? Oh, yes. I diagnosed Angus's heart condition three years ago, but he ignored my pleas to take life easy. It was a relief when your brother fired him. Once he adjusted to the ideas of retirement and a strict diet and medication regimen, he improved rapidly. Then a few months ago, he announced he was taking over the production end of the foundry again. I warned him if he did, he'd be dead in six months. Obviously, I wasted my breath."

Six months is the exact amount of time I have in mind. Suddenly, Angus's enigmatic words made a weird kind of sense.

"I can see from the look on your face, he didn't divulge his medical problems to you." Ziggy Mueller's brown eyes were sympathetic. "Don't blame yourself, Mr. Eddington. It was Angus's decision and his alone."

"I talked him into it." Josh shook his head in helpless

frustration. "If I'd had any idea . . . Damn that bull-headed old man. Why did he do it?"

Mueller shrugged. "Why does my dad work fourteen hours a day in that musty old store when he should be basking in the sun in Miami? These old workhorses don't feel alive unless they're pulling the plow."

"Mueller?" Josh stared at the doctor's gaunt face. "You're the smiling boy in the mercantile window."

"I was a lifetime ago. I left my right leg and my happy illusions in Vietnam, but I came home. That's something. Did you know Angus lost his only son in Nam?"

"No."

"We'd been friends since first grade and we were in the same artillery unit." His mouth twisted grimly. "I didn't even know he was dead till I got back to the States. He was all Angus had. His wife died when Charlie was just a kid."

"Maybe you just gave us the reason why Angus did what he did, Ziggy." Shayna's eyes misted with unshed tears. "Titusville and the people in it are his life now, and without the foundry, the town he loves would cease to exist. I think he'd risk what few years he has left to make sure it will survive."

"I know he would," Josh said. He felt sick with guilt. On Friday morning, he'd mentioned that his cousin had a buyer for the foundry. Angus hadn't commented, but remembering the bleak look on the old Scotsman's face, Josh was afraid the news had helped bring on his heart attack.

"What are his chances?" Josh held his breath waiting for the answer.

"It's too early to tell, but they look better than they did two hours ago. The next few hours are crucial. If he responds to the medication, he has a fair to even chance."

"Those aren't great odds."

"No, they're not, but he's a tough old guy. I hope seeing you will make the difference. Apparently he has something important to say to you, and he won't rest until he says it." Ziggy Mueller's sharp eyes searched Josh's face. "He's very fond of you, you know."

Josh swallowed hard. "Can I see him now?"

"Sure thing, but keep it short and don't say anything to excite him. He needs rest more than anything else right now, but I'm afraid to sedate him too heavily."

Josh left Shayna in the waiting room and followed the doctor into the C.C.U. unit. Angus was in a glass-enclosed cubicle. His face was the color of old parchment and his lips had an odd bluish hue. Tubes were attached to both arms and another fed him oxygen through his nose. He looked shrunken to half his normal size.

"Mr. Eddington's here, Angus," Ziggy Mueller said softly. "I'll leave you two alone for five minutes. That's all you should try to handle right now."

Angus's eyes were closed, but they fluttered open as Josh drew near the bed. "Joshua?" he asked weakly.

Josh caught Angus's bony fingers in his. "I'm here."

Angus closed his eyes again and lay so deathly still, Josh felt choked with fear. "Damn you, Angus, don't you dare die on me," he managed in a strangled whisper.

A faint smile played at the corners of the old man's mouth. "Just resting, Joshua. I'm kind of tired."

Josh breathed a sigh of relief. "Good. Sleep is what you need most. I'll be in the waiting room if you need me."

"Don't go yet." Angus clutched Josh's hand with surprising strength. His hooded eyelids opened half-mast. "Promise me . . ."

"Anything, Angus. You name it."

"Make that fellow who wants the foundry promise . . ."

"Promise what?"

"He'll keep it running . . . keep the men on . . . save my town."

Josh gripped Angus's hand. "I'll check him out and I won't sell unless I'm sure he'll take care of the men."

"That's all I have the right to ask of you, Joshua."

The door behind Josh opened quietly. "Ziggy sent me to tell you your five minutes are up," Shayna whispered.

Josh stood, his fingers still laced in Angus's. "I'll be back as soon as the doctor says it's okay."

"You won't forget . . . my town."

"I won't forget, and stop worrying about your town. I promise I'll take care of it for you."

Josh walked through the C.C.U. ward with Shayna's hand in his. Much as he dreaded it, the time had come to tell her his plans for their future. If she'd opened that door a minute earlier, she'd have heard Angus and him discussing the sale of the foundry. He sighed. A hospital waiting room was not the place he'd have chosen for their talk, but God only knew when he'd have her alone again.

He opened the door and, to his surprise, faced a room full of people. Beyond them stretched a hall crowded with more men and women jostling to get near the waiting-room door, and from the sounds outside the open window, the parking lot was rapidly filling with cars.

The nursing supervisor was backed into a corner, vehemently declaring, "This is against hospital rules." Not a soul was listening to her.

Siegfried Mueller pushed his way through the throng until he reached Shayna and Josh. "It appears Angus's love affair with Titusville is not all one-sided," he said drily. "Nevertheless, Sister Mary Margaret is right; this is no way to run a hospital. They're your people, Mr. Eddington. I leave it to you to persuade them to go home and let the medical staff get back to curing the sick."

Shayna walked hand in hand with Josh through the lobby of the Victorian hotel and stepped into the wrought-iron cage of the ancient elevator that serviced the penthouse. She stumbled from sheer exhaustion and Josh encircled her shoulders with a supporting arm.

Smiling up at him, she slipped her arm around his waist. He looked even more haggard than she felt. His eyes were hollow, his hair disheveled, and he had the beginnings of a scruffy beard. Only his expressive eyes still reflected the fire she'd seen kindled in them so many weary hours before. She recalled the exact moment when it had happened.

An incredible feeling of tenderness had welled within her when she'd listened to Josh commit himself to Angus and to the town the old man loved. The feeling had magnified tenfold as she'd watched him assure the crowd of well-wishers which had descended upon the hospital there was nothing to worry about, when all the time she could see he was sick with worry himself. With pounding heart, she'd faced the truth she'd been running from for weeks. She loved this complex, caring man with every fiber of her being . . . and she felt his pain as intensely as if it were her own.

Across the heads of the people crowding the waiting room, her eyes had met his, and the joyful look in his tired eyes had told her he'd instantly recognized the commitment she was making to him and returned it in kind.

Time and time again throughout the long evening of waiting until Angus was out of danger, they had renewed that silent pledge to each other, and each time it had grown deeper and sweeter. Until now, it seemed the most natural thing in the world to fulfill with their bodies what they had already promised with their hearts and minds.

Josh braced himself against the spasmodic ascension of the creaking old elevator and tightened his grip on Shayna's slender shoulders. He hardly dared believe the miracle he had been waiting for so long had actually happened, but she smiled up at him and the love and desire blazing in her azure eyes stunned him.

The elevator ground to a stop at his apartment and all at once reality pierced his euphoric bubble. The lovely woman at his side was giving herself to him openly and honestly and with complete trust. Trust he didn't deserve.

He dropped her hand and struggled to unlock the door with fingers grown suddenly clumsy. Stepping aside, he watched her precede him into the darkened entry hall of his apartment and fumbled for the light switch. "We have to talk," he said tersely. "We have to put things straight about our future before we go any further."

"Does that mean you're taking back your offer of marriage?" Shayna asked with an impish grin. "Maybe I can persuade you . . ." Stepping close to him, she slid her hands up his chest and around his neck.

Josh backed up so fast, he cracked his head on the wall. "This is nothing to joke about, Shayna. I'm serious. There are things I need to tell you, and I can't think straight when you touch me."

"Oh, no, you don't. That's my line." She advanced on him, her eyes suddenly dark and intense. "And, believe me, I'm every bit as serious as you are. Waiting in that hospital to find out if Angus would live or die brought back a lot of terrible memories. Life is a tenuous thing at best, Josh. I don't want to waste any more of mine. Maybe tomorrow, in the cold light of day, I'll feel differently. Tonight, I don't want to talk about or even think about the past or the future." She cupped his face in her hands and stared into his eyes. "I just want to love you; I want you to love me. Here. Now."

"Honey, you don't know what you're saying."

"I've never been more sure of anything in my life."

With a groan, Josh pulled her into his arms and buried his face in her silky hair. His hands roamed down her back, molding her to him, and the shudder that traveled her body echoed deep in his own. She felt boneless and fluid and unbelievably soft. A fierce, unbearable need clawed at him. Maybe she was right. Maybe this was not the time for talk. There was an elusive magic about tonight that set it apart—a perfect fragment lifted from the normal scheme of time that belonged to Shayna and to him, with no ties to reality.

There would be plenty of time to talk about reality tomorrow.

He lowered his head and covered her soft mouth with his. Her lips parted in silent, erotic invitation, and he felt her fingers slide into his hair, felt their fierce, ecstatic tug. Long minutes later, he tore his lips from hers and raised his head to gaze hungrily at her passion-flushed face. His senses reeled. Every cell in his body felt ready to burst into flames. "Show me how to please you, Josh," he heard her whisper. "Teach me how to make you happy."

The tenderness in her voice washed over him like waves washing onto sun-scorched sand. His racing heart slowed a beat and his fevered mind refocused. This was Shayna he held in his arms. His own true, generous love. Not some object of mindless lust. Gently, he smoothed her tumbled curls back from her forehead and kissed the tip of her shiny sunburned nose. "We'll learn together how to please each other," he promised.

She nodded and, slipping her hand into his, turned resolutely toward the nearest door. "I've been cautious and proper all my life," she said. "But when you touch me, I want to experience all the wonderful, exciting sensations I've only read about in novels."

Josh tugged on her hand—a queer, tender lump rising in his throat at her bold declaration. "Unless you have something really kinky in mind," he said, sweeping her up into his arms, "I suggest we use the bedroom. That door leads to the service kitchen."

"Oh!" Shayna's face flamed, and with a joyous laugh, Josh carried his daring seductress down the dimly lit hall to the darkened room beyond. He stopped beside the king-size bed where he'd spent so many lonely nights dreaming of her and, releasing his hold, let her slide down his aroused body to stand before him.

"I want to look at you," he said hoarsely, tugging her grass-stained T-shirt over her head. "I think I've been waiting all my life for this moment." With reverent care, he undressed her and held her from him, to watch the light from the hall caress the sweet, pale curves of her body and shimmer in her luminous eyes. Josh's breath caught in his throat.

"I want to see you, too," she whispered, sliding her

soft hands beneath his sweatshirt to trail her fingers over his chest and follow the vee of hair to his navel. He ripped off his shirt and jeans and reached for her again. The touch of her bare skin against his rocketed through him and he felt her trembling response. "Don't be frightened, my darling," he murmured, knowing he was fast reaching the limits of his fragile control.

"I'm not frightened—just a little nervous." Her warm lips traced the path her fingers had explored a moment before. "I love you," she whispered against his heated flesh, and the words coursed through every artery in his body.

Lifting her in his arms, Josh laid her gently on the bed and stretched out beside her. "Is this really you, Shayna," he murmured, "or am I just in the midst of another dream?"

"I think we may both be dreaming," she whispered, "but it doesn't matter as long as we dream together."

For a long moment, Josh studied the shadowed contours of her beloved face, awed by the flood of emotion that engulfed him. Then, with exquisite thoroughness he showered kisses along her slender throat, her bare shoulder, the hollow between her breasts; with the lightest touch his fingers traced a fiery path along the swell of her hip and the warm satin of her thighs . . . down the curve of her leg to end in a feathery, erotic circle of her ankle. "You're so soft and so warm," he murmured, brushing her instep with the tips of his fingers. He chuckled softly. "Except your poor little feet. They're like ice."

"My . . . my feet are always cold when I'm nervous," Shayna stammered through the haze of passion enveloping her.

"Well, we'll just have to take care of that," Josh said, and the gleam in his eyes was deliciously wicked.

He lowered his mouth to her breast, teasing first one taut nipple, then the other, with his tongue until a white-hot surge of pleasure arrowed to the very core of her being. She closed her eyes and tangled her fingers in his thick hair. The wonderful scent of him filled her nostrils and the touch of his strong fingers roaming her body left a trail of raging fire in their wake.

His hands stilled their quest and she felt him move away from her. "Josh . . ." she protested.

"Patience, sweetheart," he murmured. "More than anything else in the world, I want to see that sweet body of yours swollen with my child, but not until you have my ring on your finger."

Then, all at once, he was back and looming over her. She watched the play of light and shadow across his shock of golden hair, felt the shuddering need in his powerful body . . . and the answering hunger in her own. "I want you, Josh," she moaned. "Dear God, I didn't know it was possible to want this much."

Wonderful words of love and reassurance raced through Josh's head—words he longed to say to her before he joined his body with hers. The passion raging within him burned them from his brain before they could reach his lips. "I love you" was all he could manage before he submerged himself in her hot, welcoming depth.

He felt her tense, felt her clutch his shoulders. "Josh," she cried, arching beneath him. For one second, she went rigid. Then her body succumbed to an instinct as old as life itself, matching thrust for thrust the wild, staccato rhythm of his own.

Again she called his name, and her arms tightened convulsively around him. Her eyes were open—wide and startled. He felt the shattering force of her release, heard her ecstatic cry . . . and pleasure, so intense it was almost like pain, vibrated through him. Then together they plunged over the precipice, freefalling into joyful, mindless oblivion.

Josh surfaced slowly, aware of a deep sense of peace and well-being. For a long time, he lay still, listening to Shayna's quiet breathing. Finally she moaned softly and opened her eyes. "Hi," he said, brushing a damp curl from her forehead and replacing it with a kiss.

"Hi." Her eyes sought his, and a sleepy, contented smile wreathed her shadowed face.

He nuzzled her gently. "What are you thinking, sleepy-head?" he teased.

Her laugh was throaty, unconsciously provocative. "I'm thinking that making love with you is the most wonderful . . ." She traced his mouth with her fingertip. "I didn't know, you see . . ." She turned her head to place a tiny kiss in the palm of his hand. "It was wonderful, Josh."

"It was wonderful for me, too," he said, and something supremely masculine and exultant stirred deep inside him. He might not be the first man in Shayna's life, but her shy admission told him he was the first to take her to fulfillment. Once again, he found himself wondering what strange kind of marriage she'd had with that heroic young husband of hers.

She snuggled closer, and her foot touched his bare calf. He chuckled. "Your feet are warm now," he said, reaching over to pull her on top of him. She weighed next to nothing, and perched astride him, her eyes smiling down into his, she looked so appealing, he felt his body begin to harden again.

"Josh!" Shayna exclaimed, and he could feel her heartbeat quicken in time to his own.

"Shayna!" He laughed softly. "Tell me, my daring seductress, what do you have in mind now?"

She stared down at him, her eyes two bright question marks. "Surely you can't be thinking of . . ."

"Damned right I am," he said thickly. "I'm just following your example . . . doing my level best to be practical."

"Practical?"

He grinned. "Can you think of a better way to keep the blood circulating in those sensitive feet of yours?"

She couldn't think of a single one.

FIFTEEN

The clock in Josh's bedroom showed five minutes to four when Shayna and he finally climbed out of bed. She was still fingercombing her hair and he had yet to put on his shoes and socks when they entered the living room.

Josh was bone-tired and feeling a bit out of sorts. "This is crazy," he protested. "Megan is perfectly safe and we're as good as married. Why do we have to go barreling across town at this ungodly hour when we could be sleeping peacefully in a comfortable bed?"

"Be reasonable, Josh," Shayna pleaded. "If we arrive on Loblolly Street when everyone is setting out for work, the news will be all over town by noon."

"I feel like I'm back in that stupid potato sack race," he grumbled, hopping on one foot while he pulled a sock onto the other.

Shayna chuckled. "Are you always in such a cheerful mood when you first wake up?"

"Who's waking up? I haven't yet been asleep." Josh bent over to tie his shoes and found himself eye level with Shayna's shapely tanned legs. The memory of those legs entwined with his immediately improved his disposition.

His head was still swimming from the sheer joy of making love to Shayna. He'd expected her to be somewhat inhibited their first time together, and he'd promised himself he'd keep the fierce need he felt for her under careful control until she'd overcome her natural shyness. The matter had been taken out of his hands. From their first intimate joining, Shayna had responded to him with such passion, he'd instantly forsaken all his fine cerebral promises and abandoned himself to pure, glorious instinct.

He looked up and smiled into Shayna's eyes. "I love you, lady," he said softly.

"I love you, too, you old grouch."

"And I love making love to you," Josh added, and watched her color at his reminder of their past few hours together. The idea that she could be shy with him now when she'd been so wildly uninhibited once they'd crossed the threshold of the bedroom was strangely erotic. He felt as if the blood pumping through his arteries had suddenly turned to liquid fire.

Shayna gulped and turned away, avoiding his eyes. She glanced toward his desk and frowned. "Look at your phone, Josh," she said somewhat breathlessly.

"My phone?" Reluctantly, he forced himself to return to reality.

"A red light's flashing."

"It's my recorder. There must be a message. That's funny. I don't remember hearing the phone ring, and there's an extension in the bedroom."

"It must have been flashing when we came in. We just didn't notice it." Shayna caught her breath. "Do you think it could be the hospital?"

"God, I hope not," Josh said, retrieving his wallet and car keys from the table on which he dropped them when he entered the apartment. "Push the play button, please. We'd better find out for sure before we leave."

The words were no sooner out of his mouth than he remembered the message his cousin had relayed from the real estate office on Friday was still on the recorder. He made a lunge toward the phone, but it was too late. The tape was already rolling.

"Good news, Josh. I've found a buyer for your foundry."

Ben Hudson's brisk voice sliced through the awful silence of the room. Josh grabbed for the rewind button, but Shayna yanked his hand away and stepped between him and the recorder.

"I'm calling you at home because you said you didn't want to risk being overheard at your office. The initial offer is pretty close to the figure you mentioned last May, so I don't foresee any problems. I'll be out of town all weekend, but I'll call you Monday to set up a meeting. I know you're anxious to wrap this up so you can get back to Washington. Talk to you then."

Josh held his breath, desperately trying to get his thoughts in order. The next few words he uttered might well be the most important of his life. "Let me explain, Shayna," he said, stalling for time until some kind of inspiration filled the gaping cavity in his brain.

"Explain?" Shayna's voice sounded unnaturally shrill and her eyes were two dark circles of disbelief. "How can you possibly explain the fact that you've lied . . . that you've been lying about everything from the very beginning."

"I have never lied to you. Not once have I said I planned to stay in Titusville."

"But you knew that's what I believed, and so did all the men who liked you and trusted you—men like my father and Horace Abernathy . . . and Angus McTavish. You let us go on believing it, and that's as much a lie as if you'd put it in actual words."

"Angus has always known my plans," Josh declared, grasping at any straw that might soften the ugly picture Shayna's accusations painted.

"And you're still lying," Shayna declared in icy tones. "I heard you promise him you'd take care of his town."

"I promised I'd make certain whoever bought the foundry would keep it operating and the men employed

. . . which is more than I'm morally obligated to do. But I gave him my word and I intend to keep it."

"Come off it, Josh." Shayna gave him a withering look. "I've taken enough economics classes to know no man in his right mind is going to buy a one-hundred-year-old foundry nowadays except to bankrupt it and take a tax write-off."

The same disquieting thought had occurred to Josh more than once since he'd listened to his cousin's message, but hearing Shayna put his suspicions into words rubbed him raw. His temper flared. "If you have such a fine grasp of the problem," he snapped, "how is it you expect me to risk everything my family owns on such a losing proposition?"

"That's an entirely different matter and you know it. Four generations of Eddingtons have lived like kings off the foundry—and off the men who've worked in it. You owe it to those men to at least try to make a go of it. I thought that was what you were doing and I loved you for it."

"Stop it, Shayna," Josh declared, choked with the same frustration that had bedeviled him for the past six months. "I told Angus and I'll tell you—the fact that my name is Eddington does not automatically designate me savior of an outdated foundry and a dying town. I'll do my best to find a buyer who has the money to keep the damned thing afloat until a miracle comes along—because I don't. That's all I can do." He took a step toward Shayna. "Please try to understand, honey."

She held up her hand to ward him off and moved out of his reach. Her eyes looked huge and wounded in her ashen face. "If you planned to sell all along, why did you make such a pretense of learning the business?"

Josh swallowed hard. The answer to that question could damn him even further. "Angus gave me no choice," he said quietly. "I knew I couldn't hold the business together long enough to find a buyer without his help, and he refused to give it unless I agreed to apprentice under him.

He had some crazy idea I'd become enamored with the foundry business if he forced me to work at it for six months. I tried to tell him it would never happen, but he wouldn't listen. Naturally, if I'd known then what I know now, I'd never have agreed to his proposition."

Josh searched her face for some sign of understanding. Her expression was unreadable. "Try to understand," he said desperately. "I had to go along with him because all my plans depended on his cooperation."

"Your plans! And exactly how did romancing the daughter of one of your foremen further those precious plans of yours?" Shanya's voice sounded dangerously controlled. "What was I? Part of the smoke screen you needed to cover your manipulations until you could get safely out of town?"

"You can't believe that."

"How had you planned to end this . . . this affair of ours?" Shayna asked coldly. "Send me a registered letter from Washington?"

"What the hell are you talking about? You're not even making sense." Josh caught hold of Shayna's arms, forcing her to face him. "Maybe, as you see it, keeping silent about my plans for the foundry was tantamount to lying. As I see it, I had no choice. It was simply a business decision."

He heard her strangled gasp, but ploughed determinedly onward. "Don't confuse my plans for the foundry with my plan to marry you. One has nothing to do with the other. I have every intention of taking Megan and you to Washington with me. I tried to tell you that tonight before we made love. You were the one who didn't want to talk."

"Marry you? You're joking. I don't even know you." Shayna stared numbly at the stranger in whose arms she had lain such a short time before. "How could I have been so foolish . . . or so blind? The wonderful, caring man I imagined you to be obviously doesn't even exist." She twisted free from his grasp, sick with disgust that even now, seeing him for the coldly calculating man he was, the touch of his strong fingers could still send shivers of desire coursing through her.

"Don't do this, Shayna," Josh begged. "Don't try to turn our lovemaking into something cheap and sordid . . . and don't let your fanatic loyalty to this stupid little town destroy our chances for the future."

"My loyalty is to my family and to my friends and neighbors I've known all my life. What kind of future could I build with you in Washington, knowing you'd sold the very lives of the people I care about out from under them?"

"You're being unreasonable. Just this once, try thinking with your head instead of your emotions and you'll see that I have no choice in the matter."

Shayna tossed her head contemptuously. "Everyone always has a choice," she declared, incensed by Josh's coldly dispassionate tone of voice.

"You're right, of course. Everyone has choices of action . . . and of loyalty." Josh's eyes darkened with emotion. "You told me you loved me, but apparently your declaration didn't include the 'whither thou goest' kind of commitment a woman is supposed to make to the man she plans to marry. Are you saying now that your love is contingent upon my staying in Titusville and grubbing my life away in the Eddington Foundry?"

"I'm saying no such thing." Shayna swiped furiously at the tears scalding her eyes. "God help me, I do love you and I probably will until the day I die . . . and the only thing that my misguided feeling is contingent upon is my own blind stupidity. But I won't marry you and I don't want to see you again. For I'll tell you this, Mr. Joshua Eddington, I've just come to the conclusion I neither like nor respect you."

Josh reached for the letter opener beside his desk blotter and slit open the manila envelope marked Private and Personal. As a rule, he was the last man on the day shift to leave the production area of the foundry. Today, knowing this piece of mail was waiting for him, he'd taken off half an hour early.

He skimmed quickly through the computer printout he'd asked his Washington research assistant to send him, and groaned aloud. The detailed background report on the potential buyer of the foundry was, as he'd feared, vastly disappointing. He'd been hoping against hope his instincts had been wrong.

There'd been no logical reason for his negative reaction to the man who had arrived at the foundry two weeks to the day after his cousin's fateful phone call. He was intelligent and personable, he appeared to have a rudimentary grasp of foundry procedures, and everything from his discreetly expensive suit to his paper-thin Lucien Picard wristwatch bore the stamp of solid wealth.

Josh had disliked him the minute he stepped through his door.

It wasn't that they'd disagreed on anything. The negotiations on price and terms had been completely satisfactory, and the buyer's letter of credit from one of the country's major banks had exceeded the necessary limits. He'd even given all the right answers to Josh's questions during their cursory tour of the foundry. *He intended to honor any existing contracts and seek new ones; he'd keep the present personnel on the payroll; he'd guarantee no employee would be fired without good cause.*

It had all fallen into place so easily . . . too easily to be entirely believable.

Josh's cousin had made it plain he harbored no doubts about the buyer he'd unearthed. Looking like the cat who'd caught the world's fattest mouse, Ben Hudson had returned to the foundry the following morning with the necessary paperwork to set the sale in motion.

"Just sign on the dotted line and we'll get the ball rolling," he'd said, pushing the earnest money contract and accompanying check across the desk toward Josh.

Josh picked up his pen . . . then laid it back down. "I'll sign this later and put it in the mail to you."

Ben's mouth dropped open. "Everything's in order. Why the delay?"

"Why the rush? A few days won't make any difference." Josh sat back in his chair and studied his cousin's broad, florid face. "I'd like to run a background check on the guy before I sign away a business that's been in my family for four generations."

"A business that's on the verge of bankruptcy," Ben said sharply, shifting his massive, silk-suited body to lean forward across the desk. "Don't screw this up, Josh. Someone with that kind of money, who's willing to risk it on a foundry no one else wants, is almost too good to be true."

Josh nodded. "Exactly. Which is why I'd like to know how he made his money before I turn over the Eddington Foundry to him."

"What does it matter how he made it? It all spends the same."

"I promised someone I'd make sure the new owner would take care of the men. A lot of them are third or fourth generation employees of the Eddingtons." He shrugged. "I imagine it's difficult for you to understand how I feel."

"You're damned right it is. I stumped the bushes for four months to find a buyer for you, and this was the only nibble I got." Ben mopped his perspiring brow with a linen handerchief. "I don't appreciate your pussyfooting around on this deal, Josh, and futhermore, I don't think Kyle's going to like it much, either. He has a stake in this, too, you know."

Josh raised a quizzical eyebrow. "Since when has my brother been involved?"

"He called me last spring, right after you took over the foundry. It was his idea that I contact you and offer to find a buyer." A muscle twitched at the corner of Ben's left eye. "Kyle and I are real close. We think alike."

"Which, I assume, is your way of saying you've been reporting to him behind my back," Josh said, suddenly understanding why Shayna had felt so angry and betrayed when she'd learned of his secretive maneuvers.

"There hasn't been anything to report . . . until now. But I have to believe Kyle's lawyers will take exception to your turning down a legitimate deal for the family business just because you don't like the way the guy parts his hair."

Josh's heretofore carefully controlled temper had exploded at Ben's implied threat. He couldn't remember his exact words, but whatever he'd said had been effective enough to send his cousin scurrying from the office as fast as his unwieldly bulk would allow . . . probably to the nearest phone to call Kyle.

Josh shuddered at the thought of what that could invoke. He had his grandmother's power of attorney at the moment, but Kyle had always been able to get around the old lady. The last thing he needed right now was a family free-for-all.

The mournful wail of the five o'clock whistle parodied his wretched state of mind. It seemed everything in his life had turned sour since Shayna and he had become estranged. A hundred times he'd told himself he was better off without a woman who felt no loyalty to him, and a hundred times his empty heart and aching body had made a liar out of him.

Futhermore, his nerves were jangled from watching for some sign that the three Brenegans had been told of his plans. None. had materialized and that unnerved him even more. Shayna had so obviously chosen her family over him. Why had she kept her counsel?

All in all, the past fourteen days had been sheer hell . . . and now he had this negative report to contend with. He read it through again. On the last page, his assistant had penned a brief recap of the information. *"Your potential buyer has purchased a total of fourteen financially distressed companies. To date, not one has survived longer than eighteen months under his management. He either strips them bare and sells them piece by piece or runs them down to nothing and takes a tax loss. Hold out for top dollar on your white elephant, Josh. The guy's loaded and chances are he'll pay plenty to get his hands on a certified loser like your hundred-year-old foundry.''*

Josh slumped wearily in the worn leather chair that had belonged to his grandfather and great-grandfather before him. His assistant's advice made good sense. But he wouldn't have to visit Angus McTavis at the hospital each evening knowing he'd signed a contract that spelled the death of both the foundry and the town the old man loved.

He leaned back and closed his weary eyes. What in God's name had happened to him in the short time he'd lived in Titusville? He'd changed so much, he scarcely recognized himself.

Six months ago, he'd never have questioned the morality of a legal business transaction, no matter who got hurt along the way. Now each time he looked at a column of figures or a profit and loss statement, he saw the faces of the men whose livelihoods depended on the decisions he made.

Six months ago, he'd measured his success by his powers of persuasion. Now he judged it by the number of marketable castings the foundry had poured since they'd solved the riser problem.

Six months ago, he'd been a carefree bachelor. The idea of tying himself to one woman for life had been unthinkable. Now he knew with absolute certainty the terrible emptiness in his heart could never be filled by anyone but Shayna O'Malley and her daughter.

With a sigh, he rose, walked to the Victorian sideboard which served as a liquor cabinet, and poured himself a double shot of the Jack Daniels Kyle had stocked to serve visiting customers. Soul-searching was thirsty business.

Drink in hand, he wandered to the window to gaze at the cluttered yard below. He blinked, unable to believe his eyes. The late-afternoon sun glinted off a collage of rusty metal and discarded pallets so haphazard and so ugly, he imagined he saw a crude kind of beauty in the random pattern.

What had Angus called it in one of his expansive moments? *A junkyard sculptor's masterpiece that only a man with iron shavings in his blood could appreciate.*

Josh's heart hammered against his rib cage. Had he metamorphosed into that man in the hours he'd worked in the smoke-blackened forge? Or, as Angus claimed, had he been that man all along and simply not known it?

Whatever the reason, it suddenly dawned on him that this business about selling the Eddington Foundry was nothing more than an exercise in futility. He could no more part with it than he could quit breathing—not because of Angus or the men, not even to gain back Shayna's respect, but because he felt the same consuming passion for the hideous old monster as his ironmaster ancestors must have felt in times past.

Why had it taken him so long to recognize that truth? And what good would the knowledge do him when he'd already lost the woman he loved and jeopardized the life of a man who meant more to him than his own father ever had?

Watching the last of the day-shift men head for the motley collection of cars that would take them home to their wives and families, Josh felt engulfed by a bitter, aching loneliness . . . and a haunting sense of continuity. In just such solitary splendor must Titus Eddington once have stood at this very window over a century ago surveying his kingdom. With grim humor, Josh raised his glass to his illustrious ancester who'd started it all. "To you, sir. I've heard you weren't any luckier in love than I am."

He downed the last of his whiskey.

"And Titus begat David," he recited, "and David begat Hiram and Hiram begat Joshua . . ."

"And Kyle. Don't forget me, big brother. I'm an Eddington, too."

Startled, Josh wheeled around to find himself face-to-face with the brother he hadn't seen since he'd replaced him as head of the foundry five months before. Kyle was noticeably thinner, and the black smudges beneath his eyes and deep hollows in his cheeks gave him the appearance of a man recovering from a serious illness.

Josh put his glass down and took a step forward, profoundly shocked by his brother's appearance and not at all sure how to handle the situation. Kyle and he hadn't parted on the best of terms. "When did you get back?" he asked. "The last I heard you were in Italy with Mother."

"It didn't work out. You know Mother; at best she wasn't an enthusiastic parent. Now a thirty-two-year-old son is a positive embarrassment to her—which figures, since her latest husband is only thirty-five." He grimaced. "She insisted I call her Clarissa and she made such a point of introducing me as 'my relative from America,' I figured it was time to move on."

Josh heard the pain behind his brother's flippant words, and memories of his own disillusionment with their mother rose to haunt him. He'd idolized her as a small child and done his level best to please her, but she had never even pretended affection for her eldest son; her few capricious bursts of motherly concern had all been lavished on her youngest. Years later, when it no longer mattered, he'd learned her antipathy toward him had stemmed from his resemblance to his grandfather, whom she despised.

He felt choked with bitterness—how typical of Clarissa to fail Kyle when he needed her most.

An all-too-familiar feeling of protectiveness gripped Josh. He'd promised himself he'd never again assume the role of his brother's keeper, but old habits were hard to break. "Do you want to talk about it?" he asked gently.

"Mother and her playboy count? No," Kyle said vehemently. "The guy's a con artist. He'll stick around as long as the old girl foots the bills, but God help her if the money runs out." His mouth twisted in a tight smile. "God help us all if that happens. What would we Eddingtons be without our money?"

"We may soon find out," Josh said, and immediately regretted his words.

Kyle's face paled visibly. "Ben said he'd found a buyer for the foundry, but you were holding up the sale. Why? I should think that would solve some of our problems."

A few months before, Josh would have come up with some glib answer to appease his brother, but the man who faced him today wasn't the same whining malcontent who'd fled from his responsibilities last spring. Something about this hollow-eyed stranger demanded he tell him the truth.

"I won't sell to the fellow Ben came up with because I'm convinced he'd run out the contracts we have, then shut the place down and take a tax write-off. There are a lot of good men working for us; they deserve better than that from the Eddingtons. I intend to see they get it."

For a long, silent moment, Kyle's steady gaze probed Josh's face. "Ben said you'd gotten religion, but I can't help wondering if your decision has something to do with the fact that the Widow O'Malley is the daughter of one of those men."

"How do you know about . . . ?"

"About your involvement with her? That's easy. I still have friends in Titusville; they kept me posted."

Josh swore softly. "Your friends will have to find a new source of gossip. It's all over between Shayna and me."

Kyle's eyes widened. "You're kidding. What happened?"

"Let's just say I handled things so cleverly, I outsmarted myself."

"That seems to be an Eddington family talent," Kyle said drily. "Actually, I'm relieved. I'm not sure I could handle the lady as a sister-in-law. I couldn't even look her in the face at her husband's funeral."

Kyle's face had a furtive, haunted look. "I thought I'd gotten over my feelings of guilt, but when her brother hit me with his demands, it all came back. Talk about handling things cleverly, I spent so much money on the expensive equipment that asinine production manager insisted we needed, there was nothing left for things like leaky tanks and faulty wiring." He swallowed hard. "Tim O'Malley died in an electrical fire."

Shock ripped through Josh. For a second, the image of the sweet-faced boy in the wedding picture filled his mind and he felt sick with horror. The tortured face of his brother snapped him back to reality. "It's over, Kyle," he said softly. "If mistakes were made, they were honest ones. Don't destroy the rest of your life by blaming yourself for something you couldn't possibly have foreseen."

"I've been telling myself that ever since I left here last spring. So far it hasn't done much good. Between that and the realization that the very things I disliked most about Mother's squirrelly little count all reminded me of myself, it's been a rough five months. For the first time in my life, I've taken a really good look at myself. I don't like what I see."

Josh nodded grimly. "Join the club. To tell the truth, I think a major part of my obsession with the foundry is the hope that somewhere in that pile of rusty iron I'll find a Josh Eddington I can learn to live with." He walked to his desk, picked up the earnest money agreement and tore it in half. "Care to join me in the search, little brother? There's a lot of iron stacked out there."

Kyle's face mirrored skepticism . . . and a dawning hope. "Can we afford it?"

"Nope."

A wry grin softened Kyle's sharp features. "Well, at least we know where we stand." He hesitated. "I'm no good at production or at handling men. All things considered, I'm not even sure I could bring myself to go back in the building where . . . you'd have to handle that end of the business."

"I intend to."

"Selling's what I do best. I never had any trouble getting contracts. I just couldn't fill them."

Josh grinned. "If you can get them, I guess I can figure out how to fill them."

"Do you really think we can make it work?"

"There's a better than even chance we can't," Josh said soberly. "And that's stacking the odds in our favor."

Kyle walked to the window and stared out. "Considering my track record, those are probably better odds than I could get anywhere else."

He turned to face Josh. "Okay. Let's do it."

SIXTEEN

Shayna ripped the top sheet from her kitchen calendar and tossed it into the wastebasket. She couldn't remember when she'd been happier to dispose of a month. Between the relentless August heat and the ache in her heart, there had been times when she'd thought she couldn't make it through another day. But somehow she'd survived, and now at last it was September.

She poured herself a cup of coffee, carried it to the kitchen table, and placed it beside the folder of information she'd collected at her teachers' indoctrination session. In a few more days, she'd have the challenge of her first full-time teaching job to fill her empty days. She breathed a sigh of relief; it couldn't come too soon. She'd said her bitter farewell to Josh more than a month ago, and no matter how often she told herself she had done the right thing, her loneliness seemed to grow deeper with every passing day.

As if that weren't enough to contend with, she had to field her family's persistent questions as to why she wasn't seeing him anymore. So far, she'd managed to say just enough to confuse the issue, but she knew the truth was bound to come out sooner or later.

Actually, Megan had been her biggest problem. She'd

lost count of how many times her daughter had begged to see Josh, or how many times she'd asked her tearful question, "Why doesn't he love us anymore?"

Shayna cringed, recalling her evasive answer to that very question when Megan had asked it again just a few hours earlier. "It has nothing to do with how he feels. I'm sure he still cares very much about you, but he just can't visit us anymore."

Megan had looked perplexed and her eyes had puddled with tears, but she'd asked no more questions. Clutching the Raggedy Ann doll Josh had given her to her chest, she'd trudged down the hall to her bedroom—leaving Shayna to wonder if sticking to her principles had really been important enough to sacrifice her child's happiness.

Nothing she did made sense anymore. After all that righteous indignation she'd expressed to Josh, she couldn't bring herself to betray his plans to anyone—not even her own family. All she could do was wait each night, with her stomach tied in knots, for the Brenegan men to come home from work with the news that the foundry had been sold.

As if that weren't enough, she'd also discovered she lacked the strength of will to cut the final tie with a man she no longer respected. Heaven knows she'd tried; her failure had been both ludicrous and embarrassing. With angry determination, she'd wrestled Josh's kissing box into her station wagon the day after their quarrel and driven it to the county garbage dump . . . then driven it back home again because she couldn't bear to toss it on the malodorous heap.

Shayna pressed her fingers to her aching temples. So here she was, driving around with a wooden box poking a hole in her upholstery and a knot in her stomach that could well be the beginning of an ulcer. A sorry state of affairs if ever there was one.

She stuffed the lesson plan back into the folder without ever looking at it, hoping her mood would improve as the day wore on.

A shadow fell across her kitchen window and she looked up to see Ronnie striding toward her back door. Her heart missed a beat. What was her brother doing home at four o'clock on a Friday afternoon? Had Josh finally made his fateful announcement?

Ronnie breezed through her door, a grin spreading from ear to ear. "Hi, Sis. How about fixing me a couple of sandwiches? Ma's at her garden club, so dinner will be late at our house, and I have to get back to the foundry by six."

Shayna released the breath she'd been holding and headed for her refrigerator. "What's going on?" she asked. "I've never known you to work a split shift before."

"It's just for a couple of days." Ronnie bristled with importance. "I'm on a special project for Josh. He found a bunch of ornamental iron molds that've been stored in the pattern shop vault for seventy-five or eighty years, and the boys in the molding department cast them last week." He gave a low whistle. "You wouldn't believe the great stuff those sewer pipe jockeys turned out."

Shayna looked up from her sandwich-making. "Ornamental iron? You mean like those lacy columns in the hotel lobby or that fleur-de-lis screen in Allison's boutique?"

"That's it. And sailboats and dolphins and the oak tree Josh says is in all the iron grillwork at White Oaks and plenty more. I mean this stuff is really classy, and I'm in charge of the buffing and painting, since I'm an expert on such things after all the cars I've refinished."

Josh did this and Josh says that. Since when had Ronnie become a member of the Joshua Eddington fan club?

"I didn't realize the foundry could do that kind of work," Shayna said, making conversation to hide her turmoil.

"Neither did anyone else until Josh came across that old newspaper article in the files and showed it to Angus McTavish. It was before Angus's time, but he remembered where the molds were stashed, and Josh and Pa took it from there.''

Josh and Pa. Shayna grimaced. Dear, trusting Pop had been completely taken in by Josh—and her father was usually such a good judge of character.

Ronnie accepted the ham sandwiches Shayna had prepared and poured himself a cup of coffee. ''I suppose you heard Kyle's back. Funny thing. I never used to like him, but now that I know him better, he's really not such a bad guy. He sure has pitched in on this project.''

Shayna didn't even attempt to comment on that statement.

''He's even talked some high-priced architects and decorators from Chicago into looking at the stuff next week,'' Ronnie continued. ''He says we'll knock their eyes out because most builders nowadays think 'ornamental iron' means a bar with a few curlicues on it.''

He took a bite of his sandwich and chewed thoughtfully. ''That article Josh showed me was really something. I mean, the Eddington Foundry was pretty famous back when—even cast a lot of that fancy ironwork in the French Quarter of New Orleans.'' Ronnie's eyes glowed. ''Think of it, Sis. We're pouring metal in molds Eddington men made more than a century ago. It's almost like they're helping us keep the old place going. Horace says it gives him goose bumps.''

Ronnie's voice rose as he warmed to his subject. ''Of course, a little wrought-iron work won't keep us in business, but Josh has already come up with a couple more good ideas. I'll never figure out what a classy guy like him wants with a broken-down foundry, but thank God he does.'' He cleared his throat. ''So how about you doing your part, Sis. Give the poor sucker a break. He's already got more troubles than any man should have; he doesn't need woman troubles, too.''

Shayna glared at her brother. ''You don't know what you're talking about.''

''I know Josh sold White Oaks to the State Historical

Society and some guy from Chicago is going to auction off the furniture next Saturday."

"I'm aware of that."

"And," Ronnie continued between bites, "he's driving a company truck because he got rid of his fancy Mercedes, and he sold the hotel to a national chain. Guido Santini's sister says they're taking over the first of November."

Shayna took a shaky breath. "Josh sold his car . . . and the hotel? Are you sure?"

"Yeah, I'm sure. It's plain to see he's really strapped for money, but he's still doing his damndest to save a foundry that should have closed its doors years ago."

Ronnie looked her squarely in the eye. "The poor guy looks like death and, if you want the truth, so do you. If you're both so unhappy, why don't you get back together?"

"It's too late," Shayna said, taking a ragged breath. "He wouldn't want me after the awful things I said to him." With a strangled cry, she turned and dashed from the room before she made a complete fool of herself.

Stricken eyes in a chalky face stared back at her from the bathroom mirror. Little by little, she was coming to realize that everything Josh had said had been the truth. The Eddingtons really were in serious financial trouble. This ornamental iron project must be a last-ditch attempt to make good his promise to Angus by providing the new owner with contracts that would keep the men working. Shayna felt sick with shame. He was doing his best, and that was so much more than any other man in his place would do. And she'd told him she had no respect for him.

Dimly, through her haze of misery, she heard the telephone ring and the murmur of Ronnie's voice when he answered it. "It's Colleen Fitzpatrick," he called. "She wants to know if Megan can play."

"Megan's already playing with Colleen."

"Doesn't sound like it. You'd better talk to her."

Shayna sighed. She knew very well where Megan was, and Ronnie couldn't have picked a worse time to botch up a simple phone call. She splashed cold water on her face and hurried to the kitchen to pick up the receiver.

"Let me talk to Megan, Colleen."

"She's not here, but Mama says we can run through the sprinkler if she can come over."

Colleen was a bright child. It wasn't like her to get things so confused. "Megan left here at one o'clock with a picnic lunch for the two of you in her new school lunch pail," Shayna said with barely concealed exasperation. "What time did she leave your house?"

"I don't know, Mrs. O'Malley. Honest. Mama and me ate lunch at Grandma's. We had chili dogs."

Shayna felt a sudden twinge of fear. "May I speak to your mother please, Colleen."

"Sure, Mrs. O'Malley."

Twenty minutes later, Shayna had not only spoken to Laura Fitzpatrick—she'd called every neighbor on the street and even some as far as two blocks away. No one had seen Megan.

She paced the small kitchen, too upset to sit down. "Where in the world can she be? She never leaves the block, and I distinctly remember her saying she was going to have a picnic with Colleen."

Ronnie fell into step beside her. "Are you sure? Were those her exact words?"

"Of course I'm sure." Shayna stopped short. "Well, actually, she said she wanted to have a picnic with her best friend. I naturally assumed it was Colleen. The two of them are inseparable."

"You assumed!" Ronnie rammed his fist against the wall. "Judas Priest, Sis, you'd have to be nuts to 'assume' anything where a five-year-old kid's concerned." Anger had always been Ronnie's way of dealing with his fears and anxieties. The fury in his eyes told her, better than words, how worried he was over Megan's disappearance. With a muttered oath, he stalked to the phone.

"What are you doing?"

"I'm calling Elmer Farnsworth."

"The police! Oh, Ronnie, you don't think . . ."

Ronnie made an obvious effort to gain his composure. "I don't think anything, except Elmer and his boys can find a missing kid a lot faster than we can." He dialed 911. "So help me, if you don't blister her bottom, I will."

Shayna held her breath while Ronnie filled Elmer in on their problem. He listened a moment to the voice on the other end of the line, then turned to face her. "Elmer wants to know if there are any abandoned wells in this part of The Flats."

She gasped. "I . . . I don't think so."

"None we know," Ronnie snarled into the phone. He drummed his fingers impatiently on the wall beside the phone as he listened to the police chief. "Thanks a lot, Elmer. That's just what I needed to hear. Can you quit trying to scare the hell out of me long enough to get off your rear end and look for my niece?"

He rubbed his fingers over his eyes. "Okay, buddy. Whatever you say. We'll wait for your call."

"What did he say?"

"He said he'll get right on it and he'll call us as soon as he knows anything."

"What was that about scaring the hell out of you?"

"It was nothing. You know Elmer. He's not happy unless he's spreading doom and gloom."

"I have a right to know, Ronnie. She's my daughter."

"Judas, Sis. He just mentioned he got a report last week about a kid who was kidnapped in Indianapolis. But nothing like that ever happens in Titusville."

Shayna resumed her pacing, too miserable to talk. She had no choice but to wait for Elmer's call, but the waiting was almost more than she could bear. Over and over, she told herself Megan was all right and an hour from now they'd be laughing at themselves for panicking. But her heart was pounding like a triphammer and wisps of cold terror edged their way up her spine. When the phone finally rang, both Ronnie and she leapt for it.

She got there first. "Hello."

"Hello, Shayna." It was a woman's voice, and Shayna sagged with disappointment. "This is Millie at The Bluebell. Maybe I'm sticking my nose in where it don't belong, but shucks, I been doing that all my life."

"Please, Millie, I can't tie the phone up right now. I'm waiting for an important call."

"This'll just take a minute. It's about your kid—leastwise I think she's yours. She sure looks like you."

"Megan? You've seen Megan? Where? When?"

"She come traipsing by here a few minutes ago carrying her lunch pail and a Raggedy Ann doll . . . and her little butt was really dragging. I called her in and gave her a drink of water, but she took off again."

"Oh, Millie, thank God. Where did she go?"

"Don't know for sure, but it looked like she was heading toward the hotel. I don't mean to criticize, Shayna, but it seems to me you oughtn't to turn a little mite like that loose on her own when the day shift traffic's due to come out of the foundry. If I was you . . ."

Shayna didn't wait to hear more. She dropped the receiver and reached for her purse. "The little monkey's clear up on Main Street," she cried. "She's heading for the hotel and she has her Raggedy Ann."

She pressed her hand to her heaving chest. "Good heavens, she must be looking for Josh. I should have realized she was talking about him when she said 'my best friend.' She's been so desperately unhappy ever since . . ." She dug through her purse for her car keys. "I have to get over there before she gets caught in the shift-change traffic. Are you coming?"

Ronnie shook his head. "I'd better let Elmer know we've found her." He braced himself against the counter as if his legs were about to buckle beneath him. "I don't know why you let yourself get so upset over a dumb thing like this. I told you nothing ever happens in Titusville."

Shayna laughed, giddy with relief. "Next time I'll be as calm and collected as you," she promised, giving him a quick hug.

*   *   *

With the day shift drawing to a close, Josh found himself alone in the pattern shop. Horace had gone next door to the molding department to help John Brenegan break out the lastest batch of castings, and Kyle had left early to get ready to represent the Eddington Family at the Highlands Country Club Founders Day dinner dance.

Josh poured himself a cup of the lethal sludge Horace brewed each day in the shop coffeepot and dropped onto a nearby stool for a few minutes of peace and quiet. It had been a long, busy day and he was noticeably sagging.

Among other things, he'd tendered his written resignation to his Washington partners with his calculations of the payoff he felt he had coming to him in a buy-out of his share of the business. It wasn't that he regretted his decision; sharing his news with Angus had felt damned good. But even that had fallen flat when he'd lost the right to tell the one person with whom he most wanted to share his decision.

He was about to join Horace for the evening's stint on the new casting project when he heard Mrs. Warren page him. He took the call on the shop phone.

His first reaction to Ronnie Brenegan's "I'll be late getting back to work" was one of annoyance. "What's the problem?" he snapped.

"We've had some excitement here, and I couldn't leave my sister when she was so upset."

Josh tensed. "Shayna? What's wrong with Shayna?"

"Nothing, unless you count being scared out of her mind. Megan's been missing for hours. Packed a lunch and ran away from home, far as we can tell."

"That doesn't sound like Megan." Josh tightened his grip on the phone. "Has anyone had the sense to call the police?"

"I called them myself. Elmer Farnsworth's got his whole force out combing the town."

Fear raced through Josh like fire through dry tinder. His

knees felt rubbery, and his pulse hammered in his temples.
"Why the hell did you wait so long to call me?"

"We were checking with Megan's friends, thinking one
of them might have seen her. It wasn't until we got the
call from Millie at The Bluebell, we figured out you were
the one she was looking for."

"Say that again."

"Megan's been crying her heart out ever since you and
Sis broke up, and once we heard she was spotted on Main
Street headed for the hotel, Shayna figured out what she
was up to. She's out there now, trying to head Megan off
before the shift-change traffic hits town."

"Oh my God!" Josh dropped the phone and vaulted
Horace's drafting table. Weaving through the pattern shop
was like running a labyrinth; he made it in record time,
only barking his shins twice. He sprinted through the furnace room, past the astonished faces of the swing shift
men lining up to punch in, and hurdled the stack of iron
that stood between him and his company truck.

The truck had seen better days, but it still had a lot of
heart. Josh revved her up and took off. "Come on, Old
Lady," he begged. "My little girl's out there looking for
me, and she's only five years old."

He hit Main Street and slowed to cruising speed, his
eyes darting from one side to the other. One block, two
blocks, three blocks. The street had always seemed so
short; today it stretched on forever.

A few blocks south of the hotel, he spotted a small,
bedraggled figure in front of Mueller's Mercantile. With
a triumphant cry, he came to a screeching stop and bolted
from the truck. "Megan! Sweetheart!" he called, and
watched her tear-stained face break into a tremulous smile.

He swept her up in a joyful bear hug. She was hot and
sweaty and the corners of her mouth were sticky with
chocolate. Fresh tears welled in her round blue eyes.
"Mama said you couldn't visit us anymore, so I was coming to visit you," she sobbed. "I made you a picnic, but
I ate your cookie 'cause I got so hungry."

Josh's own eyes felt suspiciously moist. "Cookies aren't important," he said, nuzzling his cheek against Megan's flushed little face. "I've found you and you're safe and that's all that matters."

Shayna inched along Main Street, scanning the sidewalk for any sign of her daughter. Up ahead, on the opposite side of the street, a truck had stopped, and a group of spectators had gathered on the sidewalk. Her heart rose in her throat. *Dear God, please don't let Megan have been in an accident."*

Clutching the steering wheel with trembling fingers, she drew alongside the truck. Suddenly, she spotted them—the tall, golden-haired man with the black-haired child in his arms. She slammed on the brakes. "Megan!" she cried, leaping from the car to run toward them just as the five o'clock whistle blew.

Two pairs of eyes met hers—the blue ones wary, the green ones determined. "Don't scold her, Shayna," Josh said quietly. "She was looking for me."

"I know that."

"What else could she do? You told her I couldn't visit her anymore."

Shayna cringed. "I didn't know what to tell her," she stammered, the joy she'd felt at seeing them together decimated by Josh's stinging accusation. As if she hadn't already given him enough reason to despise her—now she had this to answer for.

Josh shifted Megan in his arms, and she snuggled her head beneath his chin and closed her eyes. "You can't punish a child for acting intelligently," he said, his voice husky. "I know you have a low opinion of me right now—and God knows it's well deserved—but the truth is, the three of us belong together. It's a hell of a note when a five-year-old is the only one with the sense to do something about it."

Shayna couldn't believe her ears. Despite all the stupid, judgmental things she'd done, Josh still loved her and

wanted her. For one delirious moment, she was torn between laughing and crying. She longed to throw her arms
around him and tell him she'd go anywhere in the world
he wanted to take her because she'd been dead wrong
about everything, except how much she loved him. A
glance at the growing group of spectators lining the sidewalk told her this was neither the time nor place.

"Let's go home," she said so softly only he could hear.
"Megan's big adventure has been too much for her. She's
fallen asleep in your arms. We'll put her to bed and then
we can talk. There's so much I need to say to you."

Josh felt as if a crushing weight were lifted from his
shoulders. He'd bluffed his way through the last few minutes, knowing he held a weak hand, but counting on a
gambler's luck . . . and sure enough, fate had dealt him
another miracle. After all his unforgivable blunders,
Shayna still loved him; the message in her lovely eyes
was unmistakable. If hearts could sing, his would be war-
bling like a bird.

There was so much he had to tell her. How he'd finally
realized how much the old foundry and this funky little
town meant to him. Plans he needed to share with her.
Risks he must ask her to take with him.

But all that could wait. Right now, he just wanted to
fill the aching emptiness inside him with her tenderness
and her passion . . . and send the panic he'd lived with
for the past month skittering into the dark recesses of his
memory.

"I'll put Megan down and follow you home," he said,
covering the distance to Shayna's station wagon in a few
long strides. With his free hand, he opened the rear door,
laid Megan on the seat and her doll beside her. It took
him a minute to recognize the bulky object filling the back
end of the wagon; it took him half that time to figure out
what to do with it.

Shayna saw the tenderness Josh displayed toward her
sleeping child, and her heart swelled with joy and gratitude. Whatever the future might hold, she knew all would

be right with her world as long as the three of them were together.

Josh straightened up, moved to the back of the station wagon, and opened the hatch. "You brought our kissing box with you," he said gruffly.

"Well, I . . . that is . . ." she stammered, but the explanation died on her lips when she caught the look of wonder and triumph on his face. With a sigh, she acknowledged there were times in life when a discreet silence beat the naked truth hands down.

Bewildered, she watched him remove the box, carry it to the center of the street, and set it facedown on the yellow line. "What in heaven's name are you doing?"

"Getting my money's worth out of my investment," he said smugly. "I'm not a rich man anymore. I have to make every penny count and so far, this box has been a total loss." His mouth curved in a wicked grin. "Come here, Shayna."

"I will not." Shayna felt her cheeks grow hot. The spectators on the sidewalk were jockeying for a better look, and lines of cars and pickups had formed behind both his truck and her station wagon.

"Behave yourself, Josh," she pleaded. "Look around you. We're already blocking traffic both ways. You can't put a box down in the middle of Main Street."

"Sure I can. Haven't you heard? I'm an Eddington and this is *my* town. I can do anything I want in *my* town." He crooked his finger. "Come here, woman."

His voice held the same note of arrogance that had annoyed her so much the first day she'd met him. Today it sounded endearing . . . albeit impractical. She stepped forward to reason with him and found herself swept up, plopped onto the box, and facing him nose-to-nose.

A cheer went up from the crowd and an old lady in the front row hollered, "What are you waiting for, young fella? Kiss her."

"An excellent idea," Josh murmured, as he tightened

his arms around Shayna and lowered his hungry mouth to hers.

It was the worst traffic jam in the history of Titusville. The lines stretched to three blocks north of the hotel behind Josh's truck and two blocks south of The Bluebell behind Shayna's station wagon, and life in the town was never quite the same again.

Kyle Eddington and Allison Cartwright were trapped so long in the hotel parking lot, they finally broke their three-year silence. Kyle did most of the talking, and by the time the traffic started moving, he'd convinced her to be his date for the Founder's Day dinner dance. The hotel employees peering out the windows all agreed that the way things were shaping up, Eddington-watching might well take on a whole new dimension in the months to come.

For the first time in fifty years of business, Mr. Mueller closed the mercantile early. There was no point staying open when all his customers were out on the sidewalk ogling Mr. David's grandson and his young lady. On a spur-of-the-moment decision, he decided to forego his usual lonely supper and walk to The Bluebell to partake of the Friday-night blue plate special with his son, Siegfried . . . a tradition they maintained until the day the old man died.

Ronnie Brenegan couldn't get close enough to see what was causing the tie-up. But, practical man that he was, he decided to weather it out in Grogan's Tavern where, coincidentally, the old men of the town had congregated to speculate on what fate had in store for their sons and grandsons with the new young Eddington in charge of the foundry. A few chosen words from Ronnie, and the mood was so high that the usually tight-fisted Grogan stood every man in the tavern to a free beer. It was enough to make the most cynical amongst them regain his faith in God and the future of Titusville.

Meanwhile, with the supper hour approaching and traffic at a standstill, the hungry men at the ends of the lines started such a caterwauling and honking of horns, it sounded more like New Year's Eve in Times Square than a quiet Friday in Titusville. Not a sound was heard from those at the front. In fact, they scarcely even noticed the ruckus behind them. They were all much too busy watching their favorite ironmaster kiss his lady.

SHARE THE FUN . . .
SHARE YOUR NEW-FOUND TREASURE!!

You don't want to let your new books out of your sight? That's okay. Your friends can get their own. Order below.

No. 50 RENEGADE TEXAN by Becky Barker
Rane lives only for himself—that is, until he meets Tamara.

No. 51 RISKY BUSINESS by Jane Kidwell
Blair goes undercover but finds more than she bargained for with Logan.

No. 52 CAROLINA COMPROMISE by Nancy Knight
Richard falls for Dee and the glorious Old South. Can he have both?

No. 53 GOLDEN GAMBLE by Patrice Lindsey
The stakes are high! Who has the winning hand—Jessie or Bart?

No. 54 DAYDREAMS by Marina Palmieri
Kathy's life is far from a fairy tale. Is Jake her Prince Charming?

No. 55 A FOREVER MAN by Sally Falcon
Max is trouble and Sandi wants no part of him. She *must* resist!

No. 56 A QUESTION OF VIRTUE by Carolyn Davidson
Neither Sara nor Cal can ignore their almost magical attraction.
